"I can ... you'll never recognize me."

Mark scoffed at JoJo's boast. "JoJo, you do realize I was a CIA black-ops analyst in the field for years."

"And years and years..." His daughter rolled her eyes.

Okay, maybe he wasn't going to impress Sophie.

"Observation is what I do," he continued as though Sophie hadn't interrupted. "It's how I survived. You can't get past me. Especially not with the tattoos."

JoJo held out her hand. "It's a bet, then. I do this. I get the job. You win. You get to show off your observation skills to your daughter. The only thing you're out is a half hour of your time."

"We were going to go eat...."

"Are you kidding me? I'm not leaving," Sophie said. "I want to see this."

JoJo winked at Sophie and his daughter smiled back. Great, he thought. She'd known this woman for minutes and they had bonded more tightly than he had with his daughter in months.

Still, he'd play out this little wager. What did he have to lose? It wasn't like JoJo would ever get past him.

Dear Reader,

This is my third story set in the Tyler Group world (*One Final Step,* October 2012, and *An Act of Persuasion,* March 2013) and while an author never plays favorites with her books, I have to say this was one of the most satisfying books I have ever written. I fell in love with Mark and Sophie, an absent father and his daughter, who reunited in *An Act of Persuasion.* When I thought about Mark's story and giving him his happy-ever-after, I really couldn't think about him alone.

It had to be Mark and Sophie and *their* happy-ever-after. That meant I needed the type of heroine I thought would suit them both. That's when JoJo walked on to the scene.

She's not exactly conventional and she comes with a lot of baggage. But somehow the three of them make this story work. So this isn't a story about Mark and JoJo. This is a story about Mark and JoJo and Sophie and how together they become a family.

I love to hear from readers—the good, the bad and the ugly—so check out my website, www.stephaniedoyle.net.

Happy reading!

Stephanie Doyle

For the First Time

Stephanie Doyle

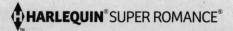

Recycling programs
for this product may
not exist in your area.

ISBN-13: 978-0-373-71881-8

FOR THE FIRST TIME

Copyright © 2013 by Stephanie Doyle

Printed in U.S.A.

ABOUT THE AUTHOR

Stephanie Doyle, a dedicated romance reader, began to pen her own romantic adventures at age sixteen. She began submitting to Harlequin at age eighteen and by twenty-six her first book was published. Fifteen years later, she still loves what she does, as each book is a new adventure. She lives in South Jersey with her cat, Lex, and her two kittens, who have taken over everything. When she isn't thinking about escaping to the beach, she's working on her next idea.

Books by Stephanie Doyle

HARLEQUIN SUPERROMANCE

SILHOUETTE ROMANTIC SUSPENSE

SILHOUETTE BOMBSHELL

Other titles by this author available in ebook format.

For Wanda
Because when I said I could never,
ever write Harlequin Superromance books,
she said let's not say *ever.*

PROLOGUE

"I NEED YOU to focus, Josephine."

She was focusing. She was focusing very hard. She knew that the man in front of her was a police detective. He had brown hair with gray mixed in on the sides. He wore brown leather shoes and khaki pants that were fraying a little around the hem. His badge number was 79134.

She'd made herself memorize it—79134.

"Tell me again everything that you saw."

Why? She'd said it all already. It wasn't going to change.

"Do it, JoJo. Tell him again." Her father paced in the living room, stopping every once in a while at the chair where her mom sat so he could put his hand on her shoulder. It only made her mom cry harder.

"We were at the mall."

"The strip mall on Springfield," her mother interjected. "It's where I dropped them off. They were supposed to go shopping, then call me to pick them up. They were supposed to stay there."

The detective nodded, and turned to JoJo. "But you decided to leave the mall instead."

"We wanted to see a movie. Two boys from our class were supposed to meet us there." JoJo winced at the sound of her father hissing. "It wasn't like a date or anything, Dad. They were just friends."

JoJo and Julia were only fourteen. They had already been told by their parents over and over that they weren't allowed to date until sixteen. Which was so stupid. All the freshman girls in high school already had boyfriends. They were, like, the only single girls in the class.

"Don't worry about that," the detective said. "Focus on what happened. You left the mall."

"The theater was just up the street a few blocks. The movie was at three forty-five." She remembered that stupid detail.

Three forty-five p.m. Why only that one?

"She was walking too slow. She always walked so slow. Then she stopped because her shoelace came undone."

JoJo could see it clearly. She was nearly half a block ahead. Julia bent down on one knee tying her shoe as if they had all the time in the world. Which, of course, they didn't because it was already three-forty. What if the movie had started when they got there? What if they couldn't find Peter and Jake? Then the whole point of doing this would be for nothing.

JoJo shouted to her to hurry. But Julia flipped her the bird instead. It actually made JoJo smile.

"Then a car pulled up along the side of the road. It was silver. A minivan. The kind where the side door slides over."

"Can you tell me the make? Was it a Toyota or a Ford?"

JoJo shook her head. She only knew the makes of cars she liked. MINI Coopers and Volkswagen bugs because they were cool. She knew the Subaru her mother drove and the Toyota her dad had driven for years. But they weren't minivans. It didn't help. Nothing she knew was helping.

"Then what happened?"

"The side door opened and this guy jumped out. It happened so fast. He just grabbed her from behind. Then she was screaming and he put her in the van."

The tears that had been falling since she had watched her twin sister be dragged into that van came faster, but they wouldn't help, either. She had to pull it together so she could tell the detective everything. It was the only way they would find her. Just like she'd told the people at the theater, and the first police officers who arrived at the scene and then her parents.

"He wore jeans. His hair was dark. I think he had a hoodie on, but I can't be sure."

"How could you tell what his hair color was if he was wearing a hoodie?"

"It wasn't on his head. The hood was down. It was gray. I'm sure it was gray. You know, like a workout sweatshirt." She just remembered that, which meant maybe there were other things she would remember. Something important that would bring Julia back.

"Then the van sped away. It made a U-turn in the middle of the street and was gone."

"Did you see the driver?"

JoJo closed her eyes. "It was just a guy. I couldn't really see. A shape behind the wheel, that's it."

"But you know that the person who grabbed your sister wasn't driving the van."

"Yes. It happened too fast. He grabbed her and the door was sliding closed and the car was moving."

"Okay, Josephine...or can I call you JoJo?"

She shrugged. Whatever. She hated to be called Josephine. Julia sometimes did it to piss her off.

"I need you to really think. When the car drove away did you see the license plate?"

Everyone wanted to know that. They kept pushing her over and over again to think about it, visualize what the numbers and letters might have looked like. If she could just remember those numbers, then they could find Julia and everything would be all right.

Only she couldn't.

"Think, JoJo!" her father shouted as he moved between her and the detective. "This is important. You have to think about what you saw and tell them the license. It's her only hope."

She lifted her face to her father. "I can't remember. I didn't see it. I don't think… Maybe it didn't have a front plate. It was fast and I was running to get her."

"That's not good enough!" he roared. "This is your sister's life! Now think!" The blow to the side of her head knocked her off the couch.

"Jonathan!"

"No," he barked at her mother. "She has to do this. You have to do this!"

"Sir, I know what you're going through right now. But this isn't the answer," the detective said, purposefully keeping his voice even and steady.

JoJo lifted herself onto the couch with a ringing in her head. That was the first time her father had ever hit her. It was so weird.

"Tell them the license plate numbers. *Tell them.* If you can't do this, it's your fault what happens to her. Do you hear me?"

Her fault? Of course it was her fault. She'd wanted to go to the movies. She had a crush on Peter. Julia knew it, too. It was probably why she was being slow. She knew it would make JoJo crazy and Julia lived to make JoJo crazy.

It was what twins did.

JoJo closed her eyes and struggled to think about what happened. The sound of the tires screeching. The vague shape of the body behind the wheel. The back of the van moving away from her as she screamed and screamed and ran so hard after them.

She couldn't remember one stupid letter of the license plate. She didn't think she even looked at it.

CHAPTER ONE

MARK SHARPE LOOKED across his desk at the latest job candidate. Her hair was slicked into a tight ponytail, with a straight heavy band of dark hair falling down her back. The nose stud she obviously sported had been removed for the interview. She wore a black turtleneck blouse that looked as if it was strangling the life out of her under her suit jacket.

Occasionally, when she fidgeted with the collar, he could see the hint of ink peeking out.

A nose stud and a neck tattoo. Who knew what else she was hiding?

"I wanted to let you know how impressed I was with your work on the Anderson case," she said.

Josephine Hatcher was the second investigator he'd interviewed. The previous one had wanted to talk about the Anderson case, too. Interviewing 101, he supposed—compliment the boss on his work. Some days, though, that case didn't feel like an accomplishment. It felt like a family ripped to shreds starting with the murder of a daughter by her own father.

"First getting the coroner's ruling of suicide overturned and then learning her father was behind the poisoning had to be shocking. He'd been free for thirteen years until you uncovered the truth."

The other candidate had said almost the same thing. Mark was a genius, a detecting marvel, a hero for justice. Blah, blah, blah...

"It took you a little long, though."

"Excuse me?" The other candidate hadn't said that.

"After you exhumed the body and were able to confirm the girl had been poisoned, the number of suspects was limited to her family and her boyfriend. Few others would have had sufficient access to her over the prolonged period of time it took to her kill her. Once you knew the method, how hard was it to eliminate suspects?"

"Not hard."

Her lips twitched. "Just saying. Can I ask why you opened the case?"

"Anonymous tip."

"Probably someone who knew her, knew the family dynamic."

"Probably," he grumbled. Who the hell was interviewing whom?

"Did you find the source of the tip?"

"No."

"Did you look?"

Yes, but he wasn't about to admit that to her. Anonymous tips were tricky. Sometimes they panned out. Sometimes they didn't. Mark always preferred identifying the source of an anonymous tip as a way of evaluating the reliability of the information. But he hadn't been able to locate the person who had sent him the copy of the coroner's report along with the plainly typed note that simply read, *She didn't do it.*

It had been enough to pique his interest. Especially when he read the report and the police file. Suicide had been a stretch, he thought. When people chose to kill themselves they wanted it done immediately.

This girl had been dying for months.

"That doesn't matter now—the case is closed. So, I should tell you I'm looking for someone with several years' experience." It was a prelude, he thought. A way to cushion the blow he was preparing to deliver.

"I've been working in the field independently for four years, and apprenticed with another investigator two years before that while earning my master's in criminology."

He sighed. He should have figured she would be the type to put up a fight. Couldn't she pick up on all the subtle *no* signs he was throwing out? It wasn't that she wasn't qualified—of course she was qualified or she wouldn't have gotten as far as this interview.

The problem was her. There was something about her that made him want to squirm in his chair. It was completely irrational. He had no idea why he felt this way. But he was a man who relied on his gut. His gut said *no*. His gut said she was trouble.

Mark really hoped that gut feeling wasn't based on the fact that when he looked her in the eyes, he had a suspicion she was smarter than he was. Because that would probably make him an ass.

"I'm targeting a certain type of clientele." Hell, that made him sound like a snob. Now he was a snob and an ass.

"I imagine paying ones."

There was no point in prolonging the inevitable. He'd made his decision almost instantly. The moment he'd shaken her hand and it fit so securely in his. A knee-jerk reaction that told him to run.

"I'm sorry, Ms. Hatcher, but I'm not sure you're the right fit."

He watched her shoulders slump. Only for a second, though, then she straightened. "Can I ask why? You have my résumé. You know I'm more than capable."

It was a ridiculously impressive résumé. A bachelor's in psychology from New York University, and that master's of criminology from Columbia—graduated top of her class in both. She'd worked for a medium-size private investigator firm for the six years since. She was changing jobs only because the firm's owner had decided to retire and she wasn't happy with the new ownership. Her former boss, Tom Reid, happened to know Ben Tyler—Mark's former boss and adversary from their days in the CIA together.

That Tom knew Ben wasn't a surprise. It seemed everybody, at some point in their life, knew Ben Tyler, who headed up the Tyler Group—a small troubleshooting firm located in Philadelphia. Ben employed a few detectives so Reid had forwarded him Josephine's résumé. Ben—recognizing that he had deprived Mark of his assistant, Anna, by knocking her up and marrying her—had sent Josephine's résumé to Mark instead.

On paper, she was exactly what he was looking for. He'd already found someone to replace Anna's duties from an administrative aspect, but his business was gaining a solid reputation and with that came more cases. Trying to make his schedule work with his daughter's was becoming a challenge. Adding a trained, licensed investigator—one recommended by someone Ben trusted—was like a godsend.

But she wasn't going to fit. Her eyes were too blue. A deep color that made him think they could see through anything—probably a great quality in an investigator but not such a great quality in a colleague.

"Can I ask you a question?" It was probably unfair to drag out the interview, especially since he'd decided not to hire her. He was curious and wanted to confirm his suspicions that she was, in fact, trouble.

"I think that's what I'm here for." She half smiled and again fiddled with the cloth around her neck.

"You've got a really impressive résumé. Did you ever consider applying for the FBI?"

"Not really my thing."

"What about your local police force?"

"Also not my thing."

Right. Trouble. Just like he suspected.

"Yet according to your list of special skills, you've spent months at several law enforcement training camps specializing in firearms and hand-to-hand combat. I guess I'm curious why you wanted to train like an agent, but didn't want to be an agent."

He watched her crack her neck as she seemed to search for an answer that was accurate, honest and didn't cost her the job—even though it was already too late.

Almost too late.

"While law enforcement—either as a police officer or a federal agent—is an honorable career path for many, I was concerned that the confines of the hierarchal structure would be too limiting. Especially for someone in the minority sex."

She didn't like authority or sexist pigs.

The sexist pigs he could get behind because she was right. While many of the government investigative agencies from the FBI to NCIS were opening their doors to more women, it was still a man's world.

But it was the authority part of her explanation he had a problem with. Since, if he employed her, he would be the authority she had a problem with.

"Can I see the tattoo?" That was for his curiosity again.

"Excuse me?"

"The tattoo. Can I see it?"

She smirked. "I have a few. In some rather interesting places so you'll have to be more specific."

"Specifically...the one on your neck."

She lifted her eyes to the ceiling, a move that reminded him vividly of his teenage daughter, then she pulled down the collar.

Black ink barbed wire. With spikes. Covering both the right and left sides of her neck. Not completely circling her skin the wires trailed off as they neared her larynx. Still, a signal to the world to back off.

"Yes, I can see where you might struggle within a—how did you phrase it?—a hierarchal structure."

"I'm a good investigator. No, check that. I'm a *great* investigator. I prefer to work on my own, but I never fail to get results. I don't see why a tattoo should be a problem in getting a job."

"Except that you know it is or you wouldn't have covered it up with the turtleneck."

"Some people are more conservative than others."

As a rule, Mark was not. In fact, a couple of months ago he wouldn't have given a rat's ass about a tattoo. But that was before the mother of his estranged daughter died in a car accident. Before he left the CIA to return to the States. Before he started the process of building a relationship with said estranged daughter…

And failed at it miserably.

Now he was trying to do everything right. He wanted the right type of company. The right type of people around his daughter. The right everything.

Nose-stud, barbed-wire-tattoo chick was not it.

He glanced at her résumé again. She'd included a list of high-profile cases she'd worked on. Some very high-profile cases. What had she said? She was a *great* investigator. That was probably true, damn it.

"Why the move to Philadelphia?"

"To get away from New York." She quickly added, "Not that there was anything bad there. Tom's brother Tim is assuming the role of president of the firm. Tim and I don't see eye to eye on a lot of things and we both knew when he took over I wouldn't stay. Tim will never make me a partner. So I figured this might be a good chance to leave the craziness of the city behind. Stop pouring all my money into rent on a studio apartment not much bigger than a closet. I considered Boston, Philadelphia and D.C. but then when Tom brought up Ben Tyler's name... Well, everyone knows his reputation. Even in New York. I came here for him, but he sent me to you. Now you're sending me away because you don't like tattoos. Is that on all people? Or on women in particular?"

Mark gritted his teeth. He would not be backed into a corner on this. "You and I both know you have problems with authority. It's why you chose private investigation and probably why you couldn't work with Tim Reid. He's former FBI as I understand."

"He might be former FBI but he's a current ass." She winced, probably knowing that calling her former boss an ass was not helping her case. "Sorry. I shouldn't have said that. For the record, I didn't have a problem with him, or his authority. He, however, had a problem with me and the fact that I have breasts. He's not a big believer in women in the workforce in general. He's an old-school, barefoot-and-pregnant kind of a guy."

"They still exist?"

"He does. Which is how I knew I would never be partner."

"Is that what you want?" Mark hadn't thought that far ahead. When he came back after Helen's death his objectives had been pretty clear. Find a way to reconnect with Sophie and find a way to make a living out of doing what he did best: gathering information. He hadn't seen much beyond that.

Everything changed so quickly when he realized that it made the most sense to have Sophie live with him. Now she was his first thought every day. Then came the business.

Strange that, despite his priorities, progress on his first objective was, to date, rather abysmal, while his second objective was prospering beyond his imagination. Hence the need for help.

"Yes, I want to be a partner. I want a piece of what I create. Eventually. I'm willing to earn it over time."

"Why not start your own business? Then nobody can tell you what to do."

"That's not practical at this point. I don't have the savings I would need for a proposition like that and, well, health care. It's a bitch. Got to have it in case one of my tattoos gets infected."

See, he thought. She was snarky. Nearly unprofessional. She'd referred to her former boss as an ass, for Pete's sake. She had penetrating deep blue eyes and she was too damn smart. All of that spelled trouble, just like he'd thought.

He was trying to establish something different in his life. Something solid and conservative. Something...that was the opposite of whatever he had been in his former life.

Because being daring to the point of recklessness wasn't something a stable father should be.

"I'm sorry."

She nodded and stood. Then she pulled out a card case from the black purse she carried—a purse he highly suspected saw the light of day only when she was interviewing—and handed a card to him.

"I'm staying downtown at the Marriott for the next few days. I figure I'll take in the city, do the tourist thing before I head to D.C. I have an interview at a firm next week. If you change your mind, you know where to reach me."

Mark had to chuckle. "I turned you down for the job, yet you're letting me know where you're going to be in case I change my mind. That's awfully ballsy."

Josephine—somehow that name didn't fit—shrugged.

"Look at my casework again. Tell me you'll find someone more qualified."

She offered her hand and he took it. Her grip was firm and confident just like it had been at the beginning of the interview. Certainly not the handshake of someone who had been rejected.

She wasn't the right fit for him, but he wasn't going to deny that inwardly he was sorry about that. The woman had guts. Guts, in his opinion, was a necessary ingredient in a successful life.

"*Lucy, I'm home!*" Mark opened the door to his condo in a city-center high-rise and wondered if tonight would be different.

Probably not.

He'd been coming home to his daughter for the past two months and not one night had she greeted him with a smile.

He set down his briefcase, one he'd recently purchased to replace the leather satchel he used to carry. The satchel made him feel like Indiana Jones. The briefcase made him feel like his father. Mark figured that was a good thing. Might make him more fatherly.

Like most Mondays, his daughter wasn't alone. The tutor he'd hired for her a few weeks ago to replace the one who had quit to go on maternity leave was here. Nancy was a nice woman in her early thirties who had proved to be an outstandingly good hiring decision. She showed up when she was supposed to, never lingered when it was time to go. Sophie's grades were being maintained at the highest level and Nancy was fairly cheap, all things considered.

Watching Nancy, wearing plain jeans and a conservative sweater, collect her books to leave made him feel better. He'd definitely made the right choice by hiring her, he thought. Which meant he'd probably made the right choice letting Josephine walk.

"Hi, Mark."

"Nancy, how are you?"

"Oh, I'm fine."

Sophie sat on a stool at the counter that separated the kitchen from the living room. She was reading a textbook and didn't look at him as he approached.

"Hey." He tried a different greeting.

"Hey."

"Did you hear me when I came in?"

"Uh, yeah. Was that supposed to be an *I Love Lucy* reference?"

"Too old?"

"Too lame, Mark."

He hated it when she called him Mark. "You know I would really prefer it if you would call me Dad."

She smiled then, but not the kind of smile he was hoping for. "Hey, I would prefer it if you had actually been a dad."

"Okay, well, I'll be going," Nancy said.

Right. Who wanted to stick around to witness such familial bliss? "Thanks, Nancy."

"See you, Sophie. Don't forget—not a word less than five hundred."

"No problem."

Mark watched Nancy leave and wondered, not for the first time, how he and Sophie must seem to her. Dysfunctional didn't begin to cover it. She probably raced home to…well, no one. He happened to know that she was single and not seeing anyone. It had been part of what he had dug up during the background check on her—that and her Match.com profile.

But no doubt she thought they were a mess. And that was the truth—he and Sophie *were* a mess. Their past—or more accurately, lack of a past—was the river that separated them. It seemed no bridge he could build would ever allow him to cross it. No matter how much he changed his life for her.

Because, in the end, for so many years he'd been nothing more than a name scrawled on the bottom of a card. Certainly not a father.

Despite that, he liked to think he hadn't been a total ass to her mother. When Helen told him she was pregnant he instantly knew he had to do the right thing and offer marriage. Only Helen knew she'd done the wrong thing by deliberately getting pregnant to hold on to a man whose life ambition was the CIA.

He thought he'd done everything right by her. He'd volunteered to refuse the CIA offer and find a more stable career—possibly with another federal agency, or scrap those plans altogether and go to law school. He damn certain had put a ring on her finger.

In the end, Helen had been the one to back away. She must have figured out that no matter how tightly she tried to hold him, he would always be looking over his shoulder wondering what kind of life he could have been living.

When he'd been stationed overseas Mark had liked to tell himself that he remained a part of his daughter's life. He'd sent her cards and presents on her birthday and holidays. He'd occasionally chat with her over the internet if he was in a place that had the capability. But no amount of justification could cover up the truth. Having spent the past fourteen years of his life outside the United States, he was the very definition of an absentee father.

Hell, he hadn't even made it home in time for her mother's funeral.

No wonder Sophie hated him.

But she was stuck with him. Dom and Marie, her grandparents, who had been in the process of selling their home to move into an assisted-living facility when Helen died, had tried to make a go of having Sophie live with them. After a few months it was easy to see that two aging grandparents in questionable health weren't up to handling a fourteen-year-old teenager.

And not just any teen. Sophie was special.

"What do you want to do for dinner?"

"Surprise me, Mark."

There it was again. That hint of sarcasm. His daughter would turn fifteen in a few months but there were times when she sounded like she was double her age. He figured it was expected. The girl was a prodigy. A piano master by age nine who had been touring the country and the world for the past five years with the most highly respected orchestras and conductors. Giving her unique gift to the world, yes. But growing up way too fast for his taste.

He'd seen her act sophisticated and gracious with some very important political and business leaders who came backstage to pay her compliments on her performance.

Mark had also seen her roll her eyes at him like he was the dumbest man imaginable. He was proud of his daughter and the way she handled herself, but he also appreciated the other side, too. It reminded him she was still just a kid.

"Okay, I'll cook."

"I said surprise me, not kill me. The last time you tried to cook it was a disaster."

"It was hot dogs," he said in his defense. "How bad could they have been?"

"They were still cold in the middle and made me gag."

"Whatever." Oh, my. Had he really stooped to responding to his daughter in her own teenage speak?

"Besides I shouldn't eat. I had a big lunch and I have to watch my figure."

The girl was tall and lithe with long straight blond hair. If there was an extra ounce of fat on her body, he didn't see it. However, he had to appreciate that she was a performer who was conscientious about how she looked onstage.

Mark decided to avoid the conversation—always a good thing when it came to women and weight—and instead went to check the mail.

In the months that they had been living together they'd fallen into a routine. He couldn't say it was a comfortable one, since Sophie was too prickly for that. However, Mark thought at least they were settling into some kind of normalcy, which he was convinced was a good thing. After all, she couldn't hate him forever. It simply wasn't practical.

She practiced every morning at a studio where he rented space. From there she usually went to rehearsal with the Philadelphia Orchestra—her current assignment—at the Kimmel Center for a few hours. Nancy came three times a week in the afternoon.

Mark wasn't sure how he felt about Sophie trying to cram what most kids did during a five-day school week into what was essentially nine hours a week. But given his daughter's grades, it wasn't like he could protest. She'd already taken a preliminary SAT test and had scored only two hundred points shy of perfection. No, he wasn't worried about her grades so much as he was the other things kids experienced in high school. Like making friends, going out to parties, getting asked to the prom. The last time he asked her if she missed that kind of stuff she scoffed at him as if all high school activities were beneath her.

Maybe they were for a girl with her mind and talents. Who knew? Mark only knew that he was starting to enjoy their camaraderie even if it was seasoned with sarcasm.

She had chores around the house, although they were simple. She was supposed to keep her room neat, help him with the grocery shopping—that being agreed upon after a totally awkward moment when he'd purchased the wrong brand of feminine products for her—do her laundry and collect the mail.

Mark hired someone to handle the majority of the cleaning, which left him with providing dinner. That mostly entailed taking Sophie out to a restaurant of her choosing or ordering in. If this was to be their life together, then he probably needed to learn how to cook something besides grilled meat and hot dogs.

Walking to the small table in the foyer where Sophie left the mail every day, Mark sorted through what was mostly garbage and stopped at a white envelope that had no addresses—his or a return—or stamps. Just his name. *Sharpe.*

"Hey, was this in the mail?"

Sophie looked at him. "Yeah, whatever was in the box downstairs I put in the dish. You know, like I've done every day for months."

He was going to have to explain to her that not every statement she made to him needed to be followed by a rolling of the eyes. The girl was going to give herself an eye condition.

Mark opened the envelope with suspicion. Maybe it was from a neighbor. He hadn't really taken the time to meet any of them, being too busy keeping up with Sophie and the business, but that didn't mean he didn't have them. Maybe they didn't like Sophie playing her electric keyboard too late at night.

There was only a single sheet of plain white paper inside. He pulled it out and saw the neatly typed sentence centered on the page.

You're going to lose her.

The instant reaction in his gut was stunning and more

powerful than anything he'd ever felt before. He lifted his eyes to his daughter, who had already dismissed him, and he thought, *The hell I am.*

This, he realized, was what it felt like to be a father.

And he kind of thought it sucked.

CHAPTER TWO

"YOU'RE SURE SOPHIE didn't do it?" Ben lifted the note in the air, looking to see if there was any imprint in the paper. Some identifying mark.

Of course Mark had already checked for that. But he hoped Ben's trained eye might pick up something he had missed. Despite the fact that Ben had been a longtime rival, Mark also knew he was the best. The truth was, after Ben resigned from the CIA, Mark had lost much of his love for the job. He'd already been making plans to leave the agency when the death of Sophie's mother sped everything up.

Ben had been his benchmark: the agent Mark intended to be someday. The man he would best someday. To set himself apart from the others, Mark had done a lot of risky stuff. One stunt nearly cost Ben and him their lives. As a result, until recently they had never exactly been friends.

Now that they were both in the States and trying to live normal civilian lives, they had forged a bond that in the past few months had strengthened into friendship. Strange, considering how they'd started. Stranger still after Mark hired Ben's assistant out from under him.

Yes, Mark had even harbored the notion of trying to steal Ben's woman—for no other reason than to resume the rivalry that got his blood pumping. But Anna was in love with Ben and had already been carrying his baby when Mark hired her.

Ben had done the smart thing by tying Anna to him

with vows and a ring. She was too easy for anyone to like. Smart, pretty, funny. Easy to be around.

For a moment Mark flashed on his interview from the day before. What was her name…Josephine? Yeah, she did not look like someone who would be easy to be around. But he had to remind himself of that because he'd been having second thoughts about letting Josephine go. Or maybe rethinking his reasons for letting her go.

Immediately, Mark shook it off. He didn't have regrets. Regrets were a waste of time.

The only thing that mattered now was the note. While Sophie played with Ben and Anna's baby—the one area of common ground Sophie and Mark shared was taking pure enjoyment out of Kelly—Mark was free to pick Ben's brain about the note.

"She said she didn't do it," Mark answered.

Ben lifted an eyebrow.

"Yes, I believe her. She's moody. She's petulant. She's constantly pissed at me. But as she told me when I asked, she's not a nut-job. If she wanted to scare me, she could find other ways to do so."

"You're sure the threat relates to her?"

"Who else could it be? Sophie's the only *she* in my life."

"What about the grandparents? Maybe it's a subtle warning that if you don't work harder to improve the relationship, you'll lose her."

Mark shook his head. "Not their style. Dom sternly lecturing me about what I'm doing wrong—yes, that is their style. They're too vocal about their disappointment in me as a father to do this."

Ben scowled. "Then we need to think of other possibilities."

That was the problem. Mark didn't want to think of other possibilities. Other possibilities potentially meant old enemies who were now in the U.S. and watching him. Threatening his daughter.

You're going to lose her.

Mark could think of a lot of Taliban leaders who would love nothing more than to cut open his chest and rip his heart out. But even if any of them were in the country, any note they left would include explicit details about their intentions for her. It didn't make sense. The government saw to it that the Taliban couldn't enter the country. Besides, now that Mark was no longer a player in the game, why would they want to hurt him? They had their hands filled with active U.S. military and paramilitary agents. He had no information that wasn't almost a year old. Information that old was useless.

Mark thought of assets he'd turned during his years on the job who might have gotten turned back. But they, too, were all overseas. There were the cases he'd solved in the year since he'd opened his business. People he'd put in jail—some fairly high-profile.

A criminal Mark had brought to justice for a scam-artist ring he'd run for years. A missing girl he'd found dead. The Anderson case. Except that Jack Anderson was dead by his own hand before he ever saw the inside of a jail cell.

With the sound of women's voices approaching, Ben turned. "There are my girls."

"Sophie is hired," Anna said. "She just changed her first poopy diaper and she didn't even flinch."

The girl sat on the couch with the baby in her arms. "I'm not going to lie. It was gross."

"I don't know that Sophie needs extra babysitting money. She's doing pretty well with her music."

Pretty good meant that any college in the country she wanted to go to was already paid for. He knew her plans included Stanford, Stanford and Stanford. In other words, the school farthest from him.

"I wouldn't charge them. I would do it because I like Kelly. You're so coarse, Mark."

Another mistake. He thought he was making an offhand joke. She thought he was an asshole. Typical.

"Can I hold her?" Mark asked. At least while holding the baby he could pretend that a child actually liked him.

Reluctantly, Sophie handed Kelly over and he cradled the nearly five-month-old in the crook of his elbow. She'd been almost a month early and to Mark she still looked impossibly small, but the doctors had all declared her perfectly healthy. Kelly seemed to be deciding whether to cry or coo so Mark helped that decision along by bouncing her gently. The cooing continued and he watched as she broke out into a large, wide smile.

So little. So precious. Mark remembered holding Sophie when she was even younger. He remembered it, because it was the last time he saw her before he left for Langley. The next time he'd seen her she'd been five years old.

Closing his eyes, he brought the baby close and smelled how fresh and lovely she was. How had he been able to leave Sophie as a baby? When he felt as possessive as a Neanderthal with her now. Now when she hated him rather than adored him as she had when she'd rested in his arms.

"Please," Sophie said. "Don't even pretend you're all about Kelly. We know what you think of babies, Mark."

Mark didn't respond to his daughter's jab. He was starting to become immune to them. Anna walked over with a sympathetic smile and took her daughter from him. "Time and patience," she whispered.

He smiled back. "Look, we should be going. My daughter probably has some more nasty things to say to me and I would rather we not subject the baby to it. It could corrupt her subconsciously. Ben, you'll continue thinking about our problem."

"I'm on it. But it might not hurt to have extra help. You should show it to JoJo."

"Who?"

"JoJo. The detective I sent to you. You said you were going to interview her. I'm assuming you hired her, so have her look into the matter. According to Tom, she's one of the best he's ever worked with."

Mark frowned. "I didn't hire her."

"Why not?"

His doubt surfaced as he once more tried to put his finger on his problem with her. "She wasn't what I was looking for. I was hoping for someone more conservative. I'm trying to create a serious agency with serious agents."

"Yes. I know. She has serious talent. It's why I let you have first crack at her."

Mark struggled with how to identify his specific issue with her. "She's got tattoos."

"You have a tattoo."

"You do?" Sophie stood with her arms folded.

Mark scowled at Ben. "It's since been removed."

"You should reconsider. Because if you're not hiring her, then I will. She's too good to let go. I figured I was repaying you for stealing Anna away."

"You didn't steal me away," Anna countered. "I chose not to go back to work because of Kelly. You two can be so full of it."

Ben waited until Anna was distracted with the baby to give Mark a small nod that said he still thought he was right about JoJo.

"I don't know if she's still in the area. She said she was sticking around for a few days before heading to D.C. for another interview, but who knows."

"Then you better act fast. The next person who sees her résumé won't be so foolish as to let her go because of a couple of tattoos."

"They're on her neck." Mark winced as he tried to imagine why a young woman might do that to herself. It had to hurt like hell.

"Totally cool," Sophie muttered.

"Don't even think about," Mark warned. "Okay. Let's make a stop on the way home."

JoJo LOOKED AT the movie list and considered what would kill time better—an engrossing thriller or some eye candy in the form of Ryan Gosling. In truth, neither was very appealing. Pounding her hand on the mattress, she considered what her next move would be.

She'd been so damn sure she would get the job with Sharpe. In her mind she had already adopted Philadelphia as her new home. She'd had a Geno's cheesesteak. What was that if not commitment?

Now she really would have to follow up on opportunities in other cities. She had exaggerated slightly when she told Sharpe he was one interview in a long line of them.

Okay, so it was a total lie. She hadn't contacted any of the other agencies she had researched because she didn't think she had to. Tom knew Ben Tyler and Ben Tyler was a man with significant influence. Since he had recommended JoJo to Mark, it should have been a lock.

Apparently not for Mark. Because he'd seen the tattoos.

JoJo got up from the bed and walked to the mirror. She'd removed the ponytail hair extension and her jet-black hair was again short and spiky. She had dyed it black a long time ago, and it brought out her blue eyes better than her natural blond. She kept it short to accent her smallish face and because it was easier to care for and to cover with a wig when she was in disguise.

Did she look a little too badass? Yes. There were times when that was an asset. Sometimes having an edge helped when she was interrogating a criminal or interviewing a witness.

But other times badass tattoos cost you a job. Two, if she counted Tim Reid's reaction to her. He never liked her, despite the quality of her work. While she blamed it on his sexism, it probably also had something to do with how she defied the conventionalities to which he adhered.

Tim had a lot in common with her father. When it was announced Tim was taking over the agency, she knew she could not work for him. They would drive each other crazy.

So where to next?

The phone rang, which startled her. There weren't a lot of people who knew she was even in Philadelphia. It was probably one of those stupid surveys about the hotel service, and she answered it out of sheer boredom. "Hello?"

"Oh, good. I caught you. Ms. Hatcher, this is Mark Sharpe."

JoJo pumped her fist in the air. Then calmly answered, "Yes, can I help you?"

"I'm downstairs in the lobby. I've had second thoughts and was wondering if I could talk to you again."

"Sure. Uh…" JoJo considered her appearance. She could change out of the jeans and sweater and into something more appropriate, but it would take her at least ten minutes to redo the hair extension. Oh, hell, it wasn't like the disguise worked anyway—he hadn't bought her conformist costume for one second. If they were going to work together, she would have to show her true self eventually. It might as well be now.

She even left the nose stud in.

MARK WATCHED THE elevators for Josephine Hatcher. When he spotted a woman with short dark hair walking toward him, he did a double take.

He would never have thought she was the same woman who had been in his office if it weren't for the tattoos around her neck. The way her hair stuck up from her head at different angles should have made her look like she'd just woken up. Instead it made her look chic and hip. She wore skinny jeans with knee-high black boots and a bulky sweater that moved with her body. Ms. Hatcher was efficiency in motion, with an edge.

She stopped in front of him and held her arms up, clearly communicating that this was the woman beneath the conservative turtleneck. The woman he would get if he hired her.

Everything in Mark recoiled. Not that she wasn't attractive in a certain sort of way, but she was so not what he needed in his life right now. Yesterday, he'd thought she was trouble. Now he knew she was more than that. She was dangerous. He could imagine what kind of example she might set for Sophie—who was already staring at the woman with awed admiration.

"Mr. Sharpe, you wanted to talk?"

Now what was he supposed to do? His gut and his brain were at war. This never happened. What was crazier was that his gut and head seemed to be taking opposite sides from what they ought to. His head should have told him that this woman was not employable and his gut should have said to take a chance on her. Instead his head was remembering her résumé, line by line, and his gut was churning with…something.

Ben said this woman was the best. Seriously?

"Uh…sorry to drop by like this unannounced, but I had second thoughts and didn't want to miss you."

"I'm glad you stopped by. Who is your sidekick? She looks a little young to be head of the HR department."

"This is my daughter, Sophie. Sophie this is Josephine Hatcher."

"JoJo," she corrected.

Sophie gave him that look of hers. "Why do you have to introduce me as your daughter? Why can't you just say I'm Sophie?"

"Well, most people like context and the crazy thing is, you are, in fact, my daughter."

"Whatever, Mark."

It was her third *whatever* of the day. He was starting to loathe the word.

He looked at JoJo—what a silly name. "As you can tell, my daughter and I have a very loving and close relationship. It's why we're here together today. She can't stand being apart from me."

Sophie sat in one of the lobby chairs and said nothing. Mark sat on a couch and gestured to a chair across from it, indicating that JoJo should sit, as well.

He didn't have a clue what he was supposed to ask, now that, once again, he was firmly against the idea of this woman working for him. She simply wasn't going to fit in his world. His old one, yes. No question she would have fit. Hell, in his old life he would have been champing at the bit to get to know the woman behind the tattoos.

But in his new world, he couldn't allow himself to cater to personal whims.

"You don't quite look like the candidate you presented yourself to be." Perfect. He could back out under the pretense that she'd misrepresented herself. Covering up her hair length…who did that?

"Sometimes people don't look past the surface. So I didn't dress to be obvious."

"*Obvious* is one word for it."

"Mark," Sophie snapped. "How uncool. Just because she doesn't look like everyone else that's somehow wrong?"

Oh, yeah. The joys of fatherhood just kept on coming. "Do you mind, Sophie? I'm conducting an interview."

"You're being a total square."

"Seriously? People still say *square*?"

"No." She smirked. "People say douche bag but I thought that was crossing a line."

"It did," he snarled.

"Uh, excuse me?" JoJo waved her hand. "My interview, remember?"

"You do understand," Mark said, "in this line of work blending in matters. Not standing out." He waved his hand to indicate her whole being as one big standout. "No offense, but you don't exactly blend."

"Is that the only thing preventing me from getting this job? You're concerned about how the way I look would affect my work?"

Not really. But what was he supposed to say? That her unapologetic style bothered him? That he felt uncomfortable merely sitting across from her? That his discomfort wouldn't be conducive to a solid working relationship? That her eyes were really, really blue?

She would be the only other investigator working for him, and he imagined them spending a lot of time consulting with one another on their cases. Something akin to a partnership. Then there was the idea of having her look into the note. That meant actually trusting this woman.

He couldn't explain all that. Instead he kept it simple. "I guess it is. I've spoken with Ben and he says I would be crazy to let you pass by. In fact, he's waiting in the wings to scoop you up if I do."

Another fact that rankled him. If he didn't hire her and

she worked for Ben, he might run into her at Ben's office. How irritating would it be to find her solving cases for Ben while he was left with someone less talented?

No doubt Ben would lord it over him.

"Okay," JoJo said, "we'll make it a challenge. I bet I can leave and, within half an hour, be in your line of sight without you realizing it's me."

"That's totally awesome. Mark, you have to let her do it."

Mark gave his daughter a wry smile. Maybe he could impress her at last. "JoJo, you do realize I was a CIA black-ops analyst in the field for years."

Sophie rolled her eyes. "And years and years…"

Okay, maybe not.

"Observation is what I do. It's how I survived. You can't get past me. Especially not with the tattoos."

JoJo held out her hand. "It's a bet then. I do this, I get the job. You win, you get to show off your observation skills to your daughter. The only thing you're out is a half hour of your time."

"We were going to go eat—"

"Are you kidding me?" Sophie said. "I'm not leaving. I want to see this."

JoJo winked at Sophie and his daughter smiled. Great, he thought. She'd known this woman for minutes and they had bonded more than he had with his daughter in months.

He did need another agent. Especially if the threat against Sophie was real. JoJo's résumé did speak for it-self.…

Not that he was worried about losing, but he conceded that, if she pulled off the impossible, it wouldn't be the worst thing from a professional standpoint.

Personal, maybe, but he could get over that. He *would* get over that.

He looked at his watch and pressed the timer.

"You have thirty minutes. You must be in my line of sight. If I identify you, I win. If I don't, you're hired. Go."

She didn't run. She didn't leave through the front door, which was what he would have done. Much better to be someone coming in that way, then coming down the elevator where he could concentrate his attention.

Instead, she sauntered to the elevators in that same efficient, but also aggressive, walk of hers. A walk that said, *Get out of my way, I'm coming through.* She stepped through the door and Mark leaned back to wait.

Thirty minutes. He wished he had a magazine to help kill the time.

CHAPTER THREE

MARK CHECKED HIS WATCH. Twenty-three minutes had passed. He watched the elevators for activity then swung his attention to the front entrance. A man and woman walked in, but a quick assessment told him the woman was well over fifty. Not that makeup couldn't do wonders, but JoJo wouldn't have had enough time to put together a costume like that.

He turned to the elevators and spied a family getting out. A mother, a father and a teenage boy who was dressed from head to toe in black and carried a skateboard over his shoulder.

At least he looked like a boy. Mark kept his attention on the kid, searching for tells. There was a tattoo on his arm, but nothing around his neck. Was that sparkle on his face a nose ring? He heard Sophie gasp—clearly she was wondering the same thing.

Had JoJo, a small woman, turned herself into an average-sized teenage boy?

The front door opened again and a single woman walked in. Tall, blond, pretty, wearing a shockingly red coat over a short skirt and high heels. Mark assessed her quickly, and decided anyone trying to blend in wouldn't wear such an eye-catching color, nor something so provocative as the short skirt. It would naturally draw the attention of any man in the vicinity. It, in fact, drew his. Her legs were fabulous.

Still, there was something about the way she moved.

Mark's gaze followed her to the desk, where she asked to use a phone. She tucked her hair behind her ear as she held the receiver to her ear. Mark could not see tattoos on her neck.

"Twenty-eight minutes," Sophie announced.

Mark stood to scope out hiding spots around the lobby where she could claim to be in his line of sight, but actually be hidden from view. The people working behind the desk hadn't changed, so she hadn't sneaked in that way. The family stood together, using the lobby computer. The boy had his back to Mark, so he couldn't check for blue eyes. Instead Mark studied the shape of his back, his height.

Close. Definitely close to JoJo's height. Had she paid the two people to pose as parents?

"Twenty-nine minutes. She's so going to win."

Mark shot Sophie a glance and started toward the kid. A motion in his periphery caught his attention. The woman on the phone had lifted a leg up behind her. He followed that beautiful leg to her shoes.

Not just high heels. Platform high heels. They raised her height by at least two inches.

Gotcha.

"Time is up. Who is she?"

Mark looked at his daughter. "Do you know?"

"I have my suspicions." Her smile was smug.

Smiling. Sophie was smiling. Mark looked at the blonde again. She had turned and he briefly caught her eye, but she bent her head and continued talking into the phone.

"You think that's her?" Mark pointed toward the kid.

Sophie's face fell a little. She obviously thought JoJo was the boy, and that he had won. He wasn't sure if Sophie was displeased that he had won or that JoJo had lost.

It had been a very short time for two people to make

such a positive connection. There were worse things than his daughter liking someone Mark employed.

He was throwing the contest, but in all of the time he had spent with Sophie, this was the most fun they had ever had. Deliberately, he went over and tapped the kid on the shoulder. The boy turned around, his Adam's apple clearly visible. "What?"

"Oh, sorry," Mark said. "I mistook you for someone else."

"Whatever."

Ah, yes, Mark's favorite word. The kid turned around and Mark could see the father shoot him a look, but Mark simply folded his arms over his chest and waited.

The blonde made her way to him sporting a victorious smile.

"Oh, my God, I totally did not guess that was you," Sophie said hopping up and down on her toes with excitement. "How did you hide the tattoos?"

"A trick I learned from Hollywood actresses." JoJo tilted her neck and peeled off a thin layer of beige tape. "They use this stuff when they're filming."

Effective, at least from a distance. Up close, Mark could see the faint outline of the tape on the other side of her neck. That was probably why she hadn't used the adhesive during her interview.

"Not bad. Hiding in plain sight. It worked."

"Did it?" JoJo asked. Their eyes met. She clearly knew she'd been caught. She wasn't counting on Mark throwing the contest.

Sophie looked at him. "Yes, totally. You won the job. Right, Mark? I mean, you're not going to back off the bet now?"

"Nope." He put his hands into his pockets. "You won fair and square. Since today is Tuesday, you can take a few days to get settled. Be at the office at eight o'clock sharp next Monday and we'll work out salary and what your billing rate will be."

JoJo held out her hand and Mark shook it. Odd for such a small hand to pack such a firm grip. She was a study in contrasts.

"Sophie, why don't you check the computer for restaurants. Find some place you want to eat."

"Okay. You should invite JoJo. It can be like a celebration dinner for beating you."

Sophie left him in a ridiculously awkward situation. He didn't particularly want to have dinner with JoJo. He would need the next few days to come to grips with the fact that he was now working with her. Maybe dinner would help with that. Maybe he would find himself less uncomfortable after breaking bread together.

"Would you like to join us? Not sure what Sophie will pick, her tastes are rather eclectic. It could be burgers, it could be sushi or it could be Thai food."

"Why did you let me win?"

Mark feigned confusion.

"You caught my eye, let me know you knew it was me. Then you tapped the kid on the shoulder. Why?"

"I guess I decided I wanted to hire you after all. Besides, it was a good costume. It *almost* had me fooled."

"You looked at my legs," she said. Not judgmentally, but merely as a statement of fact.

"That was the intention, wasn't it? For me to look at them and not at you."

"Yes. I want to make sure you're not going to have an issue working with me. Maybe the problem isn't the tattoos. Maybe the problem is I'm a woman."

Mark laughed. "Trust me. That's not the problem. I've worked with plenty of women in my career. Operatives and soldiers. I have nothing but respect for people who do their job and do it well, regardless of their gender."

"Okay." JoJo nodded slowly. As if reaching some conclusion about him.

"And if you're worried about me being attracted to you, I can promise you that *won't* be an issue."

"Okay…" she drawled.

He realized he'd basically said she was unattractive. At least unattractive to him. What phrase had Sophie used? *Douche bag?* It seemed appropriate here.

"Look, I didn't mean it like that. You're a very attractive woman. I just… For me…"

"I get it."

"Your legs were really distracting—"

"Mark, put a sock in it. This is actually a good thing. You're not into me and I would never find someone like you attractive, either. So we're cool. Business colleagues and that's it."

"That's it," Mark agreed. Although why the idea that she would never find someone like him attractive suddenly bothered him, he couldn't say.

SOPHIE HAD GONE with Mexican. The restaurant was a small place off Market Street. Not a lot of ambiance but the waiter brought out a big basket of hot chips and spicy salsa. Combined with a margarita and JoJo had all a girl needed to be happy in life.

For a second she considered passing on the drink. Not exactly a good image, to be drinking in front of the boss shortly after being hired, but she had concluded she was done playing games for this guy. She was hired. She wasn't working a case. She would have a drink and not put on any more pretenses.

She'd gone to her room to ditch the wig and the tape, but

she kept her outfit on because that was part of her, too. The vibrant red coat hung on a hook at the corner of the booth.

Neither Mark nor Sophie could refrain from checking out her tattoos every once in a while.

JoJo couldn't pretend it bothered her. After all, she'd gotten the tattoos for a very specific purpose—just like she did most things in her life. So to complain when people stared seemed hypocritical.

She also knew that with her tattoos she was writing off nice guys like Mark Sharpe, who would never be attracted to her. Solid businessman, clean-cut. Probably a conservative who wore boxers. Yes, he was definitely not her type.

Still, as she looked at him with his neatly trimmed dark hair, his barely there scruff along his chin and his dark sweater that highlighted broad shoulders, she got the impression he wasn't quite the conformist he portrayed.

Then there were his eyes. To say they were brown didn't describe them at all. They reminded her of a bird's eyes. Sharp and calculating. Assessing her like she was nothing more than a squirrel he would hunt for sport rather than food.

There was no escaping those eyes now that they were focused on her. They were like her tattoos. Badass. When he'd looked at her in the lobby and she knew she'd been made, she'd felt like prey being given a reprieve. She wouldn't be so lucky next time.

JoJo made a mental note that there wouldn't be a next time. As a rule, she wasn't intimidated by men. The experience she had with her father after her sister had died made intimidation impossible. She never feared men because she knew she could survive anything.

Mark was different, somehow. He threatened her in a way she couldn't define.

Unfortunately that threat didn't mean he wasn't someone

she might be attracted to. If anything, it contributed to the possibility. Telling him he wasn't her type had been a flat-out lie. Done out of pride because he was so completely not into her. Also because she wanted to affirm there was no way she would ever be attracted to someone she worked for.

Which was a crock. A woman couldn't control who she was attracted to. She only controlled what she did with that attraction.

She had been lucky that it was never a concern in her prior job. Even if there had been someone, she never would have crossed the line. It was hard to earn respect from your peers if they thought they could take you to bed. A perfectly logical reason to avoid interoffice dating.

Of course she'd also never had a relationship with any of the men from her last firm because she was completely and totally messed up emotionally. Every once in a while she forgot that.

"So," JoJo said, dipping a chip into the salsa. "What's your deal?" She looked at both Sophie and Mark. It was a nosy question, but she was a detective. She lived to be nosy.

Mark didn't say anything, but Sophie looked at him, clearly waiting for him to say something first. Mark just shifted in the booth and reached for a chip.

"No deal."

"Okay." JoJo was prepared to let it go, but she could hear Sophie huff.

"Uh, please. She wants to know why I call you Mark. And why we're together."

"You call me Mark to annoy me."

"My mom is dead."

JoJo heard the flat note in the girl's voice. It was as if she practiced saying it over and over again in the mirror so that when she had to say it out loud, to real people, she wouldn't crack.

JoJo was sure her own voice had the same tone when she told people her sister was dead.

"I'm sorry."

"Whatever. It was an accident that happened months ago. Actually…it's over a year now. I forgot." Sophie frowned but quickly shook away whatever bad stuff was floating through her head. "Anyway, it doesn't matter. Mark left me when I was a baby to save the world in Afghanistan and when my mom died he had to come back. I wanted to stay with my grandparents, but they're too old to keep up with me so I'm stuck with Mark."

Mark clenched his jaw and JoJo watched the muscle in his cheek spasm. "That's about eighty percent accurate."

"What part is wrong?" Sophie asked, having clearly told her story as truthfully as possible.

"You say I left you like I dropped you on the side of the road. Your mother and I reached a decision. Also, I would like to add that I have been in touch with you throughout your life."

Sophie turned to JoJo. "Sorry. He sent me cards and gifts for my birthday and Christmas. When he wasn't hiding under a rock somewhere, we would talk over the internet. Really intense conversations, too, like, 'What grade are you in now?' Mostly I saw a grainy picture of a guy with a scarf over his face. Half the time I didn't even recognize him. So emotional."

"It's sandy and windy in the Stans. Scarves are a necessary accessory for, you know, breathing."

"What—"

"—ever," Mark finished. "Yes. But you should also know I didn't come back *because* your mother died. I was coming back regardless. Your mother's death only sped up the process."

Sophie said nothing, but shook her head to show she

didn't believe it. Then she lifted her hand to her mouth and nibbled on a fingernail.

"You're not supposed to do that," Mark said.

Instantly her hand dropped and she reached for the chips.

"That's the other thing about Sophie," Mark said. "She's a child prodigy. A piano player who has toured the country and Europe performing with various orchestras. Right now she's under contract with the Philadelphia Orchestra."

"I'm almost fifteen now. We can lose the *child-prodigy* tag. Just say I play the piano."

"I would like to hear you sometime," JoJo said.

"I can get you tickets."

"Cool."

JoJo looked again at Mark. He sat back in the booth defensively, looking like he wanted to escape, but he didn't move. JoJo knew what it was like to have a broken relationship with her father. The difference between Mark and her dad was that Mark cared about what Sophie thought of him. He cared that she felt abandoned. And his expression showed that he also felt guilty.

That was something JoJo's father had *never* felt. Still didn't.

Mark excused himself to go to the restroom. "If the waiter comes—"

"You want a beef burrito," Sophie said. "Like that's news."

Mark paused and a small smile lit up his face. "You know how tempted I am to say I want fajitas?"

"Cutting off your nose to spite your face. You know you want the burrito."

His smile only grew larger. "You're right. I do."

JoJo watched him walk away and tried not to notice how nicely his jeans fit over a firm ass. Nice shoulders, nice ass. Oh, my. When was the last time she'd taken in a man's appearance like that? And of all men, it had to be her new boss?

When she looked at Sophie, the girl was biting her fingernails again. As soon as she noticed JoJo's eyes on her, Sophie dropped her hands into her lap.

"Why aren't you supposed to bite your nails?"

Sophie wiggled her fingers. "Don't want anything messing with the tools. A hangnail or infection could be death for an artist like me."

JoJo heard the sarcasm that was obviously a big part of who Sophie was. But it also let JoJo know the girl didn't take herself too seriously. Which was probably a good thing in someone so talented.

"I really am sorry about your mom. I'm not just saying it."

There was a shimmer in the girl's eyes that she would hate to know was there. A small crack. Instantly JoJo felt contrite for making the girl crack in front of company. As a concession she offered her own pain. "I lost my sister. When I was young."

"I'm sorry, too."

"It blows."

Sophie nodded. "It's like…I get up every day and I do the stuff I am supposed to do. Like nothing happened. Only everything happened."

"You feel guilty."

"Yeah. Like I should be in my room crying every day. And some days that's all I want to do, but I don't. I go to practice, I go to rehearsal. I get ready to perform. It's like this horrible thing didn't happen. Only it did. I forgot it was more than a year ago."

This was where JoJo was supposed to offer up some nice words. *You'll work through it. It will get better.* It was the least she could do.

"It will get better." JoJo choked out the words.

"Will it?"

"No," JoJo admitted truthfully. The girl was too smart and would see through any fabrication. When you removed the bullshit there was only the truth. "No, it doesn't get better. It just gets less worse."

Sophie took a chip from the basket. "She died in a car accident. The guy wasn't even drunk. It was just some stupid car accident."

"My sister was murdered. She was my twin and she was murdered."

JoJo had belched up the words—they never came out freely. But she'd played a game with a master spy and had won. Sort of. And she had gulped down a really good margarita on a stomach that was empty except for a few chips.

It felt like Sophie got it. They both knew the same pain. It was different when people died when they were supposed to because of old age or after a long illness. When they died young, the pain was sharper because it happened so abruptly. Sophie's pain was fresher, but JoJo's was no less intense.

"Murder. Oh, my God, that, like, totally sucks. I'm really sorry. Is that why you became a detective?"

"It's why I became…everything."

MARK OPENED THE door to his apartment and let Sophie pass by him.

"I was thinking of watching a movie. You up for it?"

"I'm going to read. I have work to do for Nancy that I'd rather get out of the way tonight."

She'd rather do homework than watch a movie with him. Ouch.

Still, he wasn't going to complain. Today, by far, had been their best day together. She'd been almost happy while playing with baby Kelly. She'd agreed to go with him to meet JoJo. And he knew she liked JoJo.

To quote Sophie on their ride to their apartment, JoJo was cool.

The best news of all was that she knew he preferred beef burritos. It meant they were getting to know each other. Maybe reluctantly on her part, but it was happening.

"Yeah, sure. If you're interested, maybe we could take in the new superhero movie that's coming out this weekend."

She halted. "You're into superheroes?"

"Honey, I *was* a superhero."

She rolled her eyes, but at least he got her to smile. "Yeah, sure. Okay. What—"

"Please. I beg of you. No more *whatevers*. Not tonight."

"Lame. First one up makes breakfast."

"Deal," he said, even though he knew it was a trap. Sophie had mastered the art of staying in bed until he was awake, so he would be stuck with breakfast duty. One time he tried to outwait her and ended up lying in bed staring at the ceiling until almost ten in the morning. While dinner was his responsibility, they both agreed breakfast and lunch were a free-for-all. During the week they stuck to toast or cereal.

On Saturdays he went the extra mile. They both liked egg, pork roll—a Pennsylvania tradition she'd introduced him to—and cheese on a bagel. Saturdays were quickly becoming his favorite day of the week. On Sundays they visited Dom and Marie, and while he didn't mind visiting them, he definitely liked it better when it was just him and Sophie.

It was becoming their thing. Despite her hostility, her snark factor and even her stubborn refusal to relent and fully forgive him, he was coming to like her. Loving her was automatic. But now he liked her.

He had to get her to like him in the same way. Forgoing the movie, he grabbed a beer and made his way to his bedroom, where he kept his personal computer to prevent any snooping from his daughter. Not that she would be able to get through his security, but its location added one more level of protection.

Sitting at his desk, he turned on the computer and accessed the site that would provide him with the most comprehensive information on JoJo Hatcher. A site that went beyond basic fact-checking, that some considered not completely legal.

But he wasn't messing around. The woman was now officially working for him. If he was going to ask her to help him track down whoever sent that note, he had to know everything about her. Not a single piece of information was insignificant. It was time to know exactly who he was dealing with.

CHAPTER FOUR

THIS WAS THE start of a battle. A prelude to the fight. This was a time for her to lead her people forward into the unknown. They would give their lives for her. They would sacrifice all. Where she played they would follow. With wisdom and knowledge and no fear...

"Sophie! Sophie, halt!"

The words finally penetrated and Sophie looked up from her piano, the story she'd been telling with her fingers suddenly gone.

"Yes, Maestro?" She looked up at the short, plump man standing on the raised platform with the baton in his hand. Igor Romnasky, the legendary composer and conductor from Moscow, had been chosen to direct this performance of Grieg's "Op. 16 in A minor." He claimed he'd accepted the opportunity to work with Sophie. Or so she'd been told. Instead of listening to her play however, all he ever seemed to want to do was stop her.

"You are out of pace with the orchestra, yes?"

It always sounded like a question when he said it, but it never was.

Sophie nodded, but thought that if anyone was off the pace, it was the orchestra. He should be keeping them in time with her, not the other way. It wasn't arrogance, it was the way the music had been written. The piano was king. Or in her case, queen.

"Again, yes?"

They had already been at it for three hours without a break. Her fingers were starting to get numb.

Sophie, too fast, yes? Sophie, too slow, yes? Sophie, too hard, yes?

No. Sophie was ready to take the bald man's baton and shove it up his—

"How about a short break? It's been a couple of hours. I think we all could use it."

This from the principal violinist. Sophie looked at Bay and smiled. He gave her a wink and she really hoped it didn't make her blush too horribly. She knew it made her heart race, which of course caused her palms to get sweaty. Which was gross when you were trying to play.

The maestro seemed to consider the young man with the big talent and finally relented.

"Fifteen minutes. No more, yes? Our first performance is next Friday."

Sophie pushed out her bench and stood. She hadn't realized how stooped over the keys she'd been and she nearly groaned when she stretched her back.

"You weren't off the pace."

Sophie smiled as she heard the quiet words in her ear. Turning, she smiled into Bay Tong's beautiful face. He was Korean on his father's side and Caucasian on his mother's, and so completely the most gorgeous person she'd ever met. She didn't think it was possible that someone like him would ever pay attention to her, but he did and it thrilled her every time he spoke to her.

Once a child prodigy himself, she got the feeling he tried to shelter her in ways that maybe he hadn't been. But at age eighteen he was no longer identified as special. Merely incredibly talented. Certainly talented enough to win the first chair position in the Philadelphia Orchestra.

If only he would see her as more than a kid.

Of course, it was totally understandable when she was fourteen and had first met him. But now she was nearly fifteen and they were going to be only three years apart in age. Which was practically nothing, given her level of maturity. If she really wanted to, she could test out of high school. Then she wouldn't even be considered a student.

"His hearing needs to be checked," he added.

"I know. I think he gets off on bossing me around. Whatever. I've dealt with conductors like him. They all think *they* will be the one to make me do something I've never been able to do before. It's all about their ego. All I want to do is play."

"Yes, but you can learn from them. Sometimes I know it's hard to think that way when they're yelling at you. You have to take the one piece of instruction or advice that works for you and throw the rest away."

"I spent three years at Juilliard. I know how to take instruction."

"That's different. They are trying to improve your technique. These guys care about something more. They want to pull a performance out of you and they can be ruthless in doing so. Sometimes even mean. That stuff can get to you after a while."

Sophie shrugged and lifted a shoulder. "I know."

"Just don't let him get you down."

"Protecting me again?"

He laughed softly. "Why do I think you're the type who would say you don't need anyone's protection?"

That made her beam. Because she was exactly that type of person, which meant they were getting to know each other. They had been working together since January and now, as April approached, she was starting to think that maybe things could change between them. If only he saw her differently. Her birthday was May 15 and once it came, she was sure he would look at her with new eyes.

Today she'd intentionally worn tight skinny jeans and a top that was cut low enough to reveal the tops of her breasts. She'd spent thirty-six of her fifty-dollar-a-week allowance on a push-up bra from Victoria's Secret. After weeks of owning it, she had finally worked up the courage to wear it.

Only he hadn't ogled her chest once.

"It better not be because I'm a girl." She threw her hip to one side in a pose she hoped was sexy. Then she flicked her hair—which she had spent almost twenty minutes straightening—off her shoulder. For the past few weeks she'd kept her hair loose instead of braiding it. All guys liked long hair. Everyone knew that. Well, maybe everyone except JoJo.

Braids were for little girls. It could be completely annoying when her hair got in her face while she was playing, but that was something she would have to deal with. Maybe bangs was the answer.

"Chill out, Gloria Steinem. I would do the same for any kid. Boy or girl."

Kid. That hurt. It also made her feel stupid wearing her bra. "You know, you're only three years older than me." When they'd first met, she had said she was almost fifteen, which she was—only in January that turning point had been further away than it was now.

"Three years and three lifetimes, Sophie."

"What's that supposed to mean?"

He looked at his sneakers. For rehearsal, this maestro wasn't concerned about what they wore, unlike other conductors who insisted the musicians rehearse in formal dress to better prepare for the performance.

Bay was so hot in his well-worn jeans and brown sweater

that Sophie actually came to understand how the word *mouthwatering* related to boys.

"It means I'm eighteen and you're fifteen and we're just…friends."

Sophie felt another rush of humiliation, which she immediately countered with sarcasm. "Uh…yeah. What did *you* think we were?"

He glanced briefly at her overflowing breasts, which were nearly busting out of her shirt. It was a silent message. He was letting her know he understood what she was trying to do with her clothes and her Victoria's Secret bra. She wanted to fall through the floor. She wanted to cover her breasts with her arms.

Instead she raised her hand to bite her fingernails.

"You're not supposed to do—"

"I know," she snapped. "Any other words of wisdom?"

"Sophie—"

"Hey, Sophie!"

Sophie turned at the sound of her name. Mark was walking down the aisle. "What's he doing here?"

"You never cut him any slack, do you?"

"You don't know anything about my relationship with him." Again she lashed out, still in pain from the rejection.

Bay didn't flinch. "I know he's all you've got now. I know he's here all the time trying to talk to you but you act like he's a total jerk. He's trying, Sophie. When are you going to try back?"

"I thought you said we were friends. Friends have each other's back."

"Sophie—"

"But hey, I'm just a kid, so what do I know?"

MARK CLIMBED THE steps to the stage, where everyone was milling about. He'd arrived during a break, which was great so he could talk to Sophie, but was disappointing, too, because he wouldn't hear her play today. Nothing moved him like listening to his daughter. Nothing made him more proud and, conversely, more guilty for having missed so much of her amazing life.

They hadn't been able to move her grand piano from her grandparents' house into his apartment. As spacious as his place was, it couldn't accommodate a piece of furniture that size. Instead he'd rented studio space where she could practice independently. She spent two hours there every morning before heading to the Kimmel for rehearsal. The performances would soon begin, but other than attending those, the only time he heard her play was when she messed with the electric keyboard in her bedroom.

This would have been a pre-performance treat. Maybe if the break was short, he could linger. She had informed him that she didn't care to be watched, which seemed odd since she was used to playing in front of thousands of people. Once, when she'd forgotten her purse, he came to drop off money for her lunch. She had curtly thanked him, then dismissed him. Evidently *he* was the only person she didn't want watching her.

Things were changing, he told himself. Ever so slowly, they were. He had to hold on to that.

Gone now were any rules Sophie had laid down about when he could see her. That had changed the moment he received that note. Someone made a threat against him and used his daughter to do it. If he wasn't watching her carefully, it would be someone else. Someone he would have to trust in a hurry.

Mark approached his daughter, who was talking to Bay, the violinist. Mark had met the boy before. A nice kid who had a path to success similar to Sophie's. He thought it was a great thing for her to have someone like Bay around with experience performing at this level at such a young age.

At least he had thought it was good until he saw his daughter wearing ridiculously tight black jeans and a shirt that showed her...*gulp*...breasts.

Holy jeezus, his daughter had breasts!

And they were totally out there.

"What in the hell are you—" Mark stopped when he saw her face. Tight, flushed. Ready for him to drop the hammer and call her out for wearing something so overtly and inappropriately sexual. Call her out in front of Bay, who was handsome and a friend who she talked about constantly.

"Uh, rehearsing here today?" he finished lamely. "Yeah. I figured I would stop by for a preview of the show."

"We're working the concerto," she said, her arms now fully wrapped around her thin body, her shoulders sunken in as far as she could. "You wouldn't know the composer. It's not the guy you like."

"Beethoven." Mark smiled at Bay. "I like Beethoven. I didn't know who did all that sad stuff, but it's him every time."

"Beethoven is great," Bay agreed. "Sophie does the 'Moonlight' like nobody else."

Mark smiled and as he did so felt his facial muscles contract. Was this kid flirting with his daughter? "You know, come to think of it, Bay, I don't know that I ever asked you how old you are."

He could feel Sophie shoot him the evil look of death, but after living with her for the past few months he was mostly immune to it. Her death look now brought no more than a mild sting.

"Eighteen, sir."

"Eighteen," Mark repeated, probably too loudly. "How

about that. You're legal now. It's official. An adult. Not a kid anymore."

Bay smiled and nodded as if he understood Mark's implied message. "Yes, sir. Look, I'll leave you two alone. It was good to see you again, Mr. Sharpe."

"Hey, call me Mark. After all, we're two grown men. Two men should call each other by their first names. Don't you agree, Bay?"

"Uh. Sure. Mark." He waved and walked to the string section, where the performers were starting to regroup.

"How could you?"

Mark fixed a fairly stern glare on Sophie. "Nuh-uh. Not this time. This time—" he looked pointedly at her chest "—it's on you. How could *you?* We're not going to talk about this here. I know this is your place of work—I respect that even if you are only fourteen. So we'll discuss this at home."

"Stop calling it *home.* It's not a home. It's an apartment."

"Fine. Then we'll discuss it at the apartment."

"Whatever. Why are you here anyway?"

"I told you, I had some time. I wanted to listen to you play."

Actually he wanted to check in on her. While she knew about the existence of the note, Mark was fairly sure she didn't understand its significance. To her it was some meaningless prank. To him it meant trouble. It was okay with him if she was oblivious to that—the girl had enough on her hands getting ready for opening night.

"You can do that Friday night. I told you before I really don't like to be interrupted when I'm working. I'm sorry if that sounds like diva city, but you have to respect that, too."

It wasn't said with any real heat, probably because she wasn't really mad at him. Instead, she was suffering from embarrassment and maybe a little bit of heartbreak. Fourteen and stuck smack in the middle of her first crush. And if Mark's instincts were correct, her first rejection.

Which really sucked. For her and for him.

It was easy to think that because she had just come into his life they would have all this time to get to know each other, to come to love each other, and be what a father and daughter were supposed to be to one another. Yet she was growing up—fifteen in two months. Yes, she was still young, but she wasn't exactly a kid anymore. He had to respect that her feelings were real and they had taken a hard jab that went to their soft, gooey core.

"Okay. Listen, though. Do me a favor and call me when rehearsal is over. I'll pick you up."

"Why? I usually take a cab home with some of the others."

"I know, but humor me."

"Is this about the note?"

His daughter was too damn bright for her own good. Which meant it didn't make sense to lie to her. "Yeah. This is about the note. Someone sends me a note like that and I worry."

"It was so stupid, though. It didn't say anything. I mean, lose me how? It's not like I've seen some creepy villain lurking offstage waiting to grab me."

He imagined someone making a grab for Sophie. He could see the fight she would put up. His girl wasn't the quiet or shy type. But a teenage girl didn't know what kind of evil there was in the world.

He did. He knew too much of it.

"Humor me. Call me. It will save you cab fare."

She rolled her eyes. "Fine. I've got to go."

He watched the orchestra come together onstage and took the stairs to the auditorium. She'd already told him this conductor was particularly difficult to work for. Pushing her to five, sometimes six, hours of rehearsal a day when three hours was the norm. Apparently Romnasky was a perfectionist.

Mark lingered in the dark shadows, where he knew she couldn't see him. She would probably know he was still there because the main doors hadn't opened and closed.

"Come, come, Sophie. This time perfect, yes?"

She settled on her bench and Mark held his breath as the conductor lifted his baton above his head and the music began to play.

You're going to lose her.

Words of advice from a conductor who had been working with his daughter for the past few weeks and had observed her behavior?

Mark spotted Bay in front of the row of strings, his violin tucked under his chin. Or maybe a warning from someone she considered more than a friend?

It didn't matter. In time Mark would know who sent the note because gathering information and finding answers was what he did best.

When it came to doing that for Sophie, nothing would stop him.

"Hey."

Mark stopped at the door to his office. Behind his desk sat JoJo, looking rather at home. She wore all black today. Some tights that made her legs look impossibly thin, with a wide top that should have made her seem witchy but instead showed off her impish face. A thin red belt held all the material together at her tiny waist. An elf witch. A magical fairy elf witch. With tattoos.

When he moved around the desk he saw that the Gothic ensemble was highlighted with red shoes, which transformed her style from angsty teenager to sophisticated woman.

"You do understand you're in my office. Yours is the one next door. The small one."

When he had decided to hire another detective, Mark had rented a bigger space in the same Liberty Plaza building. The new office had a reception area, two offices, a conference room and even a small kitchenette with a single-serving coffeemaker. He was intensely fond of that, as he preferred fresh coffee to stale coffee that had been forming sludge on a burner.

"I've been here for days already and you haven't given me anything to do."

JoJo had not waited until Monday to start her new job. Instead she had shown up the very next morning, on time and ready to work. He'd had no idea what to do with her so he introduced her to the receptionist, Susan, and gave her an excessive amount of paperwork to fill out.

"I checked with Susan and she said she put a bunch of new cases on your desk." JoJo stood with the files in her hand, assessing him. "You're not going to be one of *those* bosses, are you?"

"Those bosses?"

"The ones that are always telling everyone what to do and when to do it."

"Isn't that the very definition of a boss?"

She sat on the edge of his desk, her tights-wearing perfect little butt touching his phone. "I work best if I'm left alone to do my thing. Hand me the cases and I'll get you results."

"You sound confident." A self-starter. Wasn't that exactly what he wanted in a colleague? Someone who wouldn't wait around to be told what to do? "Do you always sit on furniture like that? More specifically, furniture not made for sitting on?"

For whatever reason it bothered him. The way she sat. The way her body touched his stuff. The way she seemed to take up all the space in his office. The way she called attention to her very small bottom. He could probably hold it in two hands.

No. He did *not* just have that thought. He didn't.

She stood. "Sorry. Jeez. Sensitive about people being in his office, sensitive about people sitting on his desk. I'm starting to wonder about you. I took you for the laid-back sort."

He stepped in front of her even as she tried to walk around him. "I'm not a *sort*. And you don't know anything about me."

He was sure it was the expression on his face that made her body tense. Mark knew the power of his glare well. Hell, he practiced his hard-core intimidation look. He used it to knock people off guard.

She was right. For the most part, he was a laid-back guy. Right up until the point when he wasn't.

It was time JoJo—and, really, what was with that ridiculous name?—knew that about him.

He'd sent hardened soldiers, Taliban fighters and steely covert operatives into retreat with this very expression. No doubt it would work on her.

JoJo snorted and shoved his chest. "Give me a break. You don't scare me, spy man. Now, do you want me to go over these cases or not?"

Mark was stunned by her lack of fear. Her lack of awe. Her lack of every reaction he was accustomed to. Had he become so domesticated since returning stateside that his once infamous back-the-hell-down face was no longer effective?

He sighed with disgust. It was official. He was no longer a badass. Merely the remnant of one. He supposed that was a good thing, but it felt deflating.

She still waited for him to give her enough room to pass, her arms filled with the cases he'd planned to have her go over. But he abruptly knew he didn't want her working on any of them.

A woman who could stand up to him when he was being his worst was someone who also stood a chance with Sophie when she was being her worst.

Leaving Sophie at rehearsal today had been difficult. He didn't like the idea of her without protection. But given her attitude toward him, Mark knew he needed an alternative to following her around himself. Having someone Sophie actually liked do it was the answer he was looking for.

"No, I don't want you to look at those cases. I have something more important that I need you to handle. Something incredibly important to me."

"And that would be?"

"My daughter's safety."

CHAPTER FIVE

JoJo LOOKED AT the note and felt a jab of anger behind her breastbone. Like someone had stabbed an old wound, reminding her of how real pain used to feel. The kid had lost her mother and she was building a relationship with a father she hadn't known growing up.

Now this? It didn't seem fair.

JoJo walked the few steps to her office. She felt more in control in her office. More of a problem solver and less of an empathizer. Mark followed and leaned against the door, his arms crossed.

"What are you thinking?" She sat behind her desk. Placed her elbows on its surface. Asked questions. Acted out the same role she would with any client.

"I don't know what to think."

"Old enemies, new enemies? You're starting to build a reputation in this city as someone who solves unsolvable crimes. There must have been people along the way who would want to hurt you. Hurt you through her."

"You're not going to ask me if I think she sent it?"

"No. I've met Sophie. This isn't her."

"You say that confidently. You met her this week and chatted for a few hours."

JoJo shrugged. "I know what I know. Giving your father a hard time is something I'm an expert on. While Sophie might sarcasm you to death, sneaky scare tactics aren't her style. She's too up front."

"Is that what you did after it happened? Gave your father a hard time?"

She didn't need to ask what he was referring to—any investigator by trade would certainly ferret out his employees' personal details. JoJo wondered if poor Susan knew the extent to which her privacy had been violated. It was most likely beyond what many employees would consider reasonable.

No, there was no question whether he knew about her past. But she didn't know what to say in response.

He wore a sheepish grin, yet didn't look apologetic. "It's who I am. It's what I do. I knew about it peripherally when I did the background check before I hired you. I heard you tell Sophie about it at dinner and I learned everything there was to know. I'm sorry for your loss, of course."

Right. This was the point where she nodded demurely and said thank you because it was usually the most expedient way to get people to stop talking about it. With her eyes lowered and her lips turned down in a hard frown, most people didn't press the topic. No one actually wanted to make a woman cry. Not that she had. Not for a long time.

But something about what he said rubbed her the wrong way. The way he stood in front of her thinking he knew everything, when all he had was facts from his internet search. Trying, but failing, to be apologetic for invading her privacy. It made her want to punch him in his smug face.

It made her want to cry, just to watch him squirm.

"You don't know shit about it. All you know is what you read. You don't know what happened to me. To my family. Nobody does."

"Then tell me."

"Why would I do that? I don't know you."

"But I want to know you."

Her eyes widened.

"I meant for professional reasons," he said quickly. "I need you. I need someone to watch my daughter because she won't let me. You have to be someone I can trust and that trust has to be built instantly. I agree that sometimes facts aren't enough. So tell me what really happened."

"Telling you about my family tragedy will build trust?"

"Telling me about what happened between you and your father might." Mark's expression was dour. "Okay, fine, it also might help give me some insight into Sophie. Figure out how I can change us. Fix us."

JoJo smiled sadly. "Trust me when I tell you there is nothing about what happened between me and my father that will help you to fix anything. You might say my dad and I are…permanently broken."

"It was that bad?"

"It was worse."

"I don't want to break things with Sophie. I really don't."

"Then you won't. The problem my dad and I had—and eventually my mom and I—wasn't the result of what I did. It was because of them. A kid can try to let go and parents can refuse to allow it. But if parents let go, there is nothing for the kid to do but walk away. As long as you refuse to let her go, it doesn't matter how angry Sophie gets or how snarky or how combative. That bond will still be there."

She could see him absorbing her words. Understanding what it said about her own family. What it meant.

"They had already lost one daughter. How could they let you go?"

"I spent a lot of time taking psychology courses to figure out that very thing. The truth is, murder is destructive and it has many victims. And I was not…easy."

"I really am sorry."

JoJo didn't reply. It was such a useless phrase. One that people felt obligated to offer. It didn't fix anything. It didn't change anything. It only made a person say, "Thank you." Thank you for what?

"I'll need a list of everyone you suspect might have written this note. I'll also want a list of anyone involved in any case you've solved since your return to the States. I imagine you can't put together a list of potential threats from your days in the government—security clearance and all—so you'll have to do your own work there."

"Right. And you'll—"

"I'll need to get familiar with Sophie's schedule. Her friends, teachers, et cetera. Do you want my surveillance to be covert or open?"

Mark hesitated and JoJo imagined he was weighing the pros and cons.

"Do you want to take the risk of me doing this without her knowledge, knowing at some point she might learn the truth or—"

"You can't handle covert surveillance on a teenager?"

JoJo nearly growled. "Of course I can. But should danger threaten her in some way I may need to expose myself. The girl's pretty bright. I'm thinking she wouldn't buy the story that my presence was a coincidence. Or do you want to spare the righteous teen outrage that would follow such a revelation and simply explain what's happening? A threat was made, we're checking it out, but in the meantime I'm going to be hanging around to make sure nothing happens."

Still, he hesitated.

"What did you say about wanting to fix the relationship between you and your daughter?"

"I don't want to scare the crap out of her with this. She's got enough on her plate."

"Then you need to ask yourself who Sophie is. Is she the type of kid who is going to be freaked out by this and will shut down out of fear? Or is she the type of kid who can deal with the situation and take reasonable steps to secure her own safety by accepting a necessary precaution?"

"Are you seriously trying to out-reason me?"

"I'm saying you're not a spy anymore. Getting away with a covert operation isn't the goal. Establishing trust between you and your daughter is. You know? That silly thing called trust—that thing you want to have with me. Well, I'm no expert but I'm fairly sure it's a critical component in any relationship, especially one between a father and daughter who are only starting to know one another."

"You did out-reason me," he whispered, sounding disgusted. "Okay. Come over tonight. We'll talk to her together. I'll let her know what the deal is and you can explain your role. She'll probably take it better coming from you."

"Deal."

"Did you find an apartment yet?"

"Not yet. I have some appointments tomorrow."

"To rent or buy?"

This time she was the one to hesitate, pondering how much he needed to know about her personal life. In her mind, the more space the better, especially since she realized she sort of liked him.

Not the dangerous red-zone level of like. More bordering on orange. He was funny and could trade barbs with anyone. But there was something else that made him different from other men she'd known. She'd worked for detectives, she'd trained with law enforcers. The term *swinging dick* was a staple in her descriptive vocabulary.

The difference between Mark and the other types she'd known in this profession was that he didn't have to swing his dick to prove anything to anyone.

He was a badass, and his dick was just there. Impressive without having to announce its presence.

And that is enough time thinking about the Penis. Move on.

She considered what he had said earlier. If he was going to trust her with his daughter's safety, then she could at least be honest with him about the basic facts of her life.

"Rent."

"Because you can't buy or won't buy?"

"If you're offering me a raise already…"

He sneered at her. That was the only description she could come up with for the way his lips thinned while half his mouth curled up. "I'm trying to find out if you're renting for a reason."

"Like, duh," she said, with what she hoped was enough teenage speak so he would understand.

It only made him sneer harder.

"Yes, I'm renting for a reason. Until you and I figure out if we can mesh together, I don't want to make any long-term commitments."

"Why do we have to…mesh? Why can't we simply be two people working together?"

"Dude, small office. You need to accept the fact that I'm the type who will go into your office and take the case folders if I need them. I probably need to accept the fact that, deep at heart, you're still a paranoid spy guy. If we can't do that, no meshing."

"Well, then I want to mesh." He shook his head slightly. "What I meant to say is, I want this to work out. With us."

"Ditto."

"Good. Okay, well, if you don't have a place of your own, you're probably sick of eating out. Come over for dinner."

"You cook?"

"Why did your voice go up an octave? You don't think I can cook? Is it because I'm a man? That's so stereotypical and, I have to say, a little cliché."

JoJo bit her lip because who knew? Maybe his secret passion was cooking. But she had a feeling she was being played. In fact, that was always how she felt around him. Like she was being tested or there was some hidden agenda behind everything he did and said. It constantly kept her on her toes.

The man—the real man—behind the intimidating spy or the sarcastic jokester or the seriously lost new dad, was a mystery.

Which was not a good thing because there was nothing she loved better than solving a mystery.

He's your boss. He's not a mystery. He's your boss. A boss without a Penis.

Still, a home-cooked meal—if he could deliver it—was not something a woman who ate most of her meals at restaurants ever passed up. Cooking was a luxury her job rarely afforded.

"You're on, chef."

MARK CLUTCHED THE take-out bags in one hand while he fiddled with his key. He opened the door and found Sophie where he'd left her after he had picked her up from rehearsal. Nancy was with her and the two of them had their heads down over a big book.

"Hey, I'm home."

Nancy lifted her head and smiled. "Hi."

Again, Mark was struck by the sweet nature of her smile. So open and friendly and welcoming. So unlike the woman who was coming for dinner tonight.

I want to mesh....

Where in the hell had that come from? It had been her word, but to him it conjured all sorts of lurid images. Mostly involving naked bodies and what happened to them when they *meshed.*

He wasn't even sure why the images arose. It wasn't like he was attracted to her. She was so far from what he wanted in a woman she might as well be a man. Any thoughts of meshing should be irrelevant.

That was what he needed to do. He needed to think of her as a man. A man, a fellow detective, a coworker. A hey-buddy-let's-get-a-beer-after-work dude. Or a go-watch-the-game-and-burp kind of man.

Did JoJo burp?

"What's that?" Sophie asked him.

Shifting his thoughts away from his she-man coworker, Mark set the bags in the kitchen. "This is lasagna. Home-made. Well, at least homemade by someone else. But we're going to pretend tonight. What are the odds I have a dish remotely this size?"

He started foraging through his cabinets, where he knew he'd stashed the pots and pans and serving dishes he'd bought. When he first realized that it only made sense for Sophie to live with him, he'd gone out and bought every-thing he thought a home should have. Things like kitchen implements. He was a man who owned a grater, a juicer and a whisk.

Not one of those tools had ever been used in this kitchen.

"Ah-ha!" Mark pulled out a square white ceramic dish and a saucepan and held them up to show off his discovery to the two ladies seated at the island.

"Yeah, so you have pots? I don't get it."

Mark opened the bags and pulled out a container of red sauce. He dumped the contents into the pot and put it on the stove, setting the heat level to warm.

Next action item: the delicate surgery of removing the lasagna from the aluminum container and placing it into the serving dish. What might a man need for that? Spatula.

Yes! That was a kitchen tool he was familiar with. A man had to have eggs and pancakes after all.

Sophie followed his activities with a bemused expression. "What are you doing? What is the point?"

"I think he's trying to impress someone."

Mark glanced at Nancy and saw a sad smile on her face. It was crazy, but he had the feeling he'd disappointed her by being interested in somebody else. The crazy thought occurred to him that his daughter's tutor might have a crush on him.

If so, it was flattering. She was a woman in her early thirties and attractive in a no-nonsense way. Long, ash-blond hair, pretty green eyes. Soft in all the right places. She was a woman any man would find it easy to be around. Hell, if she wasn't his daughter's tutor, he might consider asking her out.

Because wasn't that what he wanted? A nice woman. A steady woman. A woman with a lovely smile.

But she was his daughter's tutor and Sophie liked her. That was something he wasn't going to mess up. There were boundaries that couldn't be crossed if he didn't want to see Nancy storm off, leaving him hanging over something as silly as her broken heart. After all, what were the odds he could actually make a relationship work long-term?

Given his track record, his odds were on par with being able to cook lasagna on his own from scratch. And since he had no clue about what went into lasagna, those odds were basically none to none.

"Not impressing anyone," he clarified. "Just proving her wrong."

"Her." Nancy nodded. "I sort of figured."

"Who is it?"

Mark looked at Sophie. "JoJo is coming over."

He watched her face instantly change from suspicious

to excited. "Awesome. Why, though? I thought you guys were working together. Mark, you do know you can't date someone you employ, don't you? It's totally not cool."

"It's not a date. It's a work thing. But she made a crack about me cooking and well…"

"You would rather set up an elaborate scene with pots and dishes than tell her the truth. Which is that you don't cook."

"Exactly." Mark smiled. "You know, Soph, I really feel like we're getting to know each other."

"Well, I'll be going," Nancy said as she closed the book. "Let you do your…work thing. Sophie, I'll expect that report next week. See you around, Mark."

Mark ignored her doubt about the intentions behind tonight's activities. While he might appreciate her attraction, he certainly wouldn't feel obligated to explain any part of his life to her. If that put her nose out of joint, then it was her issue. He wasn't sure whether he wanted her to pursue him or not. Because when it came to him and women, it only ever went two ways. Either they chased him until he was ready to be caught, or Ben, his former rival and now friend, showed interest in a woman who Mark would then actively seduce.

It had worked every time, until Mark met Anna. Because Ben and Anna had been in love.

Love. Mark had never truly been in love. He used to worry what kind of person that made him. After years of dissecting his relationship with Helen, he'd concluded that if he'd loved her, really loved her, then staying with her and Sophie would have been more important than pursuing any life dream.

But she had betrayed him. In the worst way. She lied to him about taking birth control while actually trying to get pregnant. Trying to find a way to cage him. To keep him from doing the thing he told her he'd always dreamed of doing. They had been together for what, eight or nine months? Two young kids enjoying college and steady sex.

They hadn't even lived together. Their entire relationship consisted of bars, beers, late-night calls and finding secretive places at parties to have sex.

From that she had wanted forever. Had tried to make it happen by tricking him. A fact he would never share with Sophie.

He didn't regret the course of events. He couldn't. He had Sophie now. How could he possibly be sorry when she was so spectacularly amazing? But had Helen lived, when he returned to the States to build a relationship with Sophie, there would have been nothing but a cordial friendship between him and his ex-girlfriend.

After Helen, Mark's ideas about love and relationships changed. He was totally up front about what he wanted from a woman. Harshly, that meant sex and only sex. He liked the game. He liked the chase. Whether he was doing the chasing or someone was chasing him. And he liked sex.

There was no love involved in any of that. But lately he'd been rethinking his position. Maybe finding someone he could actually try to develop…what? After so many years of playing, he couldn't actually say he understood what a real relationship was. He couldn't fathom a scenario that he would be willing to subject not only himself to, but Sophie, as well.

"What's the matter?"

Mark shook himself out of his reverie. What the hell was his problem anyway? There was no reason to be thinking about love and sex now.

It was only JoJo who was coming over.

He transferred the lasagna to the dish then splashed the sides of the ceramic with sauce. He turned on the oven and put aluminum foil over the dish, hoping ten minutes of heat might permeate the apartment with the smell of home cooking. He didn't have to pretend with the bread. Who came home and made fresh bread? As soon as he had the garlic and butter coating ready he could throw the loaf under the broiler. Surely that would give off enough smell to convince anyone that major work had transpired in the kitchen.

"Are you serious about this?" Sophie asked as she watched him methodically set the stage.

"Like a heart attack. Here." Mark handed his daughter the garbage bag containing all evidence from the restaurant—the receipt, the trays the food came in, even the menu that had been included. "Take this to the trash shoot. Be careful on your return. If she's already at the door, double back, walk the long way around the hallway and then pretend you'd forgotten to pick up the mail."

Mark walked to the dish where Sophie had already placed the day's mail and handed it to her.

"Okay, this is officially weird."

"It's about being committed to the lie. She assumed I can't cook, I'm proving her wrong."

"You can't cook," Sophie said as if speaking to a small child.

"Hurry. In the meantime I have to look up the ingredients in tomato sauce. Tony, the rat bastard, wouldn't give up his ancient family secret. I was, like, really? It's spaghetti sauce, not life and death."

"What. Ever."

TWENTY MINUTES LATER, JoJo sat next to Sophie at the island while Mark looked on from the other side.

JoJo was oohing and aahing over every bite. Thankfully his daughter had decided to play along. Instead of ratting him out, she simply watched the two of them like she might watch one of her favorite reality TV shows. Shows she would never admit to actually watching or liking.

"This is really amazing," JoJo said around a mouthful of pasta, sauce and cheese. "You made this in such a short amount of time. Incredible."

"Oh, I didn't make the pasta or the bread." Mark leaned against the counter, striking a casual pose that declared his honesty—he hoped. "I bought both fresh. You know, this time."

"Sure. Who could make that so quickly? The sauce is the star. Such a burst of flavor. It tastes like it's been simmering for hours. I must have the recipe."

Predictable move. The girl was a private investigator. A highly successful one. Which meant she doubted everything he told her. From the moment he said he could cook.

Such suspicion in one so young. Did that come from her job? Or from what happened to her sister?

"Sorry. No can do. Family secret." Mark smiled. "Don't go looking to Sophie, either. I haven't shared it with her yet."

"That's right," Sophie said. "He's told me absolutely nothing about how to make something like this."

Mark wanted to shoot Sophie a warning look, but that would give him away. This was a game, just like the one they had played at the hotel. Mark planned to win and be up two to zero. The fact that he hadn't felt this jazzed about anything since leaving the CIA, he decided, was not a problem. Just because he was having fun didn't mean he in any way wanted to have *fun* with JoJo.

"Okay, fine. I don't really need the recipe anyway. I don't think I told you that food is a new hobby of mine. In New York I worked a case for this big-deal chef who wanted me to find the person embezzling from his restaurant. When I found out who it was—his assistant manager—he was so grateful he gave me cooking lessons for free. Can you believe that?"

If Mark had been sitting down, he was sure he would be squirming. This was not happening to him.

"Just tell me this—fresh basil or dry?"

Mark decided to base his answer on a recipe he'd read online. It wasn't possible for someone who was not a professional food critic to discern the difference in an herb. Was it?

"Dry."

JoJo's smile was victorious. Immediately, Mark knew he had been tripped up.

"Damn it! Fresh? No, wait. There is no basil is there? Freaking Tony and his damn secret recipe."

"Oh, I have no idea. You know how hard that would be to pick out a single herb from a sauce like this? That's hardcore palate stuff. No, my chef friend only told me how to make spaghetti carbonara and a risotto. Sorry," JoJo said, her lips turning down even though he knew she wasn't remotely remorseful.

Sophie laughed loudly and the sound startled Mark. It was the first time he had heard his daughter laugh at anything that hard. And it was worth his downfall. Completely worth it.

"Busted," Sophie roared. "Like, one hundred percent, total takedown."

"Yeah, fine. So you caught me."

"He even made me take the mail with me in case you caught me throwing out the restaurant bags."

JoJo chuckled and Mark could see the twinkle of mischief in her eye. As if she would have done the same thing had their positions been reversed. "It's all about commitment to the lie," she told his daughter.

It was a little weird how similar their thinking was.

After they finished eating, Sophie cleaned up. "Okay, I'm going to get started on my homework. You guys can have the living room to work."

Mark looked at JoJo. A silent agreement passed between them—it was now or never.

"Uh, actually, Sophie, we wanted to talk to you."

"Oh, great."

"Look," Mark said. "I'm worried about that note we got. I don't like the threat and I'm being supercautious. JoJo will help watch out for you over the next few days. Just until we can find out who sent it."

Sophie crossed her arms. "A bodyguard? Really."

"Not a bodyguard," JoJo corrected her. "Another pair of eyes. It's not like I would throw myself in front of a bullet or anything. Let's get real. I would call 911, like, really fast."

Mark knew JoJo was trying to make light of the situation for Sophie's sake. Cracking a few jokes. No big deal. Just a person hanging around the studio and theater. But Mark didn't buy it. Having known JoJo for even a short time, he knew she was absolutely the type to throw herself in front of Sophie to protect her.

He didn't imagine JoJo would ever again watch while another person got hurt in front of her.

"Fine," Sophie said, capitulating. "I guess I should probably show you the other one, then."

Mark felt every hair on the back of his neck rise. "What other one?"

Sophie pulled the folded white envelope out of her back pocket. "I noticed it when you handed me the mail. I didn't want you to see it and freak, but since you're already freaked out I guess there's no point in hiding it."

Mark took the envelope without saying a word. Anything he said would be filled anger at his daughter's foolishness.

He could feel JoJo coming up behind him to peek over his shoulder at what was on the plain white paper.

Just the one word.

Soon.

CHAPTER SIX

"SHE'S YOUR BODYGUARD?" Bay asked.

"I know. Crazy, right?"

"So what are these notes?"

Even from a distance, JoJo could see Sophie shrug. "I don't know. They showed up in our mail. No address or name or anything. Mark is completely freaking out. Hence the bodyguard. I mean JoJo is cool and everything. Still, I can't stand feeling like I'm being watched all the time."

And listened to.

JoJo sat at the rear of the auditorium. Far enough away to give Sophie the illusion of space. To compensate, she'd planted a small listening device in the hood of the sweatshirt Sophie was wearing. JoJo heard every word.

She felt no compunction over the intrusion. The girl needed to be watched. The second note, just like the first, offered no clues. Even the word—*soon*—was so vague that it was almost a nonthreat. Almost.

Maybe the note was from someone who wanted to mess with Mark's head but had no real intention to carry through with any actual violence. But Mark wasn't willing to take that chance and neither was JoJo. That included listening in on conversations so that she could learn about anyone connected with Sophie.

Sophie wouldn't be out of JoJo's eyesight or earshot for the duration. Mark was depending on her.

"Didn't he just hire her? You would think if he was really worried, he'd be here himself."

"Yeah, because that's what I want." Sophie snorted. "Mark sitting there watching me all day. We drive each other crazy as it is. I need to work, remember?"

"You don't need to work. You're perfect now and you'll be perfect opening night."

"Tell that to the maestro."

"He's just giving you a hard time."

"I notice he's not giving it to anyone else. He came all the way from Russia because he said he wanted to work with me specifically. Now all he does is trash me. At first I thought it was the usual ego bullshit, but now I think he might have it in for me."

JoJo agreed. She didn't need an earpiece to hear the conductor constantly berating Sophie's performance. Too slow, too fast. Not crisp enough, not sharp enough. But JoJo had never heard anything so purely perfect as the concerto Sophie had played.

It had been magnificent. Until the maestro told her to stop and then berated the girl like she was an amateur.

JoJo had been tempted to walk onstage and tell the man to back off. Something about watching him shout down from his raised platform struck a little too close to home. A short man who needed the pedestal to give himself authority.

She couldn't imagine Mark being comfortable with the conductor's behavior, either.

But she'd promised Sophie she would interfere as little as possible. The girl was a professional, albeit a young one. JoJo had to respect that.

"It's his ego talking. Don't let it get to you, Sophie. Here, have a piece of gum. Every time you want to say something to him, just bite down on it."

"Thanks. Better head back to your section. Don't want him accusing me of being lazy like yesterday."

"Hey, chin up."

JoJo had seen the young man hand Sophie the piece of gum, which she dutifully chomped on. Then he gave her a small knock under her chin with his fingers and walked to his seat. She watched as Sophie stood motionless for a second, then wrapped her arms around her waist and twisted her foot inward. She lifted a hand to her mouth, then quickly dropped it.

Sophie liked the boy. Of course she did. He was tall and handsome and talented, and Sophie was a normal teenage girl, with normal teenage hormones.

Not that she could act on any of those hormones. JoJo had already checked and learned that Sophie's friend was eighteen. The only thing they could be to each other right now was friends.

JoJo hoped Bay understood that. A fourteen-year-old girl, soon to be fifteen, who was struggling with some pretty heavy life stuff was easy prey. JoJo wanted to believe he wasn't a predator.

But she didn't trust him. Not his fault. She didn't trust anyone.

Still, she found herself a little jealous. What did it feel like to look at a boy and dream of being kissed by him? To be held by him, without any of the baggage that JoJo walked around with every day?

JoJo bet it felt good and awful and all the normal things young love and sexual desire were supposed to feel like. Something she never had as a part of her young life. It wasn't that JoJo didn't know what desire felt like—that she had experience with. Hell, she experienced it even when it was inconvenient, like it was with Mark. But she never had to act on it. She was willing to acknowledge her attraction to him, especially after seeing his face when she'd busted him on the basil. Nothing would ever come of her desire. Like nothing had ever come of it before.

Still, she kept circling to the idea that Mark wasn't like other men. That strange intangible quality made her think about him all day and all night long.

Probably the same way Sophie thought about Bay. Which was utterly pathetic.

Of course, none of JoJo's speculation took into account how Mark might feel about her. She wasn't exactly a magnet. In fact, when it came to personal dealings with men she usually assumed a confrontational stand. Better to start with the premise that any man she knew would abuse her, stop loving her…then work her way up from that. To JoJo, men were the enemy. They needed to be outsmarted, outmatched and at times taken down a peg or two.

No worries about overcoming her phobia and actually having a relationship with one of them. Not when she was constantly in battle: a battle she'd begun with her father that had never really ended.

It was enough to make her wish she was gay so she could avoid the male gender altogether outside of professional relationships.

Only she wasn't.

She had been reminded of the fact the first time she'd met Mark and felt the low punch to her stomach. Knew it again when he had been checking out her legs in the hotel lobby and it had sent a thrill through her. Most certainly knew it when he half smiled and half groaned after getting caught staging a homemade meal.

No, she wasn't gay. She was, however—at the very ripe age of twenty-seven—still a virgin.

JoJo was the girl who couldn't.

Or didn't. Or wouldn't.

Sometimes it was hard to know which of those things was true. Since knowing didn't change the fact, she supposed it didn't matter.

She turned her attention to the stage to watch and listen as Sophie went back to work and the conductor went back to yelling at the girl.

"How do you put up with that short fat dude yelling at you all day?"

"I know, right?"

JoJo had taken Sophie's key and unlocked the door to the apartment. She stepped in and started moving through the space, room to room, searching for intruders. When she returned to the living room, Sophie shook her head and plopped on the couch.

"Any creeps?"

"Nope. The place is creep-free."

"Were you a Secret Service agent or something?"

JoJo laughed at the idea. As she'd once told Mark, she and authority didn't get along all that well.

"No. But I've had some training. I know how to protect someone, if that's what you're worried about."

"I'm not worried. Mark is. They were two stupid notes that didn't even say anything superthreatening. I would be worried if they were, like, 'I'm going to chop off your daughter's hands.' Mom and I used to get crap mail like that all the time before we started having all fan mail sent to my agent for review."

"Ouch." JoJo joined Sophie on the couch. "I agree, they are vague. Why do you think you got them?"

Sophie didn't respond, and JoJo could see the girl had the sense to know that letters like those weren't common. Letters that had to be placed in her mailbox, which meant the person knew where Sophie lived.

"Hey, maybe they're from Maestro Romnasky. Maybe he's finally gone over the deep end and these notes are his warnings to me. The next one will say, 'Not right, yes? Too slow, yes?' Then we'll nail him."

JoJo understood Sophie was making a joke, but it wasn't really that funny. Not after the way JoJo had seen him treat her during the three-hour rehearsal.

"Is he always that way?"

"No. Today was a good day. Hey, I'm going to get something to eat before Nancy shows up, do you want anything?"

"No, thanks."

Nancy the tutor. JoJo knew to expect the woman because that was next on Sophie's rather rigorous schedule. Given all the practicing and performing she'd done today, no wonder she was hungry.

The doorbell rang and JoJo stood. "You make your snack. I'll let her in."

JoJo opened the door and offered a polite smile to the woman on the other side. Immediately, she could see the woman's eyes widen as she took in JoJo's appearance. It wasn't even one of her more shocking outfits. JoJo was wearing a simple black T-shirt over black jeans, but the shirt was cut in jagged strips at the top and her neck was exposed.

"Hi. I'm Nancy. I'm here to see Sophie."

"Sure, come on in." JoJo stood back.

The woman hesitated. "Are you a friend of Sophie's?"

"Not really. I work for Mark."

"Oh, you're his new detective. You're not what I expected."

JoJo raised an eyebrow. "Exactly what were you expecting?"

The woman was clearly uncomfortable with the question. She had an expression similar to someone who'd just asked a woman with a large belly when the baby was due, and learned it was just a lot of fat.

"Uh...I guess..."

JoJo decided to let her off the hook. "Don't sweat it. I know my look is...unconventional."

Nancy crossed the threshold and headed straight for Sophie, as if the girl might offer some protection.

JoJo couldn't decide if Nancy was cowardly or merely timid.

"So, what are you doing here with Sophie? Are you and Mark having dinner again?"

JoJo shoved the door and waited to hear it shut before she answered. "No, I'm here to watch over Sophie."

"Oh, well, I'm here now. I'm sure it's okay to leave."

This woman was definitely not a fan of JoJo's. She was trying to be so polite about it, too. Smiling the whole time while she waited anxiously for JoJo to head out the door. Definitely leaning toward the cowardly.

"Thanks, but I'll wait for Mark. We've got things to discuss. Work things. You understand?"

"Sure. Of course. You're his new employee. There must be many things. I'm fascinated by what you do. It must be so much more exciting than my job."

"I don't know about that. We do a lot of sitting around and watching. So why tutoring? Why not work in a school?"

"If I could, I would, but jobs are scarce in this area and I prefer this to substituting. Lucky for me, Sophie tumbled into my lap right when I needed a job."

"Lucky Sophie."

Nancy turned to the girl, who had dumped a heap of peanut butter onto white bread. "If you'll excuse me, I'll use the powder room and then we can begin."

As Nancy made her way down the hall, JoJo watched her in the same way she watched everyone. With suspicion.

The woman found the bathroom and JoJo waited until she heard the door close before wandering over to Sophie.

"I think your tutor is afraid of me."

"I know, right? It's like she's never seen anyone with tattoos before. You probably get this reaction a lot. I mean, they are intended to make you look kind of badass."

"Kind of badass?"

"Seriously badass."

"Flattery will get you everywhere."

Sophie snorted. "Let's just say I don't see you and Nancy being buds. She's okay and everything, but she's always going on about what a proper lady should do and telling me to sit straight and stuff like that. She reminds me of my grandmother."

"Well, if she warns you not to get tattoos you should listen to her."

"Really?"

"Yes," JoJo admitted. "They hurt like hell!"

Sophie laughed and JoJo joined her. As far as assignments went, this one was turning out pretty good. The kid was fun to hang out with.

Since JoJo would be able to hear everything Nancy and Sophie discussed, there was no need for the bug anymore. Patting the girl on the back in a friendly gesture, she removed the tiny device from her hood, feeling grateful it hadn't rained that day.

MARK FROWNED AT his smartphone as if it was to blame for the lack of information. He'd given the note to Ben, who was having an expert in extracting data from innocuous things like paper stock take a look at it. The scientist had come back with nothing. No prints, nothing unique about the paper or the ink. All standard office supplies.

The only thing he did know was that the font was Times New Roman, point 12.

Swell.

He opened the door to his apartment to be greeted by a smell that almost made him groan with lust.

What the heck was that? Was that actual cooking? It certainly wasn't anything Sophie could make.

"*Lucy,* I'm home."

He could hear Sophie say, "He always does that and it's so lame, but I can't make him stop."

His apartment was filled with women. Sophie and Nancy sat at the kitchen island with their heads together, working on a geometry proof. JoJo was bouncing around in the kitchen with an apron thrown over her all-black attire.

Goth meets Martha Stewart. There was a pitch for a reality TV show somewhere in that.

He realized she had every burner on his stove lit.

That was certainly a first.

"Hi, Mark," Nancy said, giving him a small wave and one of her sweet smiles. The woman really was nice and very pretty, in a quiet sort of way. It might be a good thing for JoJo to live in Nancy's orbit for a while and see how most women looked and behaved. How women *should* look and behave.

Not like Witchgang Puck in his kitchen.

"Nancy," he replied. "How's the kid doing? She learning anything with all this activity going on?"

"Yes, she is. She's doing very well. It seems all the pan rattling and pot stirring hasn't disturbed her."

JoJo stopped stirring and gave Nancy a look that suggested she didn't give a rat's ass about pan rattling.

"I got bored so I decided to show you both what real cooking is with one of the dishes I know. I save the carbonara for people who are truly special to me. Considering the kid doesn't have a problem performing onstage in front of thousands, I didn't think a little pan rattling would stunt her learning."

"Oh, no, of course not," Nancy responded. "I didn't mean that. I cook, too, so I know how fun it can be. Many dishes. I also bake. Cookies. Mark, I can make you and Sophie a batch of my favorite chocolate chip sometime."

"Sure. Sounds great." A woman in his kitchen cooking, another woman who wanted to make him cookies. All things considered, this was not a shabby end to his day.

"Okay," Sophie said, looking at Nancy. "I can't get to the end of this problem." Sophie lifted her thumb to her mouth and Nancy slapped Sophie's hand down.

"Sophie, I've told you, you shouldn't do that. It's such a nasty habit."

"I know, I know. The maestro is always on my case, too. I need to stop."

Nancy reached into her Mary Poppins bag, which always seemed to hold any textbook or supply a teacher required, and pulled out a bottle of clear nail polish.

"Use this. Put it on and anytime you bite your nail it will taste horrible. That will eventually break the habit."

Sophie took the bottle. "You sure?"

"Absolutely, I have another at home. I try to discourage bad habits in my students. My thinking is that once you allow one bad habit in your life, you're making room for others. You need to stop them before they can take hold."

"Thanks, Nancy," Mark said as he looked over JoJo's shoulder. "She needed a trick like that— What the heck is all this?"

"Mushroom risotto, lemon chicken and a watercress-and-pine-nut salad with raspberry balsamic vinaigrette. Unlike you, I can be honest and tell you the dressing is store-bought."

"For the record, I voted against the pine nuts but she said they add texture," Sophie interjected.

Mark leaned toward JoJo's ear. "You went grocery shopping?"

She turned to look at him, which made her lips incredibly close. Lips that were full and biteable. If he were a man interested in nibbling on her lower lip. Which he wasn't.

"Had it delivered. Trust me, I had eyes and ears on all day."

He gave a slight nod to acknowledge that she hadn't broken her promise. Until he knew where this threat was coming from he had to err on the side of paranoid.

"Sophie, that's our time for today. I should be going."

"You're welcome to stay for dinner," Mark said. "I assume there is enough for four."

"Absolutely," JoJo said, focusing on the risotto.

"Oh...I couldn't," Nancy said. "That's so nice that you asked, though."

"I would hate to have been sitting here smelling that good cooking and not get to eat it."

Nancy smiled and tucked her hair behind her ear. "It does smell good. I would stay, but I actually have a date. A blind date."

Mark thought about her Match.com profile. Maybe she wasn't comfortable with online dating, even though it was the modern way of meeting people. Whatever the case was, it was a good thing she wasn't putting all her hopes on him. That was a lost cause.

"Good luck."

"Thanks," she said pulling her satchel over her shoulder. "Maybe another time. For dinner?"

"Maybe," Mark said, deliberately being vague. Nancy was the kind of woman he wanted to be more interested in. But he wasn't feeling it, though he should probably try to. If he was going to pick a different type of woman to pursue, he might have to compromise on certain things.

Like desire.

While the idea of dating Nancy when she was still working with Sophie seemed off-limits, maybe as they got toward the end of the semester in a couple of weeks, he would ask her out. If Sophie was comfortable with the idea.

Do dinner. A movie. See what it might be like to be with a woman who wasn't a game player.

Nancy beamed at him. "Okay. Then. Good. Uh, Mark, can you walk me to the door? There is something I would like to discuss with you."

Mark followed her just outside the apartment door. "I think I'm paid up, aren't I?"

She blushed. "Oh, yes, we're good with that."

"Sophie is doing okay, gradewise?"

"Yes, she's quite intelligent. History isn't her favorite, but she's very adept in math, which is typical given her musical talent."

"Great."

"I'm curious why JoJo has to attend Sophie's tutoring sessions. While it really was fine to have her cooking, it is easier to work without the distraction. I don't know if this is a permanent situation, or if it has something to with my work, or—"

"No, definitely not. This isn't about you at all. It's also not permanent." Mark was reluctant to share any of the details. Still, he could appreciate how odd the change must seem when she'd been tutoring Sophie for weeks without any supervision.

"I'm working a case. There's the potential for trouble. JoJo is a precaution I'm taking until it's over."

"I see. Okay, now I have to ask, is there any potential trouble I should be worried about?"

It was a fair question. He'd all but told her that Sophie might be in danger. But he couldn't see how Nancy might be affected. "No, nothing to be worried about. Like I said, JoJo is a precaution."

"A precaution and a pretty good cook, it seems."

"I don't know. I haven't tasted her food yet. I'm with-holding judgment."

She smiled at his teasing. "I assume this means she'll be accompanying us to Chicago in two weeks."

Chicago. Mark had almost forgotten about it. The orchestra was touring, playing a three-night stint in Chicago after opening at the Kimmel. He'd asked Nancy to travel with them to keep Sophie's schooling consistent. If things weren't resolved by then, it looked like he was booking another ticket.

Thinking about it now, he wasn't sure whether leaving the area was a good thing or a bad thing. Assuming the person behind the notes wouldn't know Sophie's touring plans. On the one hand, separation might deter them from following through on the threat. On the other hand, it might delay Mark learning who was behind this.

He could only take it one day at a time.

The notes didn't offer up any clues, and this particular case was going nowhere fast.

"We'll see," he said. "It depends on how things work out."

"Of course. Anyway, I wanted to let you know I'm excited about the trip. I've never been to Chicago."

"Really? It's a great city. I'll make sure you have plenty of time to sightsee."

She tucked more of her hair behind her ear. "Looking forward to it. Good night."

"Yeah, and good luck again on that date. Who knows, he might be Prince Charming."

"With my luck, he'll be another frog. I'm not the greatest…with men. But thanks. See you tomorrow."

"Yep."

Mark watched her walk away. She wore a long jean skirt with a thick wool sweater and a bulky pair of shoes. An outfit not designed to be enticing or sexy in any way. Which it shouldn't be, considering she was coming to his place to work. He wondered if she would wear the same type of outfit on a date.

Some women tried to impress, others were more of a take-me-as-I-am type. Mark respected both. But he imagined what she might wear on a date with him, and his mind instantly pictured Holly Hobbie. Holly Hobbie was not a turn-on for him.

He was still thinking about it when he stepped into the kitchen, where JoJo was plating the food. She wasn't dressed for any kind of date in her all-black getup. Now that the apron was gone, he could see how the torn T-shirt stretched over her tiny frame and showcased her pert breasts.

"Dinner is served."

Mark noticed there were only two plates at the island. "What, you're not eating?"

"I picked while I was cooking. Trust me, it's fabulous and you will be bowing at my feet when you see me tomorrow. Just know that flowers or tears of joy aren't necessary."

"But you're not staying." For some reason the idea bothered him.

"Nope. Got plans."

"A date?"

She paused and her expression was the same as when she called him out for checking out her legs. The woman in front of him transformed from a fun and outgoing creature to a cornered animal.

A cornered animal ready to attack.

"No, not a date," she said slowly. "I'm looking at apartments, remember?"

"Oh, that's right. I forgot."

"Yeah, I'm even looking at something in this building but I'm afraid it'll be outside the budget."

JoJo in his office. JoJo in his apartment watching his daughter. JoJo living a couple of floors away. JoJo in a shirt that forced him to only look at her face so he wouldn't think about those breasts and how they might fit into his hands. *Not good. Not good.*

"More than likely. I hear they ask for your firstborn as a deposit on the rentals."

"Alas, me without any offspring to sacrifice. Okay, I'm out. Eat well and when you do…think of me fondly."

JoJo breezed out and Mark felt his apartment become more subdued. As if all the lights had suddenly been dimmed. Which was ridiculous. He was going to have to get a grip on his thoughts.

"You know, if you want you can ask her out."

"Huh?"

"Nancy," Sophie explained. "She's obviously into you. And she's nice. I know she's my tutor, but only for the rest of the school year. In three months, she'll just be a nice lady who thinks you're cute."

This was interesting. This was an actual personal conversation with his daughter. He wasn't sure he exactly liked it, but he also felt he should do anything to keep it going. "You think I should date?"

"Well, sure. You're a guy—you can't stay single forever. If you're thinking of waiting until I go to college, that's stupid. Mom dated and I was fine."

"You like Nancy?"

"She's okay. I'm not sure she's your type, though."

"So now I have a type?"

Sophie tilted her head and studied him for a minute. "Yeah, I think I'm figuring you out. I don't think Nancy would be right. I don't know if she could stand up to you when you need it. But that's what dating is all about, isn't it? Getting to know each other, seeing if you're attracted and compatible."

"Yep. That's usually the basic point."

For everyone but him. Getting to know someone had never been a priority for Mark. In fact, he couldn't even really say he had dated anyone besides Helen. Dating implied conversation, intimacy.

Any interaction with women in the past fifteen years had only involved sex. His conversations with them involved words like *harder, more, faster* and *yes, yes, yes*.

"Too bad you can't date JoJo. She, I think, would be more your type."

"You do?"

"Yes, but she's totally off-limits."

Yes, she was.

Sophie took a bite of the chicken and groaned out loud. "Oh, man. Mark, you have to taste this."

Mark took the seat next to his daughter and dug in. It was like a little bit of heaven falling on his tongue.

"Jeezus, this is good."

"Yeah, it really is too bad you can't date her. We could eat like this all the time."

Yes, Mark thought. It really was too bad.

CHAPTER SEVEN

"No, no, no. Again, Sophie, no good. You are not feeling this music. You are only playing, yes?"

"Actually, I think I am feeling it." Sophie could have bitten her tongue off.

One never defended against a critique from the maestro. Certainly not Romnasky. It wasn't done. This was his army. He was the general. If he said "Jump," the answer was "How high?" If he said "Kill," the answer was "Who?"

If he said she was playing without emotion, then she was.

Only...he was wrong. She could hear herself. She wasn't new to performing. She knew when she was on and when she was off her game.

Today was maybe her B+ game, which should have been enough for rehearsal. Her sound was clean and heartfelt. Her energy was high. She didn't know why that wasn't communicating to him. If he was frustrated, she was doubly so.

"What did you say? Did you dare contradict me? I am the maestro. I have the ear, and my ear say you no good. The prodigy. The little-girl Mozart. Such typical American hype, yes?"

Since she wouldn't win the argument, Sophie simply lowered her head, tried to shrug off the insults and to remind herself why this was important to her.

Mom was gone, Gram and Grandad were tucked away in their new home, in their new life. She didn't have school friends. Didn't have neighbor friends. Without music there would be nothing.

There would be Mark.

She dismissed the thought as irrelevant. Her relationship with him was nothing compared to her relationship with music. Music was a constant in her life. Mark was not. Who knew how long it would take him to grow bored being a father? Who knew if this time next year he would even be a part of her life? She'd looked into emancipation. As a fourteen-year-old it wasn't easy, but maybe at sixteen? If he hung in for two years, she might be able to leave him.

Wouldn't that be irony?

For now, though, she was stuck. So she would say "Yes, Maestro" and "No, Maestro" to whatever he wanted. In two days they were to have their first performance. Three sold-out events plus one matinee that was nearly full. Then on to Chicago. Where she would play for a whole new audience.

So many times when she'd been interviewed for various papers and magazines, the reporter would ask if she enjoyed performing. As if playing and performing could be separated. They didn't understand that the music by itself wasn't enough. It was the act of sharing her art that made it complete.

Like a writer who needed someone to read his book. Or an artist who needed someone to see his picture. Without the audience, the art was silent.

Yes, she loved to perform. Performing was the fun part. Yet in order to perform, she had to meet the demands of her boss. A short, fat Russian boss, who was leaving his perch to yell directly into her face.

"Maestro, maybe we should return to the rehearsal."

Sophie could see Bay standing, holding his violin at his side. Of course he would try to interfere on her behalf. Because he was the best guy she would ever know. If only she could convince him that they should be more than buddies. However, the last thing she wanted was for him to get into trouble over her.

"You have something to say, First Chair? That maybe you want…no chair, yes?"

Sophie shook her head with enough motion so Bay could get the message and sit down. It wasn't because she didn't appreciate his defense; she would probably think very hard about what it all meant later that night. It was because she could take anything Romnasky could dish out. The short man didn't scare her even a little bit.

Which was probably why he yelled so much. He knew it.

"You are lazy. You are lifeless. It is like listening to some American pop star who is all flash and no substance. I will call you Britney, yes?"

This wasn't the first berating she had ever received. It wouldn't be the last. It might, however, be the nastiest.

"I'm sorry, Maestro. I'll work harder."

He made a sound that was part sigh and part spit. She could feel the wetness on her cheek and tried to subtly wipe it off.

"Look, even now at your disgusting fingers." He grabbed her hand and held up her fingers. Even he wasn't stupid enough to use force in his grip, so she was easily able to jerk her hand away.

"I'm working on that, Maestro—"

"Work harder or I will find ways to make you work harder." He grasped her hand again and squeezed to make his point, but didn't inflict any pain.

"Hey! Back the hell away from her."

Sophie could hear a collective shifting of chairs as the shout resonated from the darkened theater.

Like some furious cheetah, JoJo leaped onto the stage and stormed in their direction. This, Sophie did not need.

"JoJo, it's fine."

"It's not fine. He put his hands on you."

Then she faced the maestro. They were even in height but JoJo looked like a Valkyrie ready to head into battle with the little Russian.

"She's leaving today's rehearsal. Now. And you're going to think about your attitude toward her before she returns."

Sophie groaned inwardly. This wasn't helping. It would make him angrier. They had only two days until opening night.

"JoJo, please. Let me handle—"

"Zip it. I've spent the past week listening to this ass-hole verbally abuse you. Today he crossed the line." She turned to Romnasky. "If you want your show to go on Friday night, then you need to think about your behavior… *Maestro.* Sophie, we're out."

"You cannot say this," he sputtered. "I say who goes. When they go. You do not control the talent."

Sophie wanted to protest but the look on JoJo's face stopped her. JoJo was protecting Sophie even if she didn't understand. Given the mood Romnasky would be in after this showdown, maybe it was best to take a break. Everyone needed to calm down.

"I'll be back on time tomorrow, Maestro," Sophie said hoping to mollify him.

"She won't be back until she gets an apology. She's a teenage girl and you're nothing but a bully. Tell that to whoever is producing this show and remind them that the sign outside has Sophie's picture on it, not yours. Let's go."

Sophie followed JoJo off the stage. Together they made their way outside the Kimmel Center to the street where JoJo hailed a cab.

"You don't understand what they are like. They're mu-sicians, they're passionate—"

"Kid, you need to let me calm down for a few, okay? I know you think it's just the way he is. I have to give you serious credit, too. You have done one hell of a job keeping your cool. But there comes a point where it's not worth it to allow yourself to be treated that way. Okay?"

"Are you going to tell Mark?"

"Sure as shit I'm going to tell him. I've been videoing the bastard and I think it's time Mark knows what you've been dealing with."

SOPHIE SAT ON the couch while JoJo played the video of Romnasky shouting at her. She could hear his nasty words all over again. What was it with classical musicians hating pop stars so much? Sophie had been forced to carry two iPods with her at all times. One for classical music and the other superhidden secret iPod for her Taylor Swift and Katy Perry collections.

If Bay knew she liked to sing "We Are Never Getting Back Together" in the shower, she would die from embarrassment.

After Romnasky's greatest-hit video ended, Mark sat with his hands clutched together and his elbows on his knees. She could feel the tension simmering in him. It was something she'd come to know about him. He could seem laid-back, like everything in the world was a joke or an amusement, but then on a dime his demeanor could change. Like a lion sitting in the sun licking his paws as if he had nowhere to go and nothing to eat, then *bam*. Prey spotted and every muscle and hunting instinct was on full alert.

Currently, she was dealing with the hungry-lion version of Mark. This version was a little scary.

She remembered her mom talking about him that way. She said it was why she fell so hard and so fast for him. Mark was the easiest guy in the world to be around, until he wasn't. Then Mark was a man of action. Sometimes he didn't always think through those actions, but her mom always knew that if she was bothered by a drunk in the bar or hassled walking to class or if anyone ever looked at her funny, then Mark would be there.

Acting on it.

"Tell me what to do here, Soph."

She faced him and could see he'd clenched his teeth, too. He looked like a guy who was holding himself on the couch through sheer strength of will when what he really wanted to do was find Romnasky and remove the man's head from his body. "You have to understand. A lot of them are like that. Temperamental, egomaniacal—"

"Assholes."

Sophie smiled as she remembered JoJo calling him that to his face. She had thought the maestro's head would explode. "It doesn't mean anything."

"He put his hands on you. He threatened you. I understand music is a big deal. I understand we're not talking about whether or not you perform in the school play. I get that this is a major show. However, I'm going to say this—I know you won't like it—I don't want you going back there."

Sophie took a deep breath. Okay, this was where she needed to be calm and rational. If she reacted to his overreaction, it would only end in them fighting. As much as she hated it, he did have some authority over her life for the next few years.

Placing her hands calmly on her lap, Sophie looked at her shortened fingernails and gulped. While the polish she applied nearly every day did taste awful, it hadn't broken her habit. Maybe she needed Nancy to find polish that tasted even more horrible.

"Okay, Mark." She used her most polite voice. The one she reserved for talking to her grandparents or to the important people who met her backstage. "I understand your concerns. Maybe we can have Roger—you remember my agent? You met him and said you liked him. We can have Roger call Mr. Radley, and ask him to tell Mr. Romnasky to back off a little. Would that work?"

Mr. Radey was the Kimmel Center's manager and all the shows performed there essentially fell under his control. Sophie had never dealt with the show's producer, but she knew Mr. Radley from the many times she'd performed at the Kimmel Center.

Sophie had never involved her agent in anything like this. She considered herself incredibly thick-skinned so mostly shrugged off these difficult personalities she occasionally worked with. The few times things had gotten out of hand, her mom had been able to take care of it for her. Usually with a few comments in the ears of the right people, suggesting she might decide to limit Sophie's touring schedule.

However, Mark didn't know those right ears. Sophie didn't, either. It was something her mother did for her. One of the ten thousand things she did that Sophie never recognized until she was gone.

Once the show opened the animosity would diminish. The maestro would stop yelling and start preening over his success. Sophie was certain of it.

"Nice try, but no. I don't think that will work," Mark said, shaking his head. "I'm going to have to talk to him, Sophie."

Exactly what she didn't want. She knew it was not a good idea. Cooler heads needed to prevail. Nothing was going to change Romnasky. She knew that. But as long as Mark knew someone said something to the conductor on her behalf, it might make him feel that he had stepped in and done his job to protect her. She could sense that was important to him.

"Please, Mark. Please. You have to trust that I've been here before. It's all bluster."

"Then the bluster will stop."

"You don't understand, he'll never give in. He'll never apologize. All he'll do is leave the show and the performances will have to be canceled."

"Your security is more important than a show."

Ugh. How very parental of him. Sophie could feel her temper rising and struggled to keep it in check. "JoJo will be there. You should have seen her today. The second he grabbed my hand she went all commando on him. I'm perfectly safe."

"I've had two notes, in two weeks, that suggest I am going to lose you. What if this man is deranged? What if he used this opportunity to conduct as a way of getting to you somehow? What if he has plans to kidnap you? Take you back to Russia?"

"Oh, please, stop with the CIA conspiracy crap. He's Igor Romnasky. He's an internationally esteemed conductor. He did not accept this assignment because he has an ax to grind with a prodigy pianist and wants to somehow take me out or kidnap me."

Mark clenched his jaw even tighter, but she felt she'd scored a point there. Best not to press for now.

"The only way I will allow you to continue to participate is if I talk to this man."

"Then that's it. You'll ruin everything. Don't you want to see me succeed?"

"I want to see you safe."

Sophie shook her head, railing at the injustice of her freaking life. "If I told you Mom would never do this, that she would never interfere directly between me and the conductor, would that mean anything to you? Because having been around me my entire professional life, she knew that what I love the most is performing."

He sighed. "I can't believe your mother would tolerate this type of treatment."

"Because she knew how this worked. She saw these men and had their numbers. She was always there, waiting in the wings. She knew I could handle myself. You know nothing! You show up in the last hour and it's all I'm-going-to-protect-you macho crap. All you are doing is ruining my career. If word gets out that a show was canceled because my *daddy* didn't like the conductor…I would be humiliated. Who is going to work with me then? Who?"

"It's just a conversation we're going to have. Man-to-man. Then I'll allow you to play."

"You'll *allow*. For fourteen years you have nothing to do with me and after less than a year, all of a sudden, you get to *allow* me to live my life. You worked for the government, Mark. Didn't they teach you about freedom there?"

Sophie was off the couch and down the hall in seconds. With as much strength as she could summon she slammed her bedroom door shut and took satisfaction that she still felt it rattling seconds afterward.

JoJo sat on the couch next to Mark, not sure what to say. No, that wasn't true. She knew absolutely the right thing to say, she just didn't know if he wanted to hear it in that particular moment.

"You did the right thing."

Mark's head dropped into his hands. "She hates me. I don't know…I don't know if I can fix this."

"She's angry with you. She doesn't hate you. She's worried about this guy's reaction. Worried about disappointing her fellow performers if the show gets canceled. Worried how they'll look at her from now on even if it doesn't. She's not wrong, either."

His head bounced up. "You think I'm overreacting?"

"No. I think you need to talk to him. I think he needs to understand that she isn't a grown woman, but a teenage girl. She's probably right, though, this guy won't change his stripes. But if he's aware there is someone always looking over his shoulder, it will force him to keep himself in check. I shouldn't have let it go on for as long as I did."

He smiled and reached for her hand. That she didn't immediately pull it away was not a good sign. She knew he only wanted to say thank you. She thought about the first time she shook his hand, when he'd interviewed her. The way his hand encompassed hers in a strong, but not forceful, grip. She remembered thinking she could trust his touch. And as cliché as it was, it had given her a little tingle. A tingle she had promptly ignored. Unfortunately, the feeling was getting harder to ignore. But she would continue to ignore it—the last reason being because she worked for him.

The first reason being because of who she was.

"Commando, huh?"

"I totally could have taken him out."

"Once again, JoJo's problem with authority rears its ugly head."

"Someday men need to learn that they can't yell and shout and stomp their feet and use brute force against someone weaker than they are. It's not right. And as much as I've seen it happen, I've never once seen it work. The fear and obedience it inspires is only temporary."

"You sound like you speak from experience."

He was still holding her hand. She shifted to let him know she was getting up. His grip only tightened.

"Who used brute force against you, JoJo?"

She sighed. She had the choice not to answer, of course.

But she knew he wouldn't stop asking questions. "My father."

"I'm sorry."

"Yeah."

It was awkward now. She shouldn't have told him. As much as he might have discovered about her past, there was something she doubted he would uncover. A trip to the hospital when she was seventeen. Victim of a car accident. Only, not really. It would be hard even for him to connect those dots. She supposed telling him was her way of reminding him that he was one of the good dads.

Good dads stopped bullies from messing with their kids. Other dads...did other things.

"I should go."

His head fell back against the couch. "Please don't. Then it'll be me and that closed door. If she comes out, I don't know what the hell I'm going to say."

"You say the truth. That you love her, you're worried about her, and there are some things a father just has to do for his little girl."

"Your father never said those things to you, did he?"

"No, he did." JoJo always knew that was what made their relationship PJ—post-Julia—that much more heartbreaking for her. Once upon a time he had been a father who loved her and worried about her and checked the closet for monsters. Julia had been the one who was afraid of monsters, but JoJo liked how it made her feel when he did his little search of the shelves. So she pretended to be afraid, too. Then Julia was taken and the only monster in the room as far as her father was concerned was her.

"Then what happened?"

"You know what happened."

"That doesn't make sense."

"No, it doesn't, does it?"

"Listen, about what I said before, about learning from the mistakes your father made to help me with Sophie…I didn't mean to make light of anything. I didn't—"

"You didn't know."

"So tell me."

JoJo shook her head. There was no reason to tell him the story. There was certainly no reason for her to relive it. And he was still holding her hand.

"Mark, you need to let me go."

He glanced at where their hands were joined and deliberately released her. "Sorry."

"Don't sweat it." JoJo bounced up and tried to pretend she hadn't been affected by his touch. "I should go."

The doorbell rang, startling both of them.

JoJo checked her watch. "It's too early for Nancy." She walked to the door and looked through the peephole. When she opened the door, she smiled at the earnest violinist. "Bay, right?"

"Yes, and you're JoJo. She said you were like her bodyguard. I didn't really believe that until today. You were pretty fierce."

"Yeah, well it's a lesson in not underestimating small women. I take it you're here to see Sophie."

"I just wanted to check on her."

"Pretty gutsy thing you did to get him to back off."

Bay ducked his head. "Not really. I let a fifteen-year-old girl shake me off. I think the guts belong to you."

"You do know she's still fourteen. Not fifteen for another few months." Mark came up behind JoJo.

"Uh, yes. I knew she had a birthday coming up, Mr. Sharpe…I mean, Mark."

"Just wanted to make sure that was clear. You're eighteen. She's fourteen."

"Yes, I know, sir. You've made it perfectly clear. I also

wanted to let you know that I never thought for one second that Sophie was in any real danger. Romnasky is all bluster. He yells and shouts and waves his hands but that's all it is. More ego than anything else. I think Sophie pushes his buttons because she's as good as she is. He's looking for a flaw to correct, and she isn't giving him one."

Mark nodded and JoJo stood back. It was up to him to decide whether or not to grant Bay permission to see Sophie. Because odds were, if he did so, that would require letting Bay enter her bedroom.

"Why don't you go say hi? It will probably help her mood."

Bay nodded. "Are you going to pull her from the performance? I'm not asking because I'm worried about my job. I would understand if that's what you decided. Romnasky doesn't deserve any less."

"No, I'm not pulling her yet. I am going to talk to this guy. Sophie is not happy with that course of action so when you open the door you might want to identify yourself quickly. No telling what heavy objects might be thrown in your direction."

"Got it." Bay smiled and headed down the hallway.

They watched as he cautiously knocked on the door, let her know who it was and then entered quietly, closing the door behind him.

Mark winced. "Did I really let him inside her bedroom?"

"He's a good kid. I can sense it."

"I was a good kid, too. And at that age I also wanted to nail anything that walked."

JoJo snorted. "I bet. You have to trust Sophie."

"Trust Sophie? Of the two I trust her the least. She's *in love*. Nothing worse than a girl in love."

"True. It's why I made it a point never to be that girl."

JoJo could see Mark's frown and for the second time that

day she wondered why she felt it necessary to tell him, of all people, the story of her life.

Her new motto with Mark was going to be: Zip It!

CHAPTER EIGHT

MARK LOOKED AT the case folder and frowned. He was making no progress with the notes involving Sophie, or Sophie herself for that matter. It was driving him insane. Which was why he pulled out the Anderson file and began to flip through the case again. Something else he hadn't been able to let go of because he hadn't found an answer he wanted.

Mark was obsessed with answers. When they eluded him, it could drive him to distraction.

"So how did it go with Bay after I left?"

Mark glanced at JoJo, taking in the dark pencil skirt and turtleneck that made her look like a librarian. She looked so prim and uptight, she should have had bifocals hanging from a chain around her neck. But there was the nose ring and the crazy hair.

She was still part punk rocker.

A man should have a conflict about being attracted to a freaky librarian.

"He lived. I must trust him."

In an effort to make amends with Sophie, he'd called off JoJo for the day. He'd driven Sophie to practice, where she was now with Bay. They were both under strict orders not to leave the studio for any reason. In thirty minutes he'd pick them up and take them to rehearsal himself. Then he'd have his chat with Romnasky. Depending on how things went he'd either stay to watch her performance, or he'd pull her from the show, essentially canceling it.

With time on her hands, JoJo had taken on a potential client interview, hence the business attire. He wasn't sure what good it did her. Sometimes it amazed him to watch how much of a chameleon she could be. The woman standing in front of him now was nothing like the person who had sat on the couch with him last night. This woman was all business.

That woman had been… It was hard to say. Vulnerable?

Unfortunately both women turned him on. He shifted in his seat and tried to focus on work.

"Did you sign the client?" he asked.

"Signed, sealed and delivered. Nothing too sexy. Just a cousin everyone in the family has lost touch with. An aunt died leaving a small estate and they want to make a good-faith effort to find him."

"Ah, an honest client. How…rare."

"What are you doing?"

"Looking at the Anderson file for the hundredth time. I've put together a list of all my closed cases. There are only four that involved sending someone to prison or to their death."

"You didn't send Anderson to his death. He offed himself. That's on him."

"He ended up dead. That's all that matters, or might matter to a person seeking personal revenge. I don't know very many people in Philadelphia unless Ben Tyler is secretly out to get me. Which, considering some of the run-ins we had, is a possibility."

"From what I know about Ben, if he wanted you in pain, you would be in pain by now."

Mark frowned. "Then I guess it's a good thing we're friends now. No, it only makes sense that if someone did want to hurt me through Sophie, they would have been impacted by the cases I've worked."

"Unless we're dealing with a complete crazy. Sophie has some professional fame. Why have you ruled out a stalker?"

"I haven't. Not entirely. Nothing is ruled out. I just get the sense that if this were a stalker, the notes would be more about Sophie and less about the impact on me."

"Okay, give me your cases."

"You haven't read through them?"

"Of course I have. I simply want to hear your perspective."

"Two were insurance frauds, Lane and Dunlap. Both are serving their sentences. Lane's in for just a few months."

"Yes, but did you hear Lane's wife filed for divorce?"

"You talked to her?"

JoJo's eyes widened as though shocked by the question. "Duh, of course I talked to her. You told me to look into this. You didn't think I'd cover every angle?"

Right. Sometimes he was so busy telling himself how much he wasn't attracted to her, he forgot the real reason he'd actually hired her. She was the best there was.

"Sorry." Mark considered that development. "So maybe Lane wants revenge? A wife for a daughter. He'd have to arrange for the notes to be delivered—not the easiest task since my personal information isn't accessible online. Also neither Lane nor Dunlap were violent men. Just cheats."

"What about Paula?"

Paula Smith was a grifter with no family connections. She'd pulled off a sting by taking an elderly gentleman for several hundred thousand dollars by cashing blank checks and then disappearing into the ether. After being hired by the man's family, Mark had found her in three weeks. Paula was still serving her sentence. Hard to imagine anyone wanting to take revenge on her behalf. She also didn't seem violent. Merely greedy.

Still, he couldn't ignore any options. But it was when

STEPHANIE DOYLE   113

he considered the Anderson case that one niggling little
doubt he had in the back of his mind surfaced. The answer
he didn't have.

"You never found the source of the anonymous tip."

"Stop doing that," Mark grumbled.

"If it makes you feel any better I'm not reading your
mind, I'm merely predicting your thoughts." As JoJo sat in
the chair across from him, she crossed one perfect leg over
another, which tightened her skirt around her hips and legs.
Holding up her hand, she rattled off her points. "Assuming
this isn't from your days in the CIA—"

"It most likely isn't." Mark had already asked his con-
tacts still at the Farm whether there was any chatter related
to him. There had been nothing. No names on the watch list
had attempted to leave Afghanistan or Pakistan. Two of the
more bitter Taliban lords he had faced were still squaring
off against American military forces. It didn't seem logical. There would be a footprint somewhere.

"Okay, then going with the theory that it might be tied
to your casework, you have three nonviolent criminals—
all still in jail—albeit one who has a bitter soon-to-be ex-
wife—"

"How do you know she's bitter?"

"That did not require a lot of investigation. It oozed out
when I made the mistake of calling her Mrs. Lane. Her bit-
terness is directed at him. Not at you for catching him. She's
got enough on her plate with the divorce, figuring out her
finances and how she's going to raise her kids as a single
mom. I didn't get the sense that concocting a revenge plot
was big on her list of priorities."

"A sense... You do that a lot, don't you? Rely on your
sense of things. It's not exactly analytical."

"My gut, my sense, is observation plus logic and reason. It makes for a pretty good algorithm. I've never been duped."

No, it was easy not to fool a person who was highly cynical and overly suspicious of all people.

A woman like JoJo wouldn't consider falling in love and having her heart broken as part of the natural ebb and flow of romance. Rather, she would say she'd been duped. Purposefully misled into giving her heart up only so it could be crushed. It explained her sometimes prickly treatment of him. He wondered if there had ever been any man who had gotten behind the barbed wire.

Not. Your. Business.

He'd told himself that about a hundred times last night while lying in bed thinking about how brave JoJo was to protect his daughter. It was sad to him that her bravery didn't extend into her personal life.

"Okay, gut-girl. What is your sense about the Anderson case?"

"I definitely don't like the anonymous caller."

"Not a caller. A letter." A plain white envelope sent to his office along with a copy of the autopsy report. A typed letter. A single sentence.

"Right. Anyway, Anderson goes free for years after killing his daughter. Why the delay? What triggered the letter? Most important, who did it?"

"I looked," Mark admitted. "For a long time. There was nothing. No prints, nothing identifiable in the paper or the ink."

"Just like the notes about Sophie."

"Just like those notes," he repeated. The coincidence wasn't lost on him, but neither was the fact that anonymous tips were, by nature, supposed to be unidentifiable. "I would have dismissed the letter outright if the facts in the autopsy hadn't been so overwhelming. When I confronted the family and was immediately stonewalled, it was more than enough to pique my curiosity. So I looked at the police report. It was regrettably sloppy. Hell, exhuming the body was just a formality. The chemicals that poisoned her were all right there on her blood report. All I had to do was find the younger brother and break him."

"You're sure it wasn't the brother who sent the autopsy report?"

"Positive. He's a fisherman who crabs off the coast of Maryland. He was out on a long haul when I got the package. The stamp date confirmed it had been mailed while he was out at sea. He would have needed a partner, which didn't seem likely. He was genuinely surprised by my arrival and questioning."

"People can be pretty convincing actors."

"You're going to doubt me? I'm a trained CIA caseworker. I spent the first part of my adult life gathering information and extracting intel from people who didn't want to give it to me. Trust me, I know when someone is lying. Sean Anderson didn't like me looking into the case at all. He was pretty young when it all went down. There was a significant age gap between them, but still I think he knew what his father had done to his sister. The sexual abuse. I truly don't think he knew about the murder. He cared about protecting his mother, who was alive, more than his sister, who was dead."

"Protecting a mother who didn't protect his sister from being raped?"

"Regina claimed she didn't know what her husband had done to Sally."

JoJo snorted. "Do you really believe that?"

Mark considered how to answer. "Yes and no. In her mind, she was telling the truth. She chose not to know her husband had been molesting her daughter for years. So, to her, it wasn't really happening. Denial is a really powerful method of mind control. You would be amazed at what the human brain can trick itself into not knowing."

"She knew it, but couldn't deal with it, so she shut it down."

"That's what I think."

"Then what happened? Why did he kill Sally?"

Mark shook his head. "Who knows? Maybe she grew old enough to want it to end."

"You think he killed his daughter because she was going to tell people the truth?"

"Again, supposition. I only know that Sean said he'd always believed it was suicide. He never wondered why she would have taken the drugs that killed her. And if he knew or suspected what his father was doing to her, then suicide might have made sense. Since we know she didn't take the poison that killed her, we can suppose that she confronted her father. Told him it was done. Told him if he didn't stop she would tell others. Jack died before anyone could find out."

"It's sick."

"It is. For years Jack and Regina lived as though grieving the tragic loss of their daughter. Sean couldn't live with the hypocrisy so he left as soon as he could. Once I found him, and showed him how unlikely it was that Sally had killed herself, suddenly protecting his mother took on new meaning."

"I called him," JoJo said.

Nothing surprised Mark at this point. He'd bet she'd called every person connected to every one of his case files.

"He wasn't happy to hear what I was calling about."

"I imagine."

"A brother lost his sister, then his father kills himself. His mother's currently *resting* at a mental health facility. It's

not inconceivable to think he'd hate the man who brought
down the house of cards."

"Nope, it isn't. It's why I checked him out, too. After he
placed his mother in the hospital he took off for Alaska.
He signed on with a fishing barge to search the Bering Sea
for bigger crabs."

"Well, I confirmed he's in Alaska. Staying at a motel
until the ship leaves port. It would be hard for him to send
anonymous notes without postage from that distance. He'd
have to be working with someone in the area. Even if he
was behind the threat, he's certainly too far away to act on
it. Revenge by proxy doesn't make a whole lot of sense."

"You're saying he's off the hook?"

JoJo wrinkled her nose. "Did you just make pun?"

"Maybe."

"Was that supposed to be clever?"

"Obviously not."

"I think that might have been the lamest thing I've ever
heard."

"Give me a break," Mark said, defending himself. "It
was fish humor. Get it—fishing…hook."

"Oh, my God, now you're trying to explain it."

Mark stood. "I'm leaving to pick up Sophie. Find someone else to abuse."

"Oh, I'm coming with you."

"You don't need to, I'll be with her."

"And miss Sharpe taking on Romnasky? Not a chance."

In the end the confrontation was anticlimactic. JoJo sat
next to Bay in the theater seats while Sophie sat very still
on her piano bench. Mark was onstage with one hand on
the maestro's shoulder speaking quietly into his ear.

In Russian.

"Is that Russian?" Bay asked, an awed tone in his voice.

JoJo nodded.

"I don't know if I've ever seen that expression on the maestro's face. I think it might actually be fear."

"I imagine Mark isn't pulling any punches." More likely he was informing him what might happen to a man's hands if a former CIA agent conducted a clandestine nighttime raid on a conductor's hotel room should he ever touch his daughter again.

Mark never raised his voice, never squeezed the shoulder where his hand was draped, but it was clear that Romnasky got the message.

"Check out Sophie. Sitting there looking so contrite, so innocent. She kills me."

"Can I ask you something, Bay? What is your interest in Sophie?"

He sighed and she could feel his body tense. "I told Mr. Sharpe…uh, I mean, Mark, I know I'm eighteen—"

"Forget that. Do you like her?"

"I… Well, let's just say if she was eighteen, maybe…but I won't let myself go there. We're just friends. The truth is I'm a little in awe of Sophie."

"How so?"

"I was her once. I did these tours. I had these egomaniacs yelling at me, too. My reaction was to go home and practice endlessly for hours. One conductor got me so worked up I actually froze onstage during a performance, convinced I no longer had the ability to play. Sophie's different. It's like she listens to what they are saying and determines for herself what is a valid criticism and what is not. But she never lets them inside her head. Not like I did."

"She's pretty amazing."

"She is. To go through what she did with her mother's death and then reuniting with her father…I hope he understands how careful he has to be."

"Why do you say that?"

"Sophie is looking for any excuse to hate him. When he doesn't provide it she tries to provoke him. As if she can dare him into leaving her. She never cuts him any slack, despite what I've told her. Heck, last night she wanted me to help her run away."

That had JoJo sitting up a little straighter.

"Don't worry," Bay said. "I talked her off the ledge. I'm only saying that if Mr. Sh—Mark isn't careful with her, he might lose her."

JoJo turned to Bay, his words sending ripples of awareness down her spine. "What did you say?"

"I said—"

"We begin now, yes?" The maestro was on the stage, tapping his baton to gain everyone's attention.

"Sorry, I have to go." Bay took his violin case and bolted down the aisle and up the steps to the stage. Mark walked toward JoJo as the sounds of Sophie warming up filled the empty auditorium.

Feeling the seat dip next to her, JoJo considered what to tell him. Bay's comments could be completely innocuous. Said as a friend who was coming to know Sophie very well. A friend who had talked her out of running away from home. Something that would have been colossally stupid given the threat she was facing.

If JoJo put Bay on the suspect list, Mark would no doubt end all contact between the teens. But JoJo didn't see any point in bringing a hammer down on the wedge his actions had recently driven between him and Sophie.

It did raise the question, though. What if the notes weren't a threat? What if Bay was simply trying to let Mark know, anonymously, that he had to be careful? JoJo watched Bay take his place on the stage, putting his violin under his chin. He didn't seem the type, but how much did she know about him?

It was enough that he would go on her list. For now. Once she knew more about him, then she could decide what to take to Mark.

"Did you make the guy shit his pants?" JoJo asked.

"Yep."

"Threatening him in Russian. Nice."

"I didn't want there to be any miscommunication."

Together, they watched as Sophie began her solo concerto and was not once interrupted by the maestro. It was a beautiful piece and her remarkable talent was evident with every note.

"She's okay," JoJo said, understanding now what Bay meant about being in awe of her. It was a remarkable thing to go through so much and come out still in one piece. JoJo couldn't say she'd been able to do the same.

"She is. And I'm not going to let anyone hurt her."

Not a threat, JoJo thought. A promise.

THE REHEARSAL ENDED without incident. Sophie walked to where Mark and JoJo were sitting. JoJo had been riveted by each note.

"I thought it was beautiful," she told the girl, not sure how to express what she'd experienced.

"I still really like the Beethoven guy."

"You only know the Beethoven guy," Sophie said, shaking her head. "Are you guys ready to go? Nancy's coming in an hour."

They made their way out of the theater. The afternoon sun bore down on them, and they had to squint to adjust their eyes from the darkened theater.

"I'll get us a cab." Mark trotted ahead of them.

"See," JoJo said, bumping her hip against Sophie's as

they walked along the sidewalk. "That wasn't so bad, now was it?"

"I guess not. I'm not sure what Mark said, but I expected more push-back from Romnasky. He didn't say anything to me the entire time. You would think he would have corrected me once just to save his pride."

"I suspect your father's presence might have had something to do with that."

"I guess. I have to admit, Mark really was kind of cool about it." Sophie quickly turned to face JoJo. "Please don't tell him I said that."

"Heaven forbid. Hey, listen, what do you know about Bay's background?"

Sophie scrunched up her face and JoJo imagined she was going to get a barrage of questions about why JoJo cared. Questions JoJo anticipated and had appropriate answers for. Instead, Sophie focused on something over JoJo's shoulder.

"What the heck—"

JoJo turned and saw a car with a darkly tinted front window coming down the street at high speed. It was hitting the parked cars along the sidewalk and taking off side mirrors. JoJo assessed the loading zone in front of where they stood, empty of parked cars. The out-of-control car was clearing a path to the sidewalk.

Without thinking, she shoved Sophie as hard as she could and watched as the girl stumbled toward the building. Before JoJo could take a step toward her, the bumper hit the back of her knees. Moving with the car's energy JoJo rolled onto the hood. The car swung dramatically as it turned to the street and she could feel herself sliding off the hood. The next thing she felt was the impact of cement.

Her hip and head slammed into the pavement and her vision went spotty as she tried to put together what happened.

"Oh, my God! Help her! Mark!"

JoJo rolled onto her side. A wave of nausea nearly had her vomiting. She blinked and through dark spots she could see Sophie kneeling over her.

"Get back."

Her voice sounded weak, but she had to make Sophie listen. The car could return.

What color was the car?

Silver.

What make? What year?

Toyota Camry, older 2000, 2001 maybe.

Did you see the license plate?

"I didn't see it," JoJo said to the stern taskmaster in her head, forcing herself to remember everything else. Tinted window. Couldn't see the driver. Silver hood. But the license plate? What were the numbers? What was the state? Pennsylvania or maybe New Jersey.

"I didn't see the plate."

"Shh. Hold on," Sophie whispered. "Dad's coming."

"Move back, Sophie."

JoJo could hear Mark barking orders. Then he was carefully checking her body, her arms, her legs, along her ribs. She moved to evade his touch, not sure how to deal with his hands all over her.

"You're moving pretty well, so I'd say there's no spinal injury. I'm going to pick you up and take you to the cab. It will be faster than waiting for an ambulance."

JoJo forced herself to take deep breaths. "Don't need an ambulance."

"Like hell."

Then she could feel herself being lifted. Despite the dull throbbing in her side and head, her body registered that this was what it felt like to be carried by a man. It was pretty nice. She hoped she wouldn't get sick on him while it was happening.

"Sophie, stay in front of me. Open the back door, then get in the front. I'll lay JoJo down, okay?"

"Yeah, got it."

JoJo wanted to say that she could sit up, but Mark wasn't giving her much choice. He laid her out on the car seat, then circled the vehicle and got in on the other side. He lifted her head carefully and settled it on his lap.

Yet another first for her.

This was JoJo. This was JoJo's face up close and personal to the Penis.

"Thomas Jefferson," he told the cabdriver. "Now."

JoJo wanted to groan. The emergency room at one of Philadelphia's biggest hospitals was bound to be a zoo. She'd be better off with an ice pack in her hotel room. Then the cab bounced over a pothole and she cried out a little as her hip jostled against the seat.

"Hold on for me, honey. Just a few more minutes."

"Mark," she said, blinking as she looked up at his face. "Did you get the license?"

"Don't worry about that now. Concentrate on breathing, it will help with the pain."

"I didn't get the license. I didn't get it. How could I do that? How could I do that again?"

"Again?"

It was the last thing she heard before she succumbed to her need to simply close her eyes and trust in Mark to make sure everything was okay.

CHAPTER NINE

"SHE NEEDS TO be woken up every few hours."

Mark nodded. He knew that much about concussions. Standing outside the E.R. room, Mark wondered vaguely if the doctor was older than Sophie. He looked like he would have to work to grow a beard. Mark decided he'd never been this young.

"Other than that, the X-rays on her hip came back fine. She has a deep hip contusion and mild concussion, but there is no need to admit her if she's adamant on leaving."

"Okay. I'll make sure to wake her then. Thank you, Doctor."

"No problem. I hope they catch the guy who did this. Drunk driver most likely."

"Most likely," Mark muttered. No point telling him that the hit-and-run may have been an attempt on his daughter's life.

He reentered the room and could see JoJo still lying on the bed. Her eyes open and focused on him. Other than looking pale, she appeared to be as fine as she claimed to be. No blurred vision, no slurry words, no memory loss. She'd been given pain medication for her head and hip and if everything went all right tonight, she could probably be on her own tomorrow.

The police officer who stood next to her, questioning her, looked even younger than the doctor. The professionals coming to his aid were children, making him feel a hundred years old.

"You said you didn't see the license plate, is that correct?"

"No, I didn't see it. I should have seen it. I know to look for it first. I don't know what happened. It caught me off guard. That's no excuse."

"Uh, hello, you were busy pushing me away and saving my life. Get over the license plate."

Mark smiled. His daughter seemed to have come through the day's events unscathed. Or at least her snark had.

"Did you see the plates?" the officer asked Sophie.

She closed her eyes, trying to recall every moment of what had happened, but ultimately shook her head. "Nothing really registered. One second I could see this car crashing into parked cars, then JoJo pushed me away. The next thing I remember was seeing was her on the ground. You really scared me, JoJo."

"Next time I'll let you get hit and I'll be scared."

"Ha, ha. Mark, are we going to tell him about the notes?"

His daughter wasn't stupid. But she connected the hit-and-run to the notes way too fast. It worried him what the fear might do to her, but rather than looking panicked, he saw resolve in her eyes.

The officer turned his attention to Mark. "What notes?"

When he'd first received the letters he never considered contacting the police. Not that he had a beef with the Philadelphia P.D. He just knew that when it came to working a case and finding an answer, he trusted himself more than any detective in uniform.

Now he figured that any help he could get he might as well take.

"I received two letters from an anonymous sender. Completely unmarked on nondescript paper. The first read,

You're going to lose her. The second said, *Soon.* I consider this a veiled threat against my daughter."

"You think today's hit-and-run is connected?"

"I have no idea."

"You must not have thought much of the threat if you didn't contact the police."

"I'm a private detective. I work cold cases. It seemed logical to pursue it myself."

"If you think a crime is being perpetrated against you, you should contact the police."

And there it was. Tone. Said with the disdain most law enforcers felt for private investigators. Especially ones who took on unsolved criminal cases.

Sad to say, the police never sent thank-you flowers after Mark solved their cases for them. A shame really.

"You're right, of course. I'll come down at some point and fill out a formal complaint for…note sending. As I said, the threat is really speculative at this point."

"Well, I'll add that to my report. If we find the car and the person driving it, maybe you'll be able to determine if they are connected. Also, if any other notes turn up…"

"I'll be sure to let you know." Mark took the officer's card and pocketed it.

After questioning and requestioning all of them again, the cop left once he was satisfied he knew as much as they did about the hit-and-run.

"What did the doctor say? Can I leave?"

"You can leave, but only if you come stay with us. I'll need to wake you every couple of hours tonight."

"Yes," Sophie said. "I mean, you don't want to be alone, right? We'll watch a movie or something together. Something romantic or funny. To take your mind off it."

JoJo smiled. "I really don't—"

"No excuses. It's the only way you're getting sprung

from this zoo. Now it sounds like my daughter is turning this into a girls' night. Since I've always wanted to know what goes on at these events, I plan to invite myself. Question number one, are we going to talk about *boys?*"

"Mark, seriously," his daughter groaned.

"Maybe do each other's toenails?"

"You could be helpful by finding a nurse to give me my dismissal papers. I understand I need those if your kick-ass insurance is going to pay this bill."

"Come on, I'm planning an evening of fun here. Oh, wait, I know. We could do one of those levitation party tricks. You know where we lift JoJo in the air with nothing but the power of our fingertips."

"You are so lame."

"Light as feather, stiff as board."

"Could you please go now? I need to get dressed."

Mark left the two women to commiserate over his lameness, satisfied that he hadn't once let them know how deeply petrified he'd been since watching JoJo, in her pencil skirt, go flying off the hood of that car.

Because the sight had been so completely jarring he hadn't gotten the license plate of the car, either. He wanted to smash his fist into a wall, and considered whether a hospital might be the best of all places to do that since he would have access to instant care.

Instead, he stood outside the room and killed time by thinking about what he would do when he got his hands on the person behind the wheel of that car.

His phone vibrated and he reached into his coat pocket. *Nancy.*

Damn. He'd forgotten to call her. She would be at the apartment by now. Probably standing on the other side of the door wondering where the hell they were.

"Nancy, I'm so sorry."

"Oh, Mark. Good, you answered. I've been so worried. I went to the apartment but no one came to the door. I tried phoning your home number but no one picked up. You've always called me when the schedule changes. I didn't know what to do."

"I'm sorry, Nancy. I didn't think. There was a small accident earlier this afternoon. I'm actually at the hospital now."

"Oh, my gosh, are you okay? Is Sophie?"

"We're fine. We're both fine. It's actually JoJo, but she's okay, too. They're about to release her."

"Oh, my gosh, thank goodness. You almost gave me a heart attack. You're sure she's all right?"

"Yes, just a little bruised."

"Okay, well, I won't keep you. I just wanted to know… but now I know. Okay. So I'll come by tomorrow?"

"Yes, that's fine. Things should be back to normal tomorrow."

"Okay, well, have a good night. Give JoJo my best."

"Will do."

Mark hung up as Sophie joined him. "I forgot about Nancy. She was a little freaked out."

"Oh, I didn't even think of calling her. We went totally A.W.O.L. on her. She's probably pissed."

"She sounded more worried than pissed."

"Well, the nurse is in there now and JoJo is signing everything she needs."

"Good. And how about you? You okay?"

"Honestly?"

"Honestly." Mark put his hands on her shoulders and let her feel the weight of his security. It might have been the longest she'd ever let him touch her. If he played his cards right, she might even let him hug her. Because after seeing that car heading directly for his daughter, he very much wanted to hug her.

"It was scary. I really thought those notes were some lame joke."

"Honey, they still might be. The person driving that car could have been a drunk who had no connection to you. I don't want you freaking out. I'm going to find the person who sent us those letters. The cops are going to find the person driving the car. There were other people walking along the sidewalk, maybe one of them caught the plates. Okay?"

"Okay."

"You trust me? I am good at what I do."

She nodded. "I do. And you speak Russian so that's sort of badass."

Mark smiled, then went in for the kill. "I don't suppose you would let a father who just suffered a very close call hug his daughter?"

She looked at him and he could see in her eyes that maybe his very strong daughter needed a hug, too. "I guess."

He wrapped his arms around her and brought her into his body. His chin rested on top of her head and when he felt her arms clasp him tight around his waist he knew that he was never letting her out of his sight again.

"Okay, you two, I'm sprung." JoJo was back in her thin heels and looked nearly steady on them as she approached. "Also shockingly, I'm hungry. So what kind of meal do I get for saving Sophie's life? I'm figuring it should at least include dessert."

"Well, it's got to be takeout since we have to get you to the apartment. Sophie, near-death-experience meal—what are your thoughts?"

Sophie bit her lower lip. "Szechuan. Or Indian. Something superhot and radical. Totally."

Mark and JoJo shrugged. "Sounds like a plan."

"IF I DRINK any more water, I will float away." JoJo laid back on the couch with her hand over her stomach.

"That's what you get for taking on the level eight spicy." Mark used his chopsticks to pull the last piece of pork from the container.

"But I was so confident after handling level seven."

"You guys are both turkeys. I went for the level ten and I'm still standing."

"Yes, but you can't see that your hair is actually on fire," Mark told his daughter. The three of them had changed into comfort clothes and decided that eating while they watched *Love, Actually* was the best way to get over the frightening events of the day.

Mark, of course, had to point out that it was highly improbable that the prime minister of England would be caught kissing a girl backstage at a school show without his protection detail being nearby. After which he'd been pummeled by pillows.

JoJo wore one of Sophie's T-shirts and pajama pants and Mark tried to pretend that he didn't realize she wasn't wearing a bra. Ogling his colleague was out of bounds. Ogling a woman in his daughter's presence was also not cool.

Ogling a woman who had recently been hit by a car made him a bad person.

Still, every time she moved, he had to force himself not to look. It was official. He was a bastard.

Beyond his prurient thoughts, there was that other feeling. The feeling that he liked JoJo lying on his couch in pajamas. He liked Sophie sitting in the chair next to them, cracking open the cookies to read everyone's fortune. He liked sitting on the floor, his back against the couch, making snarky comments about the romantic comedy that earned him hisses and boos until finally they resorted to physical violence.

He couldn't say why he liked it. It wasn't family, certainly. In fact, this felt weird to him. He tried to recall a time in the past fifteen years when he'd ever felt this… content. Contentment wasn't something you found in Afghanistan. It wasn't found in cold caves high on a mountainside. It didn't overwhelm him while hunkered on cot in a military base bunker.

He used to think shooting the shit with other agents and military personnel was his idea of camaraderie, but this was different than that. This was more personal.

By reputation, he was a lone-wolf type. Always acting on his own, taking risks nobody else took. Mark cultivated that persona. He liked the idea that he was a separate entity. He liked the autonomy it gave him. Maybe the way Helen had tried to cling to him resulted in the need to always keep a few feet of space between him and anyone else. Honestly, he didn't think so, though.

He'd simply been born that way. Which, in a way, made him want to apologize to Helen. To tell her he was sorry she felt he always had one foot out the door. Because it probably was how she felt. He knew it was how he felt.

That was what was so odd about this moment. There was no space. Not between him and Sophie. Not between him and JoJo. Yet he had no urge to get up. Instead he wanted to stay where he was. That freaked him out.

"Who wants ice cream?" Mark ran for the kitchen, telling himself it was not because he was in full-blown panic mode. But it was.

"Vanilla for me," said Sophie.

"Me, too. Maybe it will put out the level-eight fire."

"What do you want to watch next?"

"Please, something manly," Mark said from the kitchen. He wasn't sure he could handle another movie with people falling in love all around. *Love* was not in his vocabulary.

THEY DECIDED ON superheroes. Appropriately manly, without being unnecessarily upsetting. JoJo dozed off throughout the movie and when it finished she felt a hand on her shoulder, waking her.

"What's your name?"

Josephine Elizabeth Hatcher. Wow, it had been a long time since she'd thought of herself in that way.

"Come on, honey. Wake up for me. What's your name?"

JoJo couldn't imagine who might call her *honey*. She had never been a *honey* in her life. Maybe *babe,* but certainly not *honey. Honey* implied sweet and she'd spent her life devoted to not being sweet.

"JoJo."

"Where are you?"

"On the couch. We were watching movies with Sophie. It was nice."

"It was nice. Come on. Sophie's already in bed. Let me get you there, too."

"I can stay on the couch." She was fully awake now and sitting up. There was no reason to take his bed. Where he slept. Probably naked.

Now why the hell did she think that? The Penis thought was getting out of control. She knew she needed to forcibly end any thoughts about it, but tonight she didn't have the energy.

"Trust me, you're going to be sore as hell tomorrow. You'll do better if you sleep comfortably. Now are you going to stand or do I carry you again."

Carry me again.

Fortunately, JoJo didn't express that thought. No, despite the circumstances of being hit and tossed over the hood of a car she still remembered very clearly what it'd felt like to be held by him.

Safe.

She decided every woman should try it at least once, but no woman should ever get used to it. It was an illusion.

She gingerly made it onto her feet. The ice bag she'd kept on her hip all night fell to the carpet as a squishy bag of water. JoJo bent to pick it up, but Mark told her to leave it.

"I'll refreeze it tonight so you have it ready for tomorrow."

Tomorrow she would be fine. Tomorrow she would go to her hotel room. Because two days of this was too much. Too much like…something she didn't want to name.

"Do you want some ibuprofen or something? I'm not actually sure what I can give you with the concussion. I should have asked the doctor."

"No, I'm fine." Like he'd said, she was a little sore, but nothing she couldn't live with.

He followed her into his room. When she stopped in front of the bed, he stepped around her to pull the comforter down.

"I changed the sheets if that's what you're worried about."

Not really, but she obviously looked stupid standing in the middle of the room looking at the bed as if it might bite her.

She climbed in and let him tuck the comforter around her. It was such a silly gesture. She was a grown woman. Still, it made her teary.

"I'll check on you in a few hours," he said as he stood over her.

For a second she had this crazy idea that he might kiss her. Then he did exactly that, leaning over and placing a gentle kiss in the center of her forehead.

"Thank you for risking yourself to save my daughter's life. I owe you."

Uncomfortable, JoJo rolled away from him, deeper into the comfort of the bed.

It smelled like him. She knew it would, too, fresh sheets and all.

"You don't owe me," she mumbled, trying to hold on to the idea that they were only two people who worked together. "It's my job."

"Right. Sleep tight…at least for a few hours."

JoJo decided she was too uncomfortable to sleep. It didn't feel right to sleep in a bed that smelled like someone else. She'd never done it before. She would simply lie still and then pretend to wake up when he shook her the next time.

"WHAT'S YOUR NAME?"

"Hmm?"

"Come on, wake up for me. What's your name?"

"JoJo." Had she slept after all? She must have or she wouldn't be so groggy.

"Why did you get those tattoos on your neck?"

She could feel the gentlest touch of fingers caressing the side of her neck under her earlobe.

"To hurt him."

"Your father?"

JoJo nodded. "And to be different from her."

"Your sister."

"My twin. Julia."

"Okay, go back to sleep." JoJo had no problem obeying the command. She buried her face into the pillow and let his scent wrap around her as securely as the blanket.

"You smell good," she muttered.

She was asleep again before she heard his answer.

"JoJo, WAKE UP. What's your name?"

"You just said it," she grumbled. She was having a really

nice dream about soft kisses and caresses along her neck. Was this interruption really necessary?

"Where are you?"

"In your bed."

She heard a soft grunt then.

"Who am I?"

"Marky Mark?"

"Okay, now you're just being mean. Given that the sarcasm has returned, I think we can assume you're safely out of the woods. Sleep tight, we'll be here when you wake up."

We'll be here when you wake up.

Again JoJo found herself tearing up, but this time the tears slid into the pillowcase. The words sounded so nice. We. Mark and Sophie. Family.

Damn, she thought, that was the word she didn't want to use because it hurt too much.

Staying with them…it felt like family.

CHAPTER TEN

JoJo WOKE SLOWLY, stretching and bending her body every which way. Her hip still throbbed a bit but her head was clear. For moments she relaxed in the comfort of the bed, feeling deliciously content. Which was strange given how interrupted her sleep had been.

She vaguely recalled the late-night visits from Mark. In one she was fairly sure he touched her. She recalled his fingers on her neck and it brought a corresponding dull heat low in her belly.

Game over.

It was time to stop denying that she thought about him that way. The man was whip-smart. Always her first turn-on. Tall, lean and built, a deadly combination. And completely sure of himself.

Any woman's definition of hot.

Beyond those qualities there was something so much more seductive about him. It was the mystery. The idea that at any given time she didn't know which Mark she was going to get. Funny Mark. Serious Mark. Tender Mark. Badass Mark.

She didn't know if other women saw all the facets of him, but she was silly enough to want to be the only woman who did. Mark had a bad-boy quality that he held in check. Similarly, he could be compelled to lift women from the sidewalk and carry them in his arms. She'd bet when he'd been an agent, dealing with other female agents, he'd kept that tender part of himself well hidden.

It was a nice idea, JoJo thought. To think that she knew what made Mark tick. It implied he'd let her get close in this short span of time. It suggested that the trust he had in her, not only to protect his daughter, but also to show her the many sides of himself, had been almost instantly won.

There was a danger in closeness. JoJo knew that too well. The closer he allowed her to get to him, the more she risked the reverse being true. Mark knowing what made her tick.

It was scary.

It was also thrilling.

She closed her eyes and let herself do what she rarely allowed. She thought of him, about the way he made her feel. She thought about what each touch he'd bestowed on her had done to her gooey girl middle.

She thought about what it would be like to have sex.

Not sex with anyone, but with him. What his naked back would feel like under hands. What his hands would feel like on her breasts. She caressed herself under the T-shirt she wore and wondered if he'd known she hadn't been wearing a bra last night. In her life she'd never been aware of the sensation of cotton rubbing against her breasts. But she had been last night. Every time she shifted on the couch and he turned to look at her.

Cupping her breast, she felt the weight of it and tried to imagine how his hand would feel. Would his skin be rough? Would he squeeze her, or use his fingers on her like he had when he'd touched her neck?

It hadn't been a dream. She knew it hadn't. She couldn't bring the entire moment into focus, but that feel of his fingers running along her neck now made her shiver.

For a little while, she thought, only for a little while would she let herself imagine what it would be like. Her nipple under her fingers tightened and she plucked the taut flesh, imagining what he would do. He'd tug on them. Maybe a little too hard. Hard enough to make her feel it.

Then he would take a nipple into this mouth. Because that would be like him, too. Hard, then soft. Rough, then tender, so she understood there was no one Mark, but many Marks and she was in bed with all of them.

JoJo licked her finger and touched herself, wondering if this was how it would feel.

Maybe. Only stronger. More intense. She started to ache between her legs. A reminder that her sex was still a part of her body, even though she tried so hard to ignore it. It was shameful, maybe even a little sinful, that she let her other hand trail down her body, under the band of the pajama pants she wore, into her already damp panties. Because as she'd been thinking about him, she'd been trying to expand that light caress on her neck to cover her entire body.

This was so wrong. She hated to do this to herself. Hated it when her body reminded her that it wanted what she deliberately deprived it of.

She shouldn't be doing this. She shouldn't be doing this here. But oh, did it feel good to lie in a bed that smelled of Mark. To imagine she was surrounded by him. That it was his hands on her breasts, his fingers teasing her sex. To feel those things that other women did. That he'd done to other women.

Other women. Not her.

She couldn't stop. No, she didn't want to stop. She slipped a finger inside her body, pretending it was his, surprised by how wet she was, how easy it was to stroke inside her body. She turned her face into the duvet that had covered her while she slept and inhaled his scent and thought about how it might feel to have him lie on top of her, come inside her body, to thrust hard and deep.

She groaned as a surge of pleasure rippled through her body and that flicker of intense heat immediately froze her hand.

No. This wasn't right. This wasn't fair. She wasn't supposed to feel this good. Ever.

JoJo pulled her hands away from her body, laying each out to the side as far away from her body as she could, straining against a physical need she would not satisfy.

A gasp had her swinging her head to the door. Mark stood in the doorway like a piece of marble that had been sculpted. His jaw was tight, his eyes were like dark shiny diamonds. His hands were two fists at his sides. He was hitting one fist against his thigh.

For a moment neither of them moved. Then like a man breaking free of his marble cage, he forced his legs and his body to turn. Quietly, he shut the door behind him.

IT COULD HAVE been minutes or maybe an hour before he heard the sound of his bedroom door opening. It didn't matter. He was still hard.

Shifting on the couch to once again find room in his jeans for his erection, Mark clenched his two hands together and waited. He listened to her bare feet padding along the floor and thought to suggest she could borrow a pair of his socks.

But sock made him think of cock and he was trying to control himself.

Quietly, she sat next to him, dressed again in the clothes she'd been wearing yesterday. Her high-heel pumps dangling from her fingers.

Fingers he wanted to suck in his mouth. Desperately.

She'd showered. He could smell his soap on her skin. He thought about her body under a stream of hot water. He thought about him with her in that shower, naked. When he'd first heard the sound of rushing water—which he had because he'd been on the other side of his bedroom door with his head pressed against the wood in a moment of pure agony—he had actually reached for the doorknob. Something stopped him.

No, not something. He knew what had stopped him.

Shit.

This was not supposed to happen. He was not supposed to want her. She was wrong on so many levels. Except his body didn't agree.

His body was an idiot.

"So, this is a little awkward."

"Really? You think?" He cut off his sarcasm, deciding he at least needed to explain his actions. "I heard you gasp…I thought you might be in pain."

"Right. Okay. Let me start," she began as if she'd spent the time apart planning exactly what she was going to say. "First, Sophie?"

"She's with Ben Tyler. He and Anna took her for the morning. I didn't want to leave you and she needed to get to practice and rehearsal. They made it seem like they just wanted a preview of the show. She knew better, but it's fine. I think she's figured out she's not going to be out of anyone's sight until this is over."

"Okay." For a moment she said nothing. "You understand that when this is over I have to quit."

"Yeah." He didn't see any other way around it. He wanted her. Sexually. And he knew, somehow knew, that what she was doing in that bed was more about him and less about scratching an itch. The way she turned her face into the blanket as if she was taking in his scent. He closed his eyes, not to block the memory, but to hold it. Hopefully forever, because he'd never seen anything so erotic in his life.

"Sorry."

"I don't think this is something you can apologize for. It just happened."

She nodded and then must have decided there was nothing left to talk about. "I'm going back to the hotel to change, then to head over to the Kimmel Center. I can be there when Ben and Anna drop off Sophie so they can leave if they want."

She stood and it was as if a magnetic force took over his body. He reached for her wrist. His fingers circled it and held tight.

"I have questions."

She sucked in her breath and waited.

"Were you thinking of me?"

"Mark, please don't do this."

"Were you thinking of me?"

"Does it matter?"

"Yes. If you weren't thinking of me then this is just an awkward adult thing that happened. If you were thinking about me then this is something else."

"How do you figure?"

"We both agree you need to quit. I can't be your…boss. Your colleague."

"I know."

He stood and faced her, still holding on to her wrist, still not letting her go.

"But if you were thinking about me…then I can be your lover for as long as you stay in Philadelphia."

The breath whooshed out of her lungs and he could see her eyes flare at the word *lover*. He hadn't been wrong, then. She wanted him, too. She'd been thinking about him being in that bed with her. But he wanted her to say it out loud.

Then her face changed as if she were deliberately shutting down her thoughts. Her desires.

"That's not going to happen."

He didn't pursue his first line of questioning. Instead he moved on to his second question. The reason why he hadn't reopened the door. The reason why he hadn't followed her into the shower and screwed her until she screamed his name.

"Why did you stop?"

"What?"

"Before you knew I was there. Before you knew I was watching you. You stopped. You brought yourself to the edge, but you wouldn't let yourself come."

Her eyes closed. "Don't say that."

He could see he was flustering her, could see her face turning red, but he wouldn't let go until he had his answer. He never did.

This answer felt like the most important one he would ever learn because in his life he couldn't remember watching anything as painful as a woman on the brink of a beautiful orgasm forcing herself to stop.

"Tell me."

"No." She pulled at her wrist, but he held it in a firm grip.

"Then tell me why you can't be my lover. Why I can't take you back to my bed and finish what you started? Only instead of your hands it will be with my dick. Do you want that? Because that's what I want, JoJo. Really, really badly."

This time her eyes flared, but not with desire. With panic.

"I can't. I don't…have sex."

He considered what she meant but decided it didn't give him all the information he required.

"You don't have intercourse? Is it something physical…?"

"Ugh," she groaned. This time she pulled on her wrist

with enough force that he had to let her go or risk hurting her. But instead of running, she sat on the couch with her face planted in her hands.

"I don't have sex. I've never had sex. Okay. Can we just leave it at that?"

He sat next to her, not looking at her because he knew the scrutiny would make her uncomfortable, but he couldn't let this go. Not now when it seemed like every piece of information opened a whole new part of her to him. He wanted those parts. More than he wanted the sex, which seemed completely odd to him. But there it was.

"JoJo, how old are you?"

She gave him a look that told him not to toy with her. They both know the background research he'd done on her.

"Okay, of course I know how old you are. How is it that a twenty-seven-year-old woman who—"

"Looks like me?"

"Gives off a certain…vibe…is still a virgin? Because that is what you're telling me, right?"

"Wow, a vibe, is it? Even after I removed the silver tongue stud. What people must have thought of me then."

"JoJo." Mark was done playing. He needed the answers. He'd just confessed to himself and to her that he wanted to take her to bed. If he was going to have to overcome some fear or trauma she was dealing with then he needed to know that. This was his business now.

"You know what happened to my sister."

"Yes." Abducted off the street in front of JoJo, found dead in an apartment four days later the victim of a drug overdose. While the article he'd found on the web didn't go into specifics, the police report he'd dug up indicated she'd been sexually assaulted.

By more than one assailant.

"They were sex traffickers. She was young and had long

blond hair, blue eyes. We were identical. It could have been either of us, maybe both. But she stopped to tie her shoe—"

"JoJo." He grabbed her hand and held it between his. He didn't know if he wanted her to finish. He did need these answers, but not at the cost of her pain. Hell, his pain. The thought of her on that street, with those men…

It so easily could have been her.

Only it wasn't.

"They raped her for days. A steady dose of drugs and rape to, I guess, get her ready for whoever they were going to sell her to. The overdose was a mistake. It killed her, but in some ways it may have saved her from something worse. I don't know."

"I'm sorry."

She nodded, but he knew the words held no meaning for her. He wished he hadn't said them, wished instead he'd found something more important to say. Not a single thought came to him. Not one sentence that might make her hurt, a hurt he'd pulled out of her, sink back down again into her soul. There were only more questions. He was good at questions.

"Tell me what happened with your father."

"It broke him," she whispered. He was about to ask her more, thinking she was done, but it was like she stopped seeing the room around her. As if she'd gone to some other place and time. "In the beginning it was easy to forgive him for his behavior. What father could handle something so awful happening to his daughter? But then I stopped forgiving him."

"What did he do to you?"

"He drank and then he would get abusive. Not physically, not at first. But he blamed me for letting it happen. It was like every time he looked at me, he remembered I wasn't her and he hated me all over again. It was strange, too, because it wasn't like he'd played favorites before she was taken. I used to wonder if it had been me instead, if he would have been that cruel to Julia."

"You changed your appearance...."

She nodded. "I cut my hair and dyed it. I thought it might make things better but it only made it worse. He thought I was defiling her by changing. By that time I was so angry with him, I liked that it made him mad. So I did more. Pierced my eyebrow, my nose, my tongue, my belly button."

"Belly button?"

She laughed at the evident interest in his question. "Don't get excited. The belly button ring didn't last a week. I don't know how girls wear those things. It pinched and got infected. I had to walk around with my midriff exposed for weeks. He called me a whore."

"But you weren't."

"No. I couldn't. When I liked someone or thought about a boy that way I would think about what sex had been like for Julia and then I couldn't. One time because I wanted to hurt him, maybe hurt me, too, I found this biker guy with a bad attitude and a thing for 'fresh' meat. I figured if I teased him enough, provoked him enough, he would...take the decision out of my hands. Then I would know what it was like, too."

"Oh, JoJo," Mark said, closing his eyes. Imagining her as this defiant teenager trying to hurt her father and to erase her own guilt by inflicting pain on herself.

"Turned out he was a good guy with a bad reputation. As soon as I showed up at his apartment I started crying. He fed me tissues, made me drink a glass of water and drove me home on his Harley without so much as a pat on the head.

"Of course my father saw him drop me off. It was

enough proof in his mind. That was the first time he really got physical."

"Where was your mother in all of this?"

"There, but not there. She couldn't deal with what had happened to Julia any more than he could, but she didn't want see what he had become, either. That thing you said, about denial being stronger than reality, that's what it was for her. Anytime I talked to her about it, she would say he was just upset. That I should try to understand it from his perspective."

"How bad did he hurt you?"

"Black eye, bruised ribs. You're going to think this sounds sick, not that this whole story isn't disgusting—"

"Tell me." Mark could sense that at some point this conversation had changed from him needing to understand her, to her needing to tell him. He'd interrogated enough witnesses to know when they were ready to talk. Push them enough and the rest of the story would follow. Like lancing a boil, sometimes the short-term pain was worth the long-term relief.

"I relished it. I thought there, let him hit me and let everyone see what he was doing to me. Those bruises were my scarlet letter. Let the world know I stood by while they took my sister and now my father hated me. Hurt me. I liked it so much I continued to taunt him. Building on my reputation as a whore. I would leave used condoms in the bathroom where he could find them."

"Do I even want to know?"

"Egg whites with a little bit of milk."

Mark tried not to be horrified.

"Hey, you've got to commit to the lie."

"When did you know you had to leave?"

Her head fell back on the cushions. "I think it occurred

to me my senior year that suddenly there was this out called college."

"Teachers didn't report the bruises?"

"They thought it was from the crowd I was hanging with. We dressed in black so we were 'bad' kids. It was my first lesson in how you can control people's perception simply with what you wear."

Mark chuckled. "I understand your issues with authority, but I think you would have made a hell of a CIA caseworker."

"Anyway my hidden secret was that I had a 4.0 GPA with near perfect SAT scores. I applied for and was granted a scholarship to NYU. The day I found out, I got these."

She ran her finger along her neck. Her very own permanent keep-away sign.

"So you just left?"

"No, I told my parents I was going. He freaked. Because of the tattoos, because I was leaving, I really wasn't sure. How were we going to continue to punish each other with me so far away? He picked up a bat and swung. It broke my arm. My mother took me to the E.R. but when she admitted me she said I had been in a car accident. That's when I knew it was over between us. She was never going to acknowledge what he was doing. My father was never going to forgive me, and I was never going to forgive my mother. For all our sakes I needed to leave without ever going back."

"You haven't been in contact with them since?"

"No. But they knew I was at NYU for four years. It's not like they ever tried to reach me. It's better this way. None of us are innocent in this story, Mark. None of us except Julia."

It was over, he thought. Her story was told. He knew without asking it was the first time she'd ever told anyone about what her father had done to her.

"Four years of college, two more getting your master's and not one time—"

"I dated. I flirted. I thought once I could…but as soon as he got on top of me I freaked out. Needless to say, we broke up. Since then I've been about work. And for the most part there are only certain types of guys who will even look at girl like me. It's not like I'm getting hit on by Mr. America every day."

"What about therapy?"

She lifted her head and looked at him. "You have to want to fix the thing that's wrong with you for therapy to work."

"And you don't? Want to be healed?"

"Part of me feels like I owe it to her."

Mark nodded his head. In an awful way it made perfect sense.

"You understand then?"

He could see her expression was hopeful. She wanted him to tell her that her thinking wasn't warped or twisted. That she wasn't wrong to lock herself up physically and emotionally and throw away the key for the sake of her sister's memory.

Only it was. Her sister was dead. She needed to accept it and move on. She needed to live.

"Yes, I completely understand."

"Because I was thinking maybe…now that you know all of it, maybe I don't have to quit. Maybe we can just get beyond this…this…attraction thing."

"No, I'm afraid that isn't going to work."

"Why? We just agreed that nothing is ever going to happen between us."

Mark's eyebrows raised. "We certainly didn't agree to that." Mark patted her on the thigh, in a gesture meant to soothe her rather than arouse her. "JoJo, I don't want you to be alarmed but something is going to happen between us."

"What?"

"I'm going to take your virginity."

CHAPTER ELEVEN

"Sophie's okay tonight, isn't she?"

JoJo was startled to hear Mark's voice behind her. Immediately, her heart picked up speed and she could feel her face flush. She was thankful for the darkness backstage.

She should hate him for that reason alone, for making her feel like some teenage girl with her first crush, jumping at the sound of his voice. JoJo was not a jumper.

She'd been happy to have a close-up and private view of Sophie's performance. Because Sophie was a minor, Mark had access to Sophie at all times. It included her dressing room and the privilege of watching the performance from the best seat in the house. Onstage, at the edge of the curtains. Not twenty feet away. If they needed to get to her, they could.

Mark didn't clarify JoJo's connection to Sophie and fortunately the producer's assistant escorting them to the stage didn't question it. Most likely, he thought they were dating.

Which they weren't. Couldn't be.

Stagehands milled about ready to handle curtains, lights and all the behind-the-scenes activities that took place during every live performance. It really was quite astonishing, the work that went into a show with just a bunch of people in chairs playing instruments.

Once the performance started, Mark had left the stage to "assess the environment." JoJo imagined that was fancy CIA talk for checking things out, but she indulged him if for no other reason than it removed him from her "environment."

To say that she had been on edge since the moment he made his declaration was an understatement.

After he said it, patting her on the thigh like she was a small child, he quickly changed the subject toward a host of innocuous things. Did her head hurt, where they should get breakfast, had she made a decision on an apartment yet?

She'd been grateful for the distraction and had made her escape from the apartment as quickly as possible. Just in case he had the crazy idea of throwing her down on his bed and ravaging her.

In case she had the idea of letting him.

And you don't? Want to be healed?

His words came back to her and she thought about her answer. Was her virginity really a tribute to Julia? The honest answer punched her in the gut.

No. Julia wouldn't have wanted this.

The reality was, her refusal to be intimate was a result of the trauma she'd experienced at having to watch her sister be taken, and the knowing, without really knowing, what had been done to her. It was easier to believe there was some noble cause in holding on to her virginity. Some higher calling she was serving, like a nun saving herself for God.

So did she want to be healed? Should she maybe see someone who could help her?

She'd thought about it in the past, especially after taking so many psychology courses in college. At one point she'd even considered psychology as a profession. In a lot of ways it was like solving mysteries. Mental ones anyway. How ironic that would have been. Shrink, shrink thyself.

JoJo didn't want think about her answers to his questions. The combination of embarrassment over being caught touching herself in his bed, shock at discovering he was attracted to her, and exhaustion from telling him about her father was more than her mental synapses could handle.

Leaving him had been easy. It felt like a reprieve. She'd gone back to her hotel to change. He'd gone to the office to take care of some business. Simple.

Seeing him again, that was the hard part. They met up at the theater in the afternoon to watch Sophie's final rehearsal. JoJo had been nervous and edgy, but he'd been himself. His charming self. She thought the entire morning might never have happened.

Except now every time he looked at her she thought of a hungry lion. One who had the ability to pounce at will. She couldn't aspire to prey. She felt like something far more vulnerable. An injured gazelle who couldn't run or kick. He wasn't pouncing quite yet, but it felt as if the threat was always there.

The worst part was that she had to keep suppressing a tiny part of her that wanted him to do it.

Stupid gazelle.

"You didn't answer. You think Sophie's killing it, right?" Mark pointed to the stage.

"Yes, she is," JoJo finally croaked out.

"Are you going to be this way every time I get close?"

The words were said softly into her ear and she could almost feel the touch of his lips on her lobe. A sensation passed through her that defined the word *shivers*.

"I don't know what you mean. You should watch the show."

"I've already seen it."

He captured her arm just above the elbow and tugged, pulling her deeper into the shadows until it felt like they were draped in heavy curtains.

"What are you doing?" she whispered.

"I'm getting something out of the way," he muttered.

"Look, Mark, if this is about what you said, forget it. It's not going to happen. Maybe you mean well. Or maybe you don't and the idea of getting it on with a newbie turns your crank. Or maybe you think you're being generous and kind and can cure me. But I don't want to be cured. I don't want any of this."

He stopped and turned to face her. "Are you sure? Have you ever been kissed?"

JoJo rolled her eyes, even though in dark she knew he couldn't see her do it. She could still hear the music playing onstage. She could sense people standing about waiting for the next transition. But in this corner of the backstage area it felt like they were in their own world. A world where two people might take advantage of a kiss.

"Of course I've been kissed. I'm not that untouchable."

"On the contrary," he said as he wrapped a hand around her neck. Leaning close he pressed his lips to her ear. "You know when I thought about touching you here I expected to prick myself on your barbs and pull back a bloody mangled hand. Now I see, it's only soft skin."

"Mark, don't."

He raised his head and met her eyes, his lips poised mere inches above hers. "Really?"

JoJo closed her eyes.

No, not really.

Really what she wanted was for him to kiss her so she could know what it felt like with him. Because she wanted to feel that. She wanted to know what his lips felt like. What his tongue would feel like in her mouth. How it would make her feel in return.

Needy, maybe. Wanting.

But that would be okay, wouldn't it? To have a hint of sex. A sliver of pleasure.

She didn't answer him, but when he ran his thumb along her neck and waited patiently for her answer, she nodded. Enough to communicate what she wanted without committing herself fully.

It was enough.

His head dropped and suddenly she knew what his lips felt like on hers. Perfect. She surrendered to him, because it became clear very quickly that he was a master-class kisser. Tilting her head for the best angle, controlling the speed and the nature of the kiss.

Lips only. Top lip, then bottom. Then a nip of his teeth. A gentle swipe of his tongue. Finally her mouth was open and he was thrusting his tongue against hers in a way that instantly made her go wet.

It was too much. It felt too good. She could feel his body move closer, feel the contact as their chests touched and their thighs mingled together. She'd worn a cocktail dress for opening night. Red, because it was her favorite.

Red, because it was sexy and she'd done nothing but think about sex for days.

The hand not wrapped around her neck stole around her waist to her back where the red dress plunged deeply. She felt his hand on her bare skin and moaned a little into his mouth.

Had she ever been touched there, at the small of her back? He wouldn't be able to feel it, but she was sure he was touching another one of the tattoos she sported. For some reason it turned her on even more. Nobody had ever seen that tattoo and now he was touching it.

He pushed her closer to his body until she was pressed fully against him and she could feel his erection against her belly. Instinctively, she moved closer, rubbing herself against him, teasing his sex with her body. Imagining what it would feel like to have all that hardness with all his power behind it pushing inside her.

Inside her body.

Abruptly she pulled away. So hard she would have fallen if he hadn't grabbed her and held her steady.

"I can't. I can't."

"Okay," he said calmly. "Relax. This wasn't going to be anything more than kiss."

Of course it wasn't. They were in public, the show crew was milling about. The music was still playing.

She hadn't heard any of it.

"It was just a kiss," he reiterated.

Then why was she shaking?

The hands he'd used to steady her now rubbed up and down her bare arms, settling her as if she was an overexcited mare about to be mounted by a stud.

"Okay?"

She nodded again because it was easier than speaking.

"Good." He took her hand and led her back to where they had been standing before. Together they stood and watched the finale as the music built to an amazing crescendo.

His fingers intertwined with hers, his thumb rubbed along hers. She didn't think she'd ever touched a person for as long as she was touching him.

But as soon as the music stopped and the curtain came down, he let go of her.

It was crazy, because she hadn't even wanted to hold his hand in the first place, but the loss of it made her feel like he'd let her fall down a dark steep ravine.

MARK REINED IN his lust and waited for his daughter to join them in her dressing room. He thought of cold showers and kittens. He hated cats so this should be working. His erection had fortunately diminished but the part of his brain that wanted to throw JoJo down on the couch she was sitting on and take her like some crazed animal was still very much aroused. Watching her with her arms firmly crossed over her body in a gesture that said *back off,* desperately trying not to look at him, wasn't helping, either.

It only made him want her more, which didn't make a lot of sense.

Hell, it had been a kiss. Not a big deal. Just a kiss. A way to slowly ease her into the idea that they were going to be lovers. Because he truly believed that JoJo wanted to move on with her life and Mark believed that he could help her get over her irrational fear of sex.

He was being freaking altruistic in his attempt to seduce her!

Or he was being a colossal ass and the only thing driving him was his need to have her. Her, the woman he wasn't supposed to want. Her, the woman who didn't want to want him, but did anyway.

The door to the dressing room opened and Mark watched Sophie trying to back away from several musicians who were still congratulating her. He decided she was a little embarrassed by all the praise. When she finally got inside and closed the door, he heard an audible sigh and thought again how young his daughter was to handle the burden of carrying a live performance.

Which she had. She was unequivocally a star.

"Okay, please don't say no until you hear me out."

Mark didn't have to be a parent for very long to know that when a conversation started like this, his natural inclination was going to be to say no.

"This should be interesting."

"A few of the musicians are going out for a late dinner and they invited me along. I know you won't let me go on my own…."

"See, you've already had the conversation."

"But maybe you could come and just sit at another table. Please. It's opening night and no tutoring tomorrow at all."

Mark took in his daughter's hopeful expression. He had no doubt that Bay was probably going to be included in the group. Maybe the kindest thing he could do for his daughter was to tell her no. After all, whatever crush she had for the kid wasn't going to turn into anything. She was only setting herself up to get hurt.

"If you don't want to because of the car thing I understand." She was looking at JoJo when she said it, but JoJo raised her hands.

"Don't put this on me, it's his call."

Mark looked at JoJo. "You'll come with me so I don't look like a dork sitting at a table by myself?"

She smiled, her first since the kiss, and even though Mark already knew what she was going to say before she said it, he was happy that some of the tension between them had finally diffused.

"I'll come with you but I can't really help with the dork part. You're on your own there."

Sophie gave a small fist-pump. "You guys are the best. Let me just change out of my dress and we can go."

THE RESTAURANT OF choice was an Irish bar that didn't pump glaringly loud music down on its patrons and offered a nice selection of beer and fried foods. The musicians had taken up a table for ten, although the number seemed to grow as people pulled chairs up as they came in at different intervals. Mark found a booth where he could watch Sophie, but was still far enough away to give her a sense of independence.

"You're a good guy for letting her do this," JoJo said over a loaded baked-potato skin.

"Good guy, or good dad?"

She seemed to consider that. "I'm going to say both this time. You can't always bring the hammer. As we both know, I'm not the expert on great parenting, but I think letting her enjoy her success—especially with everything that's going on—is a good thing."

"Hmm," he muttered as he checked out the table where Sophie was laughing particularly hard at something Bay had said.

"You know she called you *Dad*."

Instantly he turned back to JoJo. "When?"

"When I was on the ground seeing stars after the car tossed me. She said to hold on, that *Dad* was coming."

The thought of hearing that word from his daughter filled him with something he couldn't name. It wasn't that he necessarily minded her calling him Mark. After all, it was the only name he'd ever had. It was just that he knew why she did it, to remind herself of who he was in her life and who he wasn't, and that was what hurt.

If for a second he could imagine her letting him into her life, all the way in, then he thought it was worth any price. Or maybe it was priceless.

"Don't feel guilty that it only took me getting a mild concussion to bring out Sophie's inner child. I'm cool with it."

Mark smirked, sensing JoJo was teasing him, but it still didn't detract from what had happened to her. Or the fact that she had an uncanny way of responding to this thoughts before he had a chance, or even a desire, to express them.

"I hate it that we still don't have word on the car."

"I told you, the detective said a witness got a partial on the plate. They're just running down all the potentials. We'll know something before we leave for Chicago."

Which was Wednesday. Three more performances in

Philadelphia, then everyone would fly to Chicago to become acclimated to the theater and open on Friday.

Three of the four performances scheduled there were already sold out. Sophie's fame was nationwide.

Mark checked again on his daughter, who now had one hand on Bay's arm—and was biting the nails of her other hand. Half woman, half girl. It didn't take a genius to know it wasn't going to get any easier to watch her with boys in the coming years.

His face must have given him away, as JoJo followed his gaze and turned.

"She's practicing flirting. Leave her alone."

"He likes her," Mark said grimly. "I'm trying to believe the kid when he tells me nothing will happen, but I can see the way he looks at her. Like he's a little dazzled by her. It's not all one-sided."

JoJo took a sip of her beer and Mark could see she wanted to say something but was holding back.

"What?"

"I have a theory. It's a potentially crazy theory so you can tell me I'm nuts. But if we were just investigators working a case, not two people who are desperately trying to protect your daughter, we would consider every angle."

Mark took a French fry from the plate he was sharing with JoJo, bit into it and motioned for her to go on.

"Something Bay said when we were talking about Sophie the other day. It's like he's hoping things work out between the two of you."

"So? That's a good thing, right? She likes him, she hates me, he's rooting for me, she's trying to impress him. I see win-win all the way around."

"He said he was afraid you might lose her."

Instantly the hair on the back of his neck rose, and his focus sharpened on Bay. The kid didn't look like the type to send secretive notes. There was something so earnest about him. Even now, when he was blushing at all the attention Sophie was giving him—even though he was supposed to be the older and more mature person. She was pestering him for something, and Mark could see him reach into his back pocket. Bay handed Sophie a piece of gum and she made a show of swatting her hand in front of her face to tell him the buffalo wings had been too hot.

Bay was laughing and Mark could hear it from where he was sitting. He couldn't put his head around the idea that the kid might be behind the notes.

"I don't think so."

"Hear me out," JoJo said. "Maybe he was trying to help you. We know he's been to your place at least once, so he knows where you live. We know he cares about Sophie, so there is motive. He spends most of his time with her during rehearsal breaks. Maybe he is trying to let you know that if things don't change, you are going to lose her. A totally innocuous message that you took as a threat."

"And the car that ran you down?"

"Another theory, but you had a better vantage point. I remember pushing Sophie away, but at any point did it look like the car tried to steer toward her? The sidewalk wasn't that wide—if someone was intent on harming her, was I really that much of an obstacle?"

"You're saying someone was out to get you instead?"

JoJo shrugged. "I know it sounds a little crazy. It could have been a drunk driver on the loose. But if it's inside the realm of possibility that one of your old cases wants to get back at you, then I can promise you it is totally conceivable I could have pissed off someone who wants to hurt me. I might go so far as to say likely."

"What? Someone who followed you to Philadelphia?" Mark shook his head. "I don't buy it."

"You don't know the extent to which I have pissed people off. Look, I'm just saying we should consider the idea that the two incidents might not be related. Because, as crazy as it sounds, I don't think that car was going to hit Sophie. What did you see?"

A car bouncing into other parked cars, a tinted window and JoJo and his daughter in potential danger. Nothing much after that registered, which was something he'd never experienced before. He'd been in dangerous situations. He'd been in life-threatening ones. But he'd never felt the haze of fear and panic that had completely overwhelmed him when he watched JoJo hit the hood of the car.

But she was right. Instead of continuing on a path toward Sophie, the car had turned sharply, which sent JoJo flying. Hitting someone, even if JoJo hadn't been the target, could have frightened the driver enough to deter them from continuing on to hit Sophie.

Or had hitting JoJo been the goal?

Again Mark shook his head. "No, it's too coincidental."

"This isn't the CIA. Everything is not a conspiracy plot."

"Trust me, when you know what I know everything *is* a conspiracy. I'll talk to the kid. I'll ask him directly if he sent the notes and get a read on him. We'll take it from there."

JoJo nodded.

"You know, Sophie thinks we fit."

He watched her eyes widen. "Really?"

"Not that she approves of anything happening with us. Because even at almost fifteen—that's what I'm supposed to call her now you understand, not fourteen, but almost fifteen—she knows two people who work together shouldn't have sex together."

"Then it's a good thing we're not two people having sex together."

"Yet."

She dropped the fried mozzarella stick she'd been dunking in sauce and glared at him.

"I told you it's not going to happen."

Yes, she did. Only he'd felt her respond to his kiss, felt her body melt against him, all loose and clingy. Her words, her piercings, her tats—all said back off. But there was a part of her daring him to scale that sharp fence to get to her. To touch the sweet part inside. The challenge was there. In the way she let him kiss her, in the way she kissed him back.

Like any good strategist, he backed off and tried another tactic.

"True, so maybe I should take Sophie's other suggestion."

"What was that?"

"To date Nancy."

"Nancy?"

"Yeah. She's not going to be Sophie's tutor next semester. She seems nice, dare I say interested...."

"Nancy?"

This time the mozzarella stick, now dripping with red sauce, came flying right at him.

Yeah, he knew it had been a risk to his shirt, but it was so worth it.

CHAPTER TWELVE

"I DON'T KNOW why you won't let me pay for the dry cleaning." JoJo whispered the words even though the music was peaking to a crescendo.

"I thought you said it was an accident," Mark whispered as he leaned close to her so as not to be overheard.

"It was, but I should still pay for it."

"Shh, this is the good part."

It was the Sunday matinee performance and this time Mark had suggested they watch Sophie from front row seats. By now between rehearsals and performances she had seen and heard the performance many, many times and JoJo knew exactly where they were in the production. They were twenty minutes into the final number, which meant the show would be over in a few moments. Sophie wasn't even playing at this point.

Mark was being intentionally stubborn by not letting her pay for what was an accident. Sort of.

Yes, his comment about dating Nancy had taken her off guard. And yes, something that might have felt like irrational jealousy temporarily overcame her. Which was why she threw the fried stick at him. Accidentally.

To clarify, JoJo was not that person. She wasn't someone who became territorial over a man because she'd never thought about claiming a man. Or having a man. Or a man being hers. She was now, and had always been, completely independent. She wanted it to stay that way.

Nor was she someone who acted without thought. She liked to believe she was always in control of her actions. Except for that night when she had acted on instinct and he'd ended up with a shirt full of sauce and a mozzarella stick in his lap.

After he'd kissed her!

"Also," she said softly with her lips close to his ear so she wouldn't disturb the people sitting next to them—was that aftershave he was wearing? "You have to know I one hundred percent do not care if you want to date Nancy. In fact, I encourage it. Maybe if you make her your little life mission, I won't have to find another job."

"Okay, got it," he whispered back. "You don't care."

Only it didn't sound like he believed her. "I don't!" This was loud enough to earn a shush from the woman on her right.

JoJo sank a little farther into her seat and closed her mouth, figuring it wasn't fair to those around her that she was having a bit of a mental meltdown.

Yesterday, she'd purposefully stayed away from Mark and Sophie. Only showing up for the performance and leaving after it. She had an excuse: signing a lease on her new apartment, which was month to month so she wasn't stuck with it once she was officially out of work. Sophie understood. But Mark made chicken noises when she finally turned up.

Not that he seemed to care that she didn't want to meet them for breakfast before the matinee today, either. No, he'd even suggested she take the day off completely. However, Sophie was her job and JoJo had no plans to shirk her responsibility just because she had a…thing? Crush? Attraction? Potential future relationship with said job's father?

What was she thinking? She'd never wanted a relationship. A relationship implied commitment. Two people making a life together. That came way too close to family for her.

She wanted nothing to do with family after what had happened to hers. Certainly she didn't want the responsibility or the crushing heartbreak of having children only to lose a child or see them harmed.

It was one of the reasons her celibacy didn't bother her as much as other women, who cared about things like procreation. *Celibacy,* a word completely preferable to *virgin.* *Virgin* made JoJo feel like some desperate heroine from a Regency novel who needed to be saved. She did *not* need to be saved.

No, the idea of getting involved in a committed relationship wasn't possible for her. Inevitably the question would be asked. What was the next step? Marriage. Babies. For JoJo there was no next step. There never would be.

JoJo peeked at Mark; his attention seemed to be absorbed in the musicians' performance.

So what did she want from him?

Nothing. It was all she could have. And because of the acknowledged attraction between them, they couldn't even continue to be coworkers. Which really sucked, because even though it had only been a couple of weeks she really liked working with him.

Maybe the best idea was for him to date Nancy. Maybe if he started going out with the tutor then JoJo would get over whatever this crazy feeling was. If he was over her, and she was over him, then maybe he would reconsider her employment.

There was only one problem with that scenario.

It meant he had to actually date Nancy. Become involved with her. Be attracted to her. Kiss her.

Nancy, who was in every respect the polar opposite of JoJo.

Was it possible for a man to be attracted to two distinctly different women?

Who was she kidding? A man might be attracted to someone for any number of reasons. Even a woman with barbed-wire tattoos around her neck.

The music grew louder, then they reached the end and the applause followed. JoJo felt an odd burst of pride when Sophie took her bow and the audience immediately rose to their feet.

It was silly, of course. She had nothing to do with this girl's talent. Still, she felt like she'd come to know her and through knowing her she recognized what an awesome thing Sophie did every time she took the stage. The way she captured an audience and held them in her hands simply by letting the music tell its story.

After the audience began to filter out, Mark reached for JoJo's hand.

Instantly she snapped it back. "What are you doing?"

"Leading you backstage so we can meet Sophie in her dressing room."

"You couldn't have just said that?"

"I could. But I like holding your hand. It's small and delicate. So much like you."

JoJo sneered.

"Fine. No hand-holding. I guess that just leaves kissing."

"I thought you were thinking of kissing Nancy." That didn't sound like jealousy at all.

"Nope. Dating her. Kissing you. Will you come on, I don't like having her out of my sight."

It didn't alleviate his fears that Sophie would be surrounded by fellow musicians. It was possible that one of those musicians was the author of the notes.

After making their way through the throng of stagehands and performers, they finally reached Sophie's dress-

ing room. Bay was with her, not surprisingly, and JoJo
wondered if Mark was about to confront Bay directly about
the notes. He'd already told her that he hadn't done it yesterday, with no time before the performance and afterward
Bay had left with this parents.

"Bay," Mark said as he entered the room. "I'm glad
you're here."

The young man stood from where he had been sitting
on the couch, his instrument tucked in its case next to him.

"Mr. Sharpe. Mark."

"We're going to take Sophie out to eat and we'd like you
to join us if you can make it."

"You would?" His surprise was evident.

"Really?" Sophie's beaming smile actually made Mark
flinch. JoJo figured he probably wasn't used to making
his daughter this happy and now he'd done it twice. Even
though JoJo knew this was less about getting to know Bay
and more about interrogating him.

"Yeah. Sophie can pick the place."

"Oh, my gosh, there is this new fusion place that does
both Thai and Indian—it's supposed to be amazing." The
girl was on her toes with excitement. Then she immediately
started biting on her nails. "If that's okay with you, Bay."

"Sounds awesome."

Mark shrugged. "Sounds good to me, too."

"Just give me a few minutes to change."

After everyone stepped outside the dressing room to
give Sophie her privacy, Bay turned and offered a hand to
Mark. "Thank you, sir. I appreciate you allowing me to be
part of Sophie's life…as a friend."

Mark smiled, but JoJo could see there was something
feral in it. She wanted to tell Bay to run, but she also wanted
her theory about the notes addressed. She was sure Mark

would get his answers, the question was how much he would damage Sophie's trust to get them.

"What are you planning?" JoJo asked as soon as Bay turned the corner of the hallway.

Mark looked at her and she really didn't like his expression. The smile was gone, replaced by a coldness she'd never seen in him before, even though he'd told her it existed.

Mark sighed then as if a great weight had been placed on his shoulders. "I'm going to do what I have to. You need to understand that about me. It's not that I can be ruthless, it's what I *am*."

"Are you trying to scare me?" Which she would never admit to him, but if he was, it was working.

"No, I'm trying to warn you."

LESS THAN AN hour later they were settled into a booth with ten different plates on the table. Sophie had ordered what seemed to be one of everything, but no one was complaining since the food tasted so good.

JoJo waited for Mark to pounce on Bay but for the most part he kept the conversation pretty innocuous. They were seated together on the same side of the booth and JoJo had to work to make sure no parts of her touched any parts of him. Every once in a while she would feel his thigh bumping hers but given the limited size of the booth it was hard to know if it was intentional or not.

At one point, when his thigh lingered and seemed to rub against hers, she concluded it was intentional and shot him a dirty look. He, of course, feigned innocence. When she turned back to the food she could see Sophie looking at her. Then at Mark, as if assessing their nonverbal communication.

"Greg! What a surprise!"

Mark jumped to his feet. A tall lean man with dark hair approached the booth.

"Mark, good to see you." The man smiled.

"Please pull up a chair, we've got so much food ten people couldn't eat all of this."

Greg pulled up a chair at the end of the booth and settled his length into it. JoJo could now firmly feel Mark pressed against her side and it distracted her from thinking about who Greg was.

"Greg and I know each other through Ben. He works for the Tyler Group."

JoJo instantly ran down the list of people she knew who were contracted with the Tyler Group. She had done research on the team when she thought she was going to interview with the legendary Ben Tyler before being passed along to Mark. She knew each member of the group and their particular talents. The part-troubleshooting, part-investigating group contracted with a number of really smart people for various tasks. Some were investigators, some were subject matter experts and one person in particular was a former psychologist who also happened to be an expert in the physiology of lying.

What a coincidence.

"Greg, that's my daughter, Sophie, and this is Bay... her friend."

Greg nodded to both of them. Then turned his attention to JoJo sitting in the corner. "And you are?"

"We'll get to JoJo in a second," Mark said, halting the introductions. "Bay, Sophie may or may not have told you about some notes I received."

Bay looked at Sophie and shifted uncomfortably. "She did, sir. I don't know if she wasn't supposed to say anything, but we talked about it a few times, trying to think of why someone might send them. Stuff like that."

Mark looked at Bay, directly dismissing his daughter's distress.

"Bay, did you write those notes?"

"Mark, what are you doing?"

"Sophie, I need you be quiet for a second."

"Bay, did you send me a note saying that I was going to lose her?"

His jaw fell open and he stammered for a few seconds before saying, "No, I didn't send them."

"Them. How do you know there were two?"

"She told me. She said it was why you were so freaked out and why JoJo and you showed up for every rehearsal. JoJo is supposed to be her bodyguard, right?"

"But you didn't leave them in our mail as some kind of warning to me about my relationship with my daughter."

"What relationship?" Sophie snapped.

"No, sir. I...I didn't."

Mark turned to Greg.

"He's not lying."

"He's stammering like crazy," Mark pointed out.

Greg reached across the table to bring a plate closer to him and investigate its contents. "Yes, but he's not lying."

"Like, who are you again?" Sophie asked Greg.

"A friend." Greg shrugged and decided on the plate with some snap peas dressed with a garlic paste. "Oooh, good."

"I'm sorry, Bay. I had to ask you straight up."

"No, you didn't have to ask him, you should have asked me and I would have told you."

Mark didn't look at Sophie. "I had to ask."

"Can I get out?"

"You can't leave the restaurant," Mark told her.

"Can I go to the bathroom? Is that allowed...Mark?"

Bay scrambled out of the booth to allow Sophie to get

out. As she stormed off down the narrow space between the tables to the bathrooms, Bay remained standing.

"I'll go follow her." Then he stopped. "I know you don't know me. I guess you don't trust me, either. But I would never do anything like send notes or anything. It's not who I am."

"Okay." Mark nodded. "Thanks."

As Bay followed Sophie to the back of the restaurant, Greg slid into the booth seat and started eyeing up the rest of the plates of food. He went for the shrimp first.

"JoJo, this is Greg Chalmers. He…"

"I know who he is." JoJo reached over the table and offered a hand, which Greg shook. "I'm just surprised you had to call in someone with his talents. You told me you were this badass interrogator, but you didn't think you could pick up on whether or not the kid was lying. Hell, he blushed."

"I didn't want my emotions regarding his feelings toward my daughter to distract me. I needed impartiality. Hence Greg. Thanks for coming."

Greg popped another shrimp. "Thanks for feeding me. So what's the deal with the neck tattoos?"

JoJo gasped and instinctively put her hand around her neck to cover them. "Fashion statement," she muttered.

"Not likely. You just started working for Mark?"

"A couple of weeks ago."

"How is it working out between you two?"

She waited a beat for Mark to answer and when he didn't, she said, "Okay." Then squirmed in her seat. Not a comfortable thing lying to an expert lie detector.

"Mark seems to be under a different opinion," Greg said, leaning back in the booth.

JoJo shot Mark a vile look. "You talked to him about us?"

"I talked to him about you," Mark corrected her. "He's one of the best psychologists in the country.…"

"Ex...not a psychologist anymore. No license."

"I thought if you wanted someone to talk to..."

JoJo's jaw dropped as Mark's words sank in. "Are you for real? Did you just set up Bay and me at the same time?"

"Two birds. One stone. It was efficient. Plus, he works for food." Mark pressed against her and lowered his voice. "You need to talk to someone, JoJo. He's the best there is."

"What did you tell him?"

"Nothing you wouldn't have wanted me to. I only let him know that you might need some help."

"You ass." Fury had her shaking in her seat. "Let me out."

"JoJo...I think it would be good for you."

"No, you think it would be good for you. Isn't that the real truth?"

He sighed. "I want you to heal."

"You want to get laid. Now. Let. Me. Out."

Mark slid out of the booth and stepped back.

"Tell Sophie I'll be by tomorrow to pick her up and take her to the studio." JoJo practically jogged out of the restaurant, moving between customers and staff until the crisp fresh air of spring was hitting her face.

She got to the corner of the city block and realized she had no sense of where she was. No thought of what direction she should be heading in to get back to her place.

He'd set her up. Not just Bay—that was ruthless enough. To do it to her, when she was unprepared to defend herself, that was beyond ruthless. It was hurtful.

Shaking her head, JoJo focused on searching for a cab. She didn't know where she was, but she knew where she wanted to go. Back to her apartment, where she would be safe. This was what came from making connections with people. They got to know you, they thought they could heal you. Fix you. He didn't understand. Fixing her meant losing the one constant connection to Julia she still had. Her sacrifice.

"Hey, JoJo!"

Closing her eyes, she turned at the sound of a man's voice calling to her. If it had been Mark she would have ignored him, but it was Greg. His long strides ate up the distance between them pretty quickly.

"Look, Greg, if you're going to try to convince me…"

He held up a hand to stop her. "I'm not. Despite what Mark believes, I'm not into forced therapy."

"Then what are you doing out here?"

"He asked me to watch you get safely into a cab. He couldn't leave Sophie."

"I'm a big girl. I can take care of myself." JoJo turned her back to him and lifted her hand in the air waiting for some yellow cars to flock to her.

"I've known Mark awhile now. We've gotten together a few times with Ben for drinks."

"Good for you." The last thing she wanted to talk about was Mark. She couldn't remember the last time she felt so betrayed. Unfortunately, that wasn't true. She knew exactly when it had happened before and who it had happened with. That Mark now had something in common with her father made things even worse.

Greg moved around her so that she had to face him. "Mostly, from what I've gathered during my time with him, he's a cold ruthless jerk. Funny as hell because of it, though. Never pulls any punches. Always says what he means. So he's fun to hang out with."

"Why are you telling me this?"

"In the past couple of months, I've noticed his interactions with men and women are completely different. With men he's brutally honest and like I said that can mean being a bit of an ass. With women, however, he's…shallow. Everything is on the surface. Except when he talks about his daughter. Then it's all anxiety and worry. But still he hasn't penetrated any of the really deep emotions with her. Mostly because she won't let him."

"Your point?"

"When he asked me to come here today and why, it was a no-brainer that he would do anything to protect Sophie. I'm afraid it's because he feels like safety is the only thing he can give her. When he also asked me to see if I could get you to talk, that surprised me. It meant you were more than a colleague. More than any other woman has been to him since I've known him. If for no other reason, I wanted to meet you because of that. To see who you might be."

JoJo held her arms out to the side. "Well, you've seen me. Get a good look because as soon as we put this thing with Sophie behind us, I'm out of here."

"Nah, I'm not seeing you. Not *you*. Just the part of you that you show everyone else. But the woman behind the tats, you must have shown her to him. And he must have shown you something, too, or he wouldn't be so torn between coming after you and leaving his daughter behind."

"You can't defend him."

"Puh-leeze, did I mention what a jerk he was? He's always asking me to play poker even though he knows I'm a gambling addict. Wants to see if he can bluff me. No, I'm not defending him. I'm explaining him. I don't know what you meant when you said he only wanted to get laid, and I'm not going to ask unless you ever decide you do want to talk to someone. I can only tell you, this isn't about sex with him. It's about something else."

JoJo nodded but only to make him stop talking. She didn't want to think about something else. She was having a hard enough time thinking about sex. Or not thinking about sex with Mark.

Greg lifted his finger into the air and his towering height brought a cab immediately to her corner.

"Show-off."

"It's one of my many talents."

"You're not going to do something stupid right now, like give me your card." JoJo was suddenly afraid she might take it. Talking to Greg was easy. Like he was a person she instantly knew even though she'd only just met him.

"I told you, I don't have a practice. If you want to talk, Mark has my number. If you don't want Mark to know we're talking then find a way to get the number without him knowing. You're a private eye so it should be easy for you."

JoJo walked to the cab. "Thanks. I'll…consider it."

Greg smiled and she found herself warming to that smile. He seemed like a truly nice guy.

"Great, I'm going to go and finish your dinner. You don't have a problem with that, right?"

"Go eat with my blessing. And tell Mark—when Sophie's not around—that I said, go to hell."

Greg smiled. "Nice play. It will keep him on edge."

JoJo got into the backseat and gave the driver directions. As she sat back, it occurred to her that she had been playing with Mark since the moment they'd met. When she'd worn a turtleneck and hair extensions and had tried to convince him she was someone else.

He'd seen through that disguise. So she'd put on another.

Maybe that was the problem with them. Maybe it was time for the *games* to end.

CHAPTER THIRTEEN

"OH, MY GOSH, I'm going to get sick."

Mark smiled at Nancy's fear, but also her excitement at standing on what felt like the top of the world. They were on the Skydeck in the Willis Tower and Nancy had braved the glass balcony to look straight down on the city.

It wasn't a sight for people with acrophobia. Hell, it wasn't a sight for anyone who didn't like roller coasters, but Nancy was braving it out. For about five seconds. Then she hopped out and Mark offered her his hand.

"Wow. That was... I'm not sure if I liked it...but thank you. I never do things like that. Daring things."

"You're welcome."

They made their way to the elevator and descended to the city streets. Wandering in the direction of the hotel but stopping occasionally so Nancy could window-shop.

"I want to thank you for the whole day." Nancy beamed at him from under a red hat that matched her sweater. While nearly April, the city of Chicago didn't seem to be aware of it. "First the brat sandwiches and the walk along the lake and now this. I feel like I really got to see Chicago."

A twinge of guilt surfaced and Mark tamped it down. "It worked out. JoJo was on top of Sophie's schedule all day. Since Sophie isn't speaking to me, I figured it best to make myself scarce. Besides, it was a lot to ask for you to come out here and keep Sophie on schedule with her class work. I wanted you to enjoy the experience."

It almost sounded like the truth. And it partly was. It was nice of her to agree to the trip and to help keep Sophie's schedule routine.

It was also true that Sophie didn't want anything to do with him. Neither did JoJo.

Nancy seemed like his best bet if he wanted anyone to speak to him today.

Except he couldn't avoid the fact that he was using her. JoJo wasn't speaking to him but JoJo knew where the hell he was and who he was with. He'd made sure of it.

When Greg came back to the restaurant, he'd let Mark know that JoJo had gotten a cab and was headed back to her place. While Bay stood watch over Sophie's very long bathroom break, Greg continued to clean up all the remaining food and in between bites told Mark that he was screwing up with JoJo.

You like her. Admit it. Stop making this a competition between the two of you and treat her like a woman you want in your life.

Which was part of the problem. Since Helen, Mark never had a woman in his life. A woman in his bed, sure, but not his life. Suggesting honesty and openness was so like Greg. Pathetic. Instead he chose to ignore her as much as she was ignoring him. On the plane, with the three of them seated in the same row, he pretended it was perfectly natural to go two hours without saying a word.

Which was why over breakfast he'd told Sophie about his plans to take Nancy sightseeing. Sophie, who had been sitting with JoJo. No doubt Greg wouldn't approve. Mark was still playing games. Only this time with Nancy. It wasn't fair.

"Can I ask you a question?"

"Sure." Mark was wondering how the hell he was going

to get them both back to the hotel without her thinking this had been a date.

"Was this a date?"

So much for that plan.

"I'm sorry?" There it was. Classic asshole maneuver. Invite a woman out, show her the city, feed her some brats, but then act shocked that she should suggest it was exactly what it was.

"Oh. Gosh. I'm sorry. Maybe that was presumptuous…"

Mark watched her flush and fidget with her gloved hands. He hung his head in self-disgust. He was getting close to forty and he was still completely and totally clueless when it came to women.

Why the hell did it have to be so hard? What the hell was wrong with him that he couldn't behave like a normal man, in a perfectly normal situation? It was like he didn't know how to be a good guy even if he tried.

Because you're not normal. Something broke inside a long time ago and instead of fixing it, you plastered over it.

Sadly, that sounded about right. He wanted to kick himself in the ass again for what he'd done to JoJo. Not Sophie or Bay. He didn't blame himself one bit for eliminating Bay as a suspect. Not only did he need to know that the threat was still out there and it was real, but he also needed to assure himself that the kid who spent more time with his daughter than he did was on the up-and-up. Greg's confirmation was all the proof he needed.

But suggesting to JoJo that she needed help, needed psychology when he was completely messed up in the head, too, was condescending.

So now he was a condescending asshole. At least he could fix part of this.

"Nancy, stop," he said, reaching out to take one of the hands that was fidgeting with her jean skirt. Which was shorter than others he'd seen her wear. Outdated maybe, but paired with the red sweater and the black knee-high boots, he could tell she'd dressed for her version of a date.

"Mark, I didn't mean to imply anything. It just took me off guard that…"

"This was a date. In every aspect this was a date."

"Oh."

He pulled her off the busy street and into an alleyway between two city buildings. It was quieter and Mark realized it was because the buildings sheltered them from the brisk wind that he'd gotten used to over the course of their walk.

"Look, I feel really bad," he said.

"You didn't have a good time. Of course you didn't. You were probably bored. It was just a stupid high-rise building. You've probably seen it a ton of times."

"No, no. Today was nice." *Be a man. But don't be a jerk.* "I…I guess I wanted to see maybe what it might be like for us on a date."

"Okay."

"Unfortunately, I think my head isn't all the way into this. I think I shortchanged you."

"Because you maybe have feelings for JoJo?" Her eyebrows were high on her forehead and Mark considered that the woman wasn't a fool. It was actually one of things he liked about her. She was smart without having to try to prove it all the time.

Unlike him.

He was pretty sure he should lie at this point. He didn't want Nancy to think she'd been used. He didn't want Sophie to know about any *feelings* he may or may not have for JoJo, although he hoped Nancy wouldn't share that kind of information with a pupil. However, he also didn't want to mislead her. He'd been enough of a dick to her as it was.

"Maybe. I don't know."

She smiled then. A little sadly, but it was easy to tell she wasn't crushed. She'd known the whole time where he stood. "JoJo and I are not alike."

He snorted. Understatement of the year. Nancy was calm, and sweet, and nice. Easy to be with. Mark was never easy around JoJo. "No, you are not."

"I think that's why I asked you the question. I had a feeling you and JoJo were more of each other's type. So when this started to feel like a date...I was curious."

"You're anyone's type, Nancy."

And she was. He'd done his normal research when he hired her, but there wasn't a hell of a lot to learn about her past. She'd been adopted at a fairly late age, but that wasn't altogether unusual. She grew up with a very sedate middle-class couple. Went to state college, became a teacher and was laid off because of state budget cuts. He'd found no debt other than a car payment and a small student loan and no outstanding warrants. The most exciting thing about her was her Match.com page because it suggested she wasn't entirely averse to taking a risk.

She was warm and pleasant to be around. She had a nice smile and would make a great date for anyone who wanted to ask her out. Which made his reaction to her, a reaction that could best be described as nothing, stupid.

This would be so much easier!

It was his brain talking. Sadly men rarely let their brains rule when it came to sex.

Nancy shrugged. "That's nice to say but it hasn't always been my experience."

"No luck on the blind date?"

He'd remembered her mentioning it. He also remembered thinking it would be a good thing if it did work out for her and her anonymous friend. Then he could completely ignore the logical part of his brain, which insisted that a relationship with a very steady, very safe person would be a good idea to establish stability in his life. Because ultimately, that wasn't what he wanted.

"No. It was okay. But he never invited me on a second date. I think he was seeing someone else later in the week. He mentioned another email. I guess things worked out with her better. I don't ever seem to be the first pick, you know. Always second."

"Listen, let's go grab something to eat. We can talk about how it sucks to be single."

Nancy reached out and grabbed his hand. He could feel the stiffness of the leather gloves she wore around his fingers. "Look, Mark, you're a nice guy. And maybe I was curious, too. But we both know we're much better off with you as my boss and me as your daughter's tutor."

"And friend."

"Okay," she agreed as if considering that option. "Friend."

"So as my friend, will you come eat with me?"

She shook her head. "Friendship doesn't just happen. You have to earn it. Work for it. I actually don't have a lot of friends in my life for that reason. I don't really do casual acquaintances and my best friend, she was like a sister to me...well, I lost her a long time ago. It changed me."

"I'm sorry."

Her eyes were unfocused and he guessed she was thinking about her lost friend. Missing her. "People always say that. *I'm sorry.* But you didn't do anything to hurt her. I'm never sure why people say that."

Mark remembered thinking the same thing when he'd said the same words to JoJo. How pointless they really were. "Maybe because it's the only thing we can say."

"Maybe. Walk me back to the hotel?"

"Absolutely."

They made their way back into the bustle of the street and Mark considered the idea of having to work for a friendship. He didn't really have many friends, either. Ben and Anna certainly qualified. Maybe even to an extent Greg, although because Mark liked to bust the man's balls simply for the fun of it, he wasn't sure if Greg felt the same way about him.

Then there was JoJo. JoJo didn't necessarily feel like a friend.

It was odd. Completely bizarre that the thought should occur to him, but when he thought of JoJo his instant reaction was to place her in context with Sophie.

When he thought of JoJo, he thought of...family.

AFTER SLIDING HIS key card into the door of the hotel suite, Mark walked in to the sound of laughter.

"Shut up!"

"No, seriously, I want those shoes."

"They are totally tacky."

"Tacky is the new black. I'm ordering them online and you will see."

Mark paused for a second, taking in the two women on the couch. JoJo and Sophie were both sitting in the common area between their two rooms. Mark had one bedroom. Sophie and JoJo were in the other.

He couldn't ask for better protection for his daughter and the truth was he couldn't ask for a better friend for her, either. Talk about something that neither one of them had to work for. It was like Sophie and JoJo had fallen into friendship headfirst. Although he could see Sophie still respected JoJo's role. She was a professional. Sophie gave her that credit. However, Sophie was also going to tell JoJo when she thought her shoe choice was tacky.

He coughed into his hand to let them know he was there.

At the small sound, they both picked their heads up out of the magazine they were reading and looked at him. Sophie immediately stood up and went to her room. The door was heavy, so it was hard to slam, but somehow she managed.

"My daughter. The door slammer."

"She really makes an art of it."

"What about you? Forgive me yet?"

"No, I just have no desire to leave the couch. How was your *date* with Nancy?"

Mark took off the heavy peacoat he'd worn to protect him from Chicago's ridiculously cold spring weather. He sat next to her on the couch in a heavy slump. He felt parts of her body pressed up against his and he liked that she didn't move.

"Please tell me I made you jealous."

"Why would I tell you that?"

He smiled inwardly, knowing that what she was really thinking was *why would I tell you that...even if it was true.* At least that's what his sometimes delusional brain came up with and it satisfied him.

"So that I might have at least accomplished one of my missions today because the other was a colossal failure."

"You wanted to make me jealous?"

"I did. I know it makes me a jerk. You may or may not have started to detect that's a theme with me. But I liked the idea of knowing you didn't want me going out with Nancy. I liked better the idea of you thinking about me all day."

She didn't say anything for a while, just let the silence close in around them.

"What was your other mission?"

"To see if I could stop thinking about you and start thinking about Nancy. Because she's safe and easy and stable, which are all the things I want in my life now that I'm with Sophie."

184 FOR THE FIRST TIME

In general, honesty was always a risk. He really hoped Greg was right about this shit. He thought JoJo might prefer it to subterfuge, which was his normal operating agenda.

"It didn't work?"

He was sure he heard smug satisfaction in her voice. He couldn't blame her for it. She was right.

"Nope."

"Doesn't really get us anywhere, does it? I'm still not going to be with you and you're still going to fire me."

Mark reached out and put his hand on her thigh. She was wearing stretchy pants with black leather boots similar to Nancy's, only JoJo's black boots turned him on while Nancy's had barely registered with him.

The fabric hid nothing from his hand. He could feel the strength of the muscle. The way it tensed at his touch, but also the way after a minute it relaxed. He just needed to do that with her whole body.

"You need to know I didn't ask Greg to meet us at that restaurant because I want to screw you."

"No?"

"No. I'm trying to be completely honest with you about everything so I need you to trust what I'm going to say now. I called Greg because I thought he could help you. I know he could help you. He's easy to talk to and since there is no point in lying to him most people don't. It makes his method of therapy-slash-nontherapy very effective."

"I told you I don't want help."

Mark shook his head. "I don't buy that. I don't buy that because you've been letting me touch you for the last few minutes without trying to move away. You want to be touched, JoJo. It's okay to feel that way."

She squirmed a bit, but he didn't release her. Instead he moved his hand down so that instead of being on the front of her thigh it curved around the inside. Slowly he let it slide down a bit toward the center of her.

He stopped when she fidgeted again, listening as her breathing sped up. For moments he held it, letting the intimacy of his touch register.

"It's okay to feel the swish of I-don't-know-what in your belly. I don't know if it feels the same for a woman. I know I'm feeling it, just having my hand here. So close to where you were touching yourself. I see you on my bed and it makes me crazy. Does it feel good?"

She didn't answer. Her eyes were closed. But he could see an almost imperceptible nod.

"Does my hand feel a bit possessive? Like I can touch you here but nobody else can. Like I can touch you here…"

He moved his hand, again sliding it up her thigh and cupping between her legs. He could hear the air pushing in and out of her nose so quickly it squeaked. But simultaneously, he could feel her body relaxing on the couch as the warmth of his hand covered her most intimate part. It seemed to fill her with a lethargy, which was as much a part of sex as the urgency that came with it.

She'd had one foot on the floor and the heel of her other boot placed precariously on the edge of the couch. It lost its hold on the material and now both legs were on the floor and his hand was rubbing her subtly between her legs. Just enough to stir her desire, not enough to satisfy it.

Not unless he pushed his hands into her pants, past her panties, to where she would be slick and his fingers might be able to…

A thump from the other room had him snatching his hand away.

"Holy shit, I forgot she was there."

Instantly, JoJo stood, crossing her arms over her chest, and one leg over the other as if to shield what he'd so recently had access to. "That was… I can't…with her in the next room…"

Mark stood and put his hands on her shoulders to steady her. It almost wasn't fair. He could feel her shaking and he knew in many ways he was torturing her. He was constantly proving her attraction to him. Doing it in public where he thought it was safe. This time he hadn't considered his daughter in the next room, much to his embarrassment. But the outcome was still the same.

JoJo wanted him. She wanted the feelings he was forcing on her. Which meant the conflict between her fear and her desire would only grow stronger. Agitate her more.

"That was my fault."

She shook her head tightly. "Not just yours. Mine, too. I own it. You're not some evil seducer, you know. I know what I'm letting you do. Why I'm letting you do it. It's just that I don't know if I can finish it. I don't even know if I want to."

"Then I'll back off."

"You will?"

He had to. Otherwise he would be what she said he wasn't: a seducer. A man who used the knowledge of what sex did to a person, how it enticing it could be, how debilitating to rational thought. He could use it to push her into something she wasn't ready for and didn't even know if she wanted to experience.

He was a jerk sometimes. But he wasn't a scumbag.

"I have to. This can't be about me or what I want. As much as that sucks. This is me not lying again. I want you and I think if you let me I could get past your defenses. That's the sex god in me talking."

"He's a confident fellow."

"He's been around the block. My point is, with you none of that is going to work. I don't want to wake up next to you one morning and have you look at me like I stole something you wanted to hold on to. So the choice is going to be yours. Completely."

"Thank you."

"And if your choice isn't me…"

"You think I'm going to have sex with someone else?"

Crazy how the idea irritated him. He wasn't possessive with women. Ever. Mostly because there was no reason to be possessive about someone who he knew he wasn't going to hang on to for the long-term. Women were always temporary. Who they slept with before him and who they slept with after him never concerned him.

Only for JoJo there was no one before him. For the first time, he didn't like to think of anyone after him, either. Certainly he didn't like the idea of someone else instead of him. Again, that wasn't his call.

"I don't know. I can't believe how corny this is going to sound, but all I know is you have too much passion. Passion inside of you that shouldn't be locked down behind your barbed-wire fence. You deserve someone who sees that. Who can bring it out of you. If it's not me—yes, that would royally piss me off but I would get over it—then it should be someone else. Someone you care about. Maybe you can get there talking to Greg, maybe you can't. But it was important enough to me to try. I care about you, JoJo."

She looked away from him. "You probably shouldn't."

"I know I shouldn't. I wish I saw you like I saw Nancy. I wish I could work beside you and not think about you in all the ways I do, but I can't. What I'm trying to say is, this feeling that I have isn't just about getting in your pants. It's bigger than that. So I'm going to back off. No more touching, no more kissing."

He took some hope from the fact that her face scrunched

up like a kid who had just been told there was no more dessert.

"If you want me, you know where I am."

"'Kay."

He nodded. "Good. Now in a few minutes I'm going to attempt to win back the love and support of my cherished daughter."

"Why wait?"

"I don't want to be thinking about my penis when I do it. I sort of do that a lot around you."

JoJo gave him a solid clap on the back. Nothing sexual in that touch, just a solid offer of camaraderie.

"Good plan. Now go get her...Dad."

SOPHIE HEARD THE knock and knew she could ignore it. He wouldn't open the door without her agreement. Would he? He wasn't completely barbaric.

The door opened and her eyes narrowed. Right. He was just that barbaric.

"I didn't say you could come in."

"I was doubting you would and I want to talk. Harder to deny me in person."

Sophie sighed and looked to the ceiling. He was wearing the puppy-dog face she'd come to know. That look that said, *I can't be all bad.* Which reminded her that sometimes he wasn't.

"It's not fair. It's not like I can lock the door because JoJo's stuff is here, too."

"Then I guess you have to accept that sometimes I'm not going to wait for you to invite me in."

"That sucks."

"Pretty much." He made to sit down on the bed across from her, but then as if he was wigged out by sitting on JoJo's bed he sat on the edge of hers. "If it makes you feel any better, I've always had a thing about trying to get into rooms that were barred to me."

"Right. Spymaster Mark."

"Something like that. Look, I know I upset you but by confronting Bay…"

"Confronting him? How about ambushing him?"

"Let's not get overly dramatic. I asked a question."

"With a human lie detector at the table."

"It was efficient. If you can look at it from my perspective, I was trying to eliminate him as a suspect."

Sophie wanted to shout, but her head was pounding from being angry for hours on end. Instead she tried for calm outrage. "He's not a suspect. He's my friend. You could have asked me that and I would have told you."

"I wanted an impartial opinion," Mark muttered.

"You embarrassed him, humiliated me. You're so sure these notes are threatening. They don't even say anything like that. You're a spy, you spent your life paranoid. They could be anything. They could have come from the maestro…"

"Is he giving you a hard time again?" Mark asked, pouncing.

"No," Sophie huffed. "He barely even looks at me anymore. I could be sucking it up big-time and he wouldn't even comment."

"I highly doubt you're sucking it up big-time."

"I'm just saying it could be anyone I work with. I checked with Mr. Radley and he told me there is a directory with all of the musicians' names and addresses. If I needed it he could email it to me."

Mark smiled at her. "Look at you, following up like that. Your own little investigation."

"Don't get crazy. It's not like I broke into the producer's office."

Mark held his hands up. "I would have been so proud."

"My point is, you don't get it. There are so many people who might do something like this as a sick joke just to get under my skin and rattle me."

"To clarify the point, the notes appeared to be addressed to me. To get under my skin. But why do you think it could be so many people?"

Sophie shrugged. She didn't want to think about how many people sitting behind her day in and day out resented the hell out of her, but she knew he didn't understand that part of the business.

"Because a lot of musicians hate the whole prodigy thing. They think it's a gimmick. They think the only thing drawing in the crowds is my age. Ask Bay. He was the focus of any show he performed in until he hit seventeen and he didn't look like a kid anymore. His talent didn't change. His lead billing did. I get why they resent me."

Sophie lifted her fingers to her mouth and bit down. When she tasted the sour nail polish on her tongue she cursed softly.

"Is it working?" Mark indicated to the nightstand, where the glass of clear polish sat.

"I guess. It doesn't take more than one bite, that's for sure. But the stuff is so foul." She wondered if it was the cause of her stomachaches. Food was no longer appealing and out of nowhere she was getting waves of nausea.

More likely it was just a cold or flu that was coming on. Which sucked, timing-wise. They were only here for a limited time. She wanted to be able to give her audiences here her best. Sophie quickly put it out of her mind. She couldn't control how she felt. All she needed to do was to get through the next three performances. Then they would head back to Philadelphia for a two-week break before flying to Los Angeles. She'd been sick before and had performed. Hanging on for another few days was nothing.

"I'm sorry your colleagues resent you. It must be hard to make friends. Harder still because most of them are older. I didn't really think of that."

"Mom was always trying to protect me from it. She'd bring me to the theater, let me perform, then get me out of there before anyone had a chance to make their feelings known. Before I started to question why all the musicians would do things after shows, but nobody ever invited me."

"Last week? Was that the first time you were asked to an after-show hangout?"

Sophie nodded. She couldn't help smiling when she thought about it. It had been the...*Best. Night. Ever.*

"I didn't know I should be protecting you from them. Just one more thing that sucks about living with me, I'm sure."

Sophie could have let him live a little with that guilt but it didn't exactly seem fair. While she understood why her mother wanted to protect her, the older she got the more her mother's hovering had chafed. Sophie had to accept that there were going to be haters and move on. Because beyond the haters there were also going to be people she missed out on having friendships with if she isolated herself entirely.

The truth was, if her mother was still alive she doubted she would have had a chance to really get to know Bay. She certainly would not have been allowed to go out with him and the other musicians.

Sophie didn't want to think about what that meant. She wasn't happy her mother was gone. She would give anything to have her back. She just wondered how her mom would have adjusted to her getting older. It would have been a struggle with her in some ways, just like it was a struggle with Mark in others.

"No, I'm sort of cool with how you handle things. I'm almost fifteen. I need to be able to interact with other people in the show. That's why I liked Bay so much when I first met him. He's been where I am, but now he's part of the team. They accept him and he sort of brings me along... so they have no choice but to accept me. This has been the best show by far to work on."

"But you still think someone might have sent those notes."

"I know Bay didn't, but that's all."

"Well, now I know Bay didn't, either. How about this, I'm done with surprises. If I'm going to do something related to the notes that might impact you or your relationships with anyone I promise to give you a heads-up."

"How about a say in *what* you're going to do?"

Mark winced. "Not going to happen. But I'll listen to you. I'll consider what you have to say. I just can't guarantee it will impact any action I plan to take."

Sophie closed her eyes and fell back on the bed. "Ugh. I want this over."

"Me, too, honey."

Mark stood up and Sophie figured their fight was over. She wouldn't admit it, but she didn't like fighting with him. She didn't enjoy not talking to him out of spite. It made her feel too isolated. Too cut off from everything. As long as they were talking, she knew that she still had family. Family that cared. It was hard to imagine that she had actually considered emancipation. She could handle a few more years with Mark.

Unless he screwed something else up, which was not entirely unfeasible. Could she keep forgiving him if he did?

"That was the first time you called me *honey.*"

Mark turned back to her. "I know, right? It sort of fell out of my mouth. Like no effort at all."

"Well, *honey* is fine. But don't start getting crazy. Like *kiddo* or *baby doll*."

"Got it. No *kiddo* or *baby doll*. What about *sweetie pie?*"

She rolled her eyes and stifled the laugh he'd almost elicited. They had made up, which was cool with her, but she wasn't going to encourage him beyond that. He might start to think she liked him.

He might start to think maybe there was even more than that between them.

"THANK YOU, DETECTIVE."

JoJo looked up as Mark shut Sophie's door behind him. "All good?"

"We're speaking. I consider it a monumental victory."

"Well, then we can celebrate with some good news. The cops found the car."

Mark's body went on instant alert. "Do they know who it's registered to?"

JoJo was already opening up her laptop. "Don't get too excited. It was reported stolen that same day."

"Where did they find it?"

"Junkyard. Burned up inside so no prints, no DNA."

"It's what I would have done. Stolen the car, trashed it, set it on fire. That doesn't sound like some random drunk. There is a deliberateness to it."

JoJo agreed. It was possible a person might have sobered up and realized what had happened. Then wanted to get rid of the evidence. But the fact that the car was stolen first was too much of a stretch. No, the person who hit her stole that car with the intent to do damage.

"What are you doing?"

JoJo wiggled her eyebrows. "You hired me because I have skills. Allow me to impress you."

She typed in the name of the person who had reported

the car stolen. She tracked that to a home address, a business address and two email accounts. She plugged the information into the program she'd built to cross-reference data related to cases Mark had previously investigated. Then, she waited.

After dismissing a few random bits of information that scrolled on the computer screen, she stopped. "That's interesting."

Mark sat down next to her on the couch. She looked at him, or more specifically, at his hands. He held them up for display. "No tricks. I promise. We're working now."

She turned the laptop toward him.

"What am I looking at?"

"Regina Anderson's address."

"What about it?"

"When I started looking into potential suspects I included information related to any of the cases that you had taken since you got to Philadelphia. Names, addresses, phone numbers. Any data you had from the case file. Then if we found something we could cross-reference the new information with your casework and see if anything popped."

"Something popped?"

"The car was stolen from somebody who lives on the same street as Regina Anderson."

Mark stared at her and she could see his mind spinning, wondering what the odds were that it could be a coincidence.

"You said you checked and she was still in the mental health facility."

"Yep," JoJo confirmed. "On lockdown, too. They wouldn't let me speak to her. Only immediate family."

Mark nodded. "That leaves the son. Call the hospital. See if anyone's called for Regina. If it is Sean and he's doing this for his mother he might want to let her know what he's accomplished."

"Okay, but based on my last conversation with Sean, he should be in the middle of the Bering Sea. Assuming he was telling the truth, of course. I'll call the hospital and I'll also get confirmation from the motel where I tracked him to see when he left."

Mark got off the couch. "And I'll call Ben. Have him check the Anderson house out for us. See if there are any signs of life in case Sean chose to come home instead."

JoJo picked up her cell but heard a knock on the door. Mark turned at the sound and frowned. The interruption was unexpected. JoJo didn't have to be a mind reader to know Mark wouldn't like anything unexpected right now.

"It might be Bay. You know he's staying in the same hotel with his parents. Sophie would have given him our room number."

"Oh, great," Mark groaned. "I get to once again let him hang out with my daughter in a room with a bed in it. Parenting…what a hoot."

He walked over and opened the door, but JoJo could see it wasn't Bay. Instead, it was a hotel worker in uniform. Who passed something to Mark.

"This was left downstairs at the front desk with specific instructions that it be hand-delivered to you."

When Mark shut the door, the look on his face suggested he wasn't pleased.

"What is it?"

"A plain envelope."

JoJo moved the laptop and got up to stand next to him as he studied the envelope. He held it up to the light and they could both see a note inside.

Mark opened it and pulled out the paper. JoJo could see

the words neatly typed in the center, similar to the other notes.

I'm sorry.

"For what?"

Mark folded the note and JoJo could sense the anger vibrating throughout his body. It was odd that she felt the same way. Sophie wasn't hers, but it felt like whoever was threatening her, whoever was putting this anger and fear into Mark, was coming after her, as well. She wanted to hit something. Or someone.

"Whoever it is, is in Chicago." Mark's voice was a low hum.

JoJo's mind raced as she tried to the think of all the possibilities. "You don't know that. It could have been mailed to the hotel."

"Then it's someone who knows her damn schedule! Where the hell she stays when she's here."

JoJo didn't flinch at his bark because she knew it wasn't directed at her. She needed to focus for him. He wasn't capable of it in this state.

Although he was right. Whoever sent the note knew at least where the musicians were staying, if not Sophie specifically. It would be an easy assumption to make that she would stay in the same hotel. Whoever sent the note didn't have to know their room number, only that it needed to be delivered to Mark Sharpe.

They needed to make new reservations. Finding another hotel would at least limit Sophie's vulnerability. JoJo would do a simple internet search to find out how easy or hard it would be to follow the orchestra's schedule. The producer could tell her if they frequently used this hotel.

But first things were first. "You stay with Sophie. I'm going to go question the hotel staff."

She moved past him, but he reached out to grab her arm. "I should go."

JoJo knew she was dealing with a highly volatile man right now. She'd seen so many sides to Mark and looking up into his face, she knew this was the scary side. The deadly one. It was a stark reminder that it would always be a part of him, no matter how far away he was from Afghanistan.

JoJo was on board with this side. Sophie should be protected by all the fierceness that Mark could offer her. Without a specific target there was no place to take his fire. Instead he needed to rein it in by focusing on the tasks ahead.

"Listen to me," she said, not trying to pull away from him, but instead moving closer, toward his tight muscles and humming temper. "You're not thinking clearly. You're angry, upset. It will be easier for the staff to talk to me."

"What I am…is violent."

Yes. She felt it in the hand still wrapped around her upper arm. It clenched and unclenched with systematic intent. Not to hurt her or inflict pain, but simply to suggest he was of a mind to hurt someone.

She rested her hand on his chest and they both looked at it as if neither could explain her instinct to soothe the savage beast. "I know. You have reason."

"You're not afraid." It wasn't a question, but a statement.

He was right. She wasn't. When she'd confronted her father in his rages she always sensed the harm he'd wanted to inflict. She countered the animal instinct that always told her to flee by standing still instead. Even before he'd started to hit her.

With Mark she didn't sense any urgent need for flight. He wasn't going to hurt her. There was control behind all of his actions. Even his touch. But if she didn't solve the puzzle of the notes soon, she wasn't certain how much longer his control would hold.

"No, not of you."

He shook his head. "Maybe you should be. I've never felt like this, JoJo. I've never felt this kind of..."

"Fear."

His eyes met hers. "Is that what this is?"

Her lips tweaked at his astonishment. "I think so."

"If you knew the things I could do right now to the person who sent this note. Things I've done in the past. To men. To women..."

He was trying to scare her again. Maybe even push her a little, test her strength against the onslaught of his ugly past. She'd seen his ruthlessness by springing Greg on both her and Sophie. Now he was trying to tell her there was an even darker side.

"Yeah, I know. It's what made you a badass agent. But it doesn't scare me."

Oddly, it had the opposite effect. She could imagine the lengths he would go to protect Sophie. JoJo could imagine the lengths he would go to protect her, too. Despite her past, despite his past, instead of being frightened she felt safe. She also knew that by accepting Mark as...what, she wasn't even sure of yet. But she had to accept all the parts of him.

"It should scare you."

"Too late. You're already the guy who tried to fake cooking a pasta dinner. How much of a threat can you really be?"

With that she felt some of the tension leaving him. His hand dropped from her arm and she shivered a little as the warmth left her.

"We don't tell Sophie about this note. She's got enough on her plate, we don't need to add to it. Plus she has it in her head that it might be one of her fellow musicians."

"Seriously?"

"I think she understands that not everyone appreciates her top billing. She doesn't see the subtle nature of what these notes say...*I'm sorry.* It's like he's already hurt her."

"He hasn't."

"Right. Anyway, she doesn't look good to me and I can't tell...I can't tell because I don't know my daughter well enough...whether it's because of stress or she's coming down with a cold. So let's keep this between us."

JoJo nodded. "We'll need to make another reservation. A different hotel so no one knows where we are."

Mark nodded. "We'll tell her there was a problem with the room and the hotel manager found us accommodations at one of the nearby hotels. We'll pack while you ask around."

"Okay." JoJo was about to step around him when something he'd said stopped her. Instead she lifted her hand to his cheek. She could feel his five-o'clock shadow and it occurred to her she'd never touched a man this way. With tenderness. Never wanted to.

"You're a good father."

He sighed, then put his hand on top of hers, as if absorbing her words, her comfort, through his skin. Then he pulled away and let her go.

His jaw ticked. "Just so we're clear. I don't want *you* to think of me like a father."

That made her laugh. "Trust me, the last thing I think of you as is my father."

"Excellent. What's the first?"

That was a very good question.

CHAPTER FOURTEEN

"THERE'S DEFINITELY BEEN someone in the house recently." Mark tightened his grip on the cell phone as he listened to Ben describe what he was seeing.

JoJo had already returned from her excursion. Interrogating the staff had yielded no information. A manila envelope had been left at the front desk when no one was manning it. A window of time the clerk estimated as no longer than two to three minutes. One of the new clerks had a bathroom emergency.

When a clerk coming off break returned, he opened the manila envelope, saw a printed note inside that requested hand delivery to Mr. Sharpe. He called a bag boy over to handle it.

The letter hadn't been mailed. It had been left. By someone who must have been in the lobby waiting for an opportunity to drop it off. A person who wanted to hurt Sophie. A person who potentially had already hurt JoJo. A person who had followed them to Chicago.

Someone close.

Sophie hadn't questioned why they had to pack up and change hotels. She'd been annoyed more than suspicious. And probably disappointed she wasn't going to have any chances to run into Bay randomly throughout their stay.

Luckily, Mark had found another suite a couple of city blocks away—a little nicer and more costly, but it was worth any price. Once they were settled, JoJo and Sophie curled up on the couch to watch a movie on the wide flat-screen TV. He closed the door to his room and called Ben.

"Any problems getting into the house?"

"Is that supposed to be a joke?"

Mark winced. It wasn't that he'd forgotten who he was dealing with, it was simply that he was more rattled then he had ever been in his life. "What are you seeing?"

He waited for a response, imagining Ben methodically making his way through the darkened home. With a small pinpoint flashlight, so as not telegraph his home invasion, as his only illumination while making his way from room to room. It was what Mark would have done had he been there.

"Nothing overt. But there is a table in the foyer covered with picture frames. I can see from the dust that some of them have been shifted. Normal things. High school grad-uations, a family-reunion-type picture, a kid in a football uniform."

"Nothing normal about that family," Mark reminded him.

"The dust has been disturbed more under one in par-ticular. It's him. Anderson, with his daughter sitting on his lap. She's smiling in the picture but there is a look in her eyes...."

"How old?"

"Fourteen maybe. Fifteen."

"He'd been molesting her for years at that point. My guess is she was sixteen when she decided to end it. When he started to slowly poison her."

"Whoever it was didn't have a key. The back door lock was jammed open. A crowbar maybe. Nothing subtle. But whoever did it has had access to the house since. None of the electronics have been touched. TV, stereo, computer. Whoever did this had no intention of stealing anything."

"Except a car..."

"What?"

"Never mind. It's what I needed. Whoever is sending those notes is connected to the Anderson case. I just need to find out who and why."

"Let me know if there's anything else you need."

"JoJo and I have it covered. You've done enough, thanks. Tell Anna I'm sorry for making you leave her in the middle of the night to go spying."

"It's not my first experience with strange late-night calls. She's pretty cool about that. Now if you want me to apologize to Kelly that's something else. I didn't get to read her a bedtime story tonight. No doubt she won't be speaking to me in the morning."

Mark smiled at Ben's dry humor. "You know she can't talk, right?"

"We communicate without words."

For a moment, Mark wondered what that was like. To have established that type of connection with Sophie from the beginning, instead of always feeling like she was trying to squirm away from him.

He thought about the fear that had blazed through him when he realized whoever was threatening them had followed them to Chicago. Fear like he'd never experienced before. Fear that he hadn't even realized he was capable of feeling.

Mark had jumped out of helicopters, had been caught in gun battles, had escaped certain death a number of times. He thought he was immune to fear.

No, he had been immune to it. He just wasn't anymore.

"Ben, can I ask you…"

"Anything."

"Kelly. If she was ever in trouble or hurt how do think you would respond?"

There was a definitive moment of silence.

"I can't answer that. I can't think about her being hurt or in trouble because if I do my mind shuts down. I become an irrational creature and irrational creatures are not thoughtful enough to know how they might respond in such a crisis."

Oddly, Ben's words made him feel better. Under pressure, Ben was the coolest man Mark had ever met. Cooler than him. If Ben would lose it, then Mark didn't worry he was completely crazy by acting like this. Feeling like this.

"And if it was Anna…"

"There's no difference. Anna and Kelly are mine. With them I function. Without them, I don't. Not properly. It's as simple as that. You saw me after she fell into the coma when delivering Kelly. You know."

Mark closed his eyes on the memory. Ben covered in blood and broken in ways he'd never seen him. Yes. Now he understood that expression on Ben's face. Like he'd lose himself if he lost Anna.

"Can I ask something else? When Anna worked for you—if nothing had happened, if you hadn't gotten sick and she still worked for you—do you think you ever would have admitted to yourself how you felt about her?"

"I don't know. I hope so. Otherwise I would be the dumbest jackass on the planet. Why do I feel like we're not talking about me and Anna?"

He shouldn't have said anything to Ben. He was too damn intuitive. "It's nothing. I was curious. Forget I said anything."

"Mark," Ben drawled through the phone. "You're not actually starting to develop feelings for someone, are you? That would be a novelty for the legendary player, Mark Sharpe."

"You did it," Mark grumbled, feeling defensive.

"I did. When I never believed I could. If that's where

you are, believing you're not capable of those feelings because you've never had them before, I can tell you this—"

"Yeah?" he asked, impatient for whatever pearl of wisdom Ben was about to bestow.

"—they suck."

Okay, Mark thought. Not exactly the answer he was hoping for.

"Don't get me wrong. They're wonderful, amazing and also life-changing. But having them, acknowledging them and living with the fear that someday something could happen to Anna or Kelly, this…love…that I feel is the hardest thing I've ever lived with."

"Right."

"I also wouldn't change it for anything."

Mark understood what Ben was saying. He just wasn't sure he was prepared to open himself up like that. He felt like he'd already given everything he could give to Sophie. He'd come home to her, brought her to live with him. Had come to genuinely like her. But somehow he knew there was more. Some deeper connection that they were both holding back from feeling.

That Sophie would hold back made perfect sense. It was natural she would be wary of him when he'd missed most of her life.

For him, there was no reason to hold back. Except that he wasn't sure he knew how to let himself feel so strongly for another person. It was crazy that as he was trying to figure that out with his daughter, a woman had come along who affected him like no other woman ever had.

Letting JoJo in, letting her get to him on more than a physical level, shouldn't have made sense to him. Only it did.

"Thanks, Ben."

"Should I post a watch on the house? In case the person returns?"

"Don't bother. The person is in Chicago."

Mark hung up the phone and joined JoJo and Sophie, who were halfway through the movie. JoJo looked at him, but he shook his head to indicate they would talk about it later. He sat on the couch next to Sophie and dug into a handful of popcorn she'd made from the suite's stacked kitchenette.

"This place is the bomb. I've never stayed anywhere so swanky. Do you think Hollywood people stay here when they come to Chicago?"

Mark nodded. "I'm very certain Angelina and Brad were the guests right before us."

Sophie rolled her eyes. "Yeah, right. Hey, we need to tell Nancy where we are. I have lessons tomorrow."

Mark felt a tightness in his chest. Right now only three people knew where Sophie was. Mark had even checked in under one of his aliases. It was an old habit to keep a set of backup identification and credit cards with him at all times.

Until she was onstage, it would remain just the three of them. "I'll call her tomorrow, but any tutoring should be done in her room, okay?"

"Why? There's more space here."

"I think your dad doesn't want to show off our nice digs. Makes us look like jerks," JoJo chimed in. Then she also reached for Sophie's bag of popcorn. "Can we talk about this later? We're getting to the good part."

Mark inwardly applauded her distraction technique. "What am I watching?"

"CIA agent turned traitor, turned counterspy, turned rogue killer," Sophie elaborated.

"Awesome. I love it when Hollywood gets the CIA right."

Mark looked at JoJo, who was staring at him instead of

the television screen. There were a hundred questions in her eyes and he wanted nothing more than to answer them. To share with her what he knew. Get her impressions and thoughts. He'd known her for only a few weeks and yet he felt more in tune with her as a partner than anyone who had come before.

It really was a shame she was going to have to quit after all this was over.

After an hour of car chases, highly improbable gun standoffs and a thrilling secret revealed, Sophie was ready to call it a night.

"I need to sleep if I'm going to have enough energy for tomorrow night," she announced, struggling to get off the couch.

Mark stood and placed his hand on his daughter's forehead. "You don't look good to me. You're face is all flushed."

She looked skeptical. "Do you even know what you're feeling for?"

"Excessive heat?"

"I'm fine. It's just a cold. I'll take some medicine and that will knock me out so I can sleep."

"Okay."

Mark watched her walk to the bedroom and shut the door behind her quietly. He smiled as he thought how nice that it wasn't slammed. They really were making progress.

"It could be the schedule that's wiping her out. It never ends. It's a lot, you know?"

Mark turned to JoJo, who was still wearing the same black stretchy pants he'd been so fond of earlier. He hadn't noticed the loose top that covered her to her hips. Probably because he'd been so enamored with her pants. With her legs curled up under her and the bag of popcorn now cold, sitting in her lap, she didn't look much older than Sophie.

Yet he trusted her to watch over and protect his daughter without question. A testament to her brains, her strength and her tenacity.

"I know it's crazy," he said. "What I don't know is how much control I have over that. This is her life and she loves it."

"I get that, but at some point she should have a chance to be a kid. Maybe meet a nice boy who isn't eighteen years old and go out on a... What's that thing called again?"

"I believe the word you are looking for is *date*. And don't encourage her. I like it this way—I'm starting to become the most important man in her life. You know, after Bay."

Mark sat on the couch with a heavy sigh. Their bodies bumped together. This time he kept his hands to himself. He'd made a promise to her that whatever happened next between them would come from her initiative. He would honor the promise. But he couldn't suppress the thought that he would like nothing better than to put his head in her lap and let her soothe away this new strange emotion in his life known as fear.

Never in his life had Mark put his head in anyone's lap. Not even his mother's.

Was this what a relationship felt like? As if he could turn over control to someone else and let them carry his burdens for a time? Instinctively, he rejected the notion. He would carry his own burdens. He would solve his own problems. To do anything else would only open him wider to...what? He wasn't sure, but it couldn't be good.

Despite what Ben had said, he didn't know if he had it in him.

It was probably the worst trick to play on JoJo. To seduce her. To introduce her to sex and pleasure and intimacy. All the while never once really giving her anything of himself other than his dick. The only thing he'd ever given to anyone.

"I suck."

"At what?"

"People."

JoJo nudged him with her shoulder and settled herself more fully against him. "I don't know. I used to think I sucked at people, too, but we seem to be doing all right together."

"Maybe that's the magic between us. You're not willing to take. And I'm not willing to give. We make quite a pair."

JoJo was quiet for a time and Mark realized how insensitive he'd sounded. "I'm sorry…"

"Don't. You're right. Tell me what Ben said."

"Someone has been inside the Anderson home. Broke the lock on the back door, but stole nothing. Some dust under pictures in the foyer had been disturbed. Someone was looking at a picture of Anderson with Sally—the daughter he molested—on his lap."

"Well, when I called the mental facility was closed. I'll call again in the morning. I also checked on Sean. According to the motel owner where he last stayed, he did leave on a catch. Put a few things in the motel's safe for storage. Not that it means much. He still could have bailed on his ship at the last minute. I'm not going to be able to get access to the major airlines' passenger lists to see if I can track him on any flights out of Anchorage, but he would have needed a private plane to get off the smaller islands. I'll look into that."

Mark shook his head. "I'm not feeling Sean. Sean knows his father was a molester, if not a murderer. The person who would direct their anger at me and not at Jack Anderson is someone who has to deny what Anderson was, what he did to his daughter. It's the only way I become the villain, a target of revenge."

"A daughter for a father."

"A little biblical for my tastes, but yes. I uncovered the truth and because I did, Anderson killed himself. Someone is upset enough by that to come after my daughter."

"Which means we need to take a harder look at the Anderson family in general. Cousins, aunts, uncles. Friends of the family. Anyone who might have never believed what Anderson did to his daughter."

"Yep. We'll get started tomorrow." He patted her leg, innocently, but as soon as his hand found her body a bolt of lust shot through his body. He decided he was a sick human being. His daughter in jeopardy. A case up in the air. A woman who didn't even know what she wanted from him sexually and still he was lusting after her like a teenager with no control.

He stood and rubbed his hands against his jeans as if he could erase the memory of what it felt like to touch her.

"We'll talk tomorrow. Determine a plan of attack."

JoJo nodded, but she didn't say anything. Instead she was staring at him as if he had the answer to a very important question. Mark felt devoid of answers.

"Okay," he said. "See you."

"Mark?"

He stopped on his path to his room, but he didn't look at her. He was fairly certain that if he turned and looked at her he would end up picking her up, taking her to his room and laying her down on his bed. The thought of sinking into her, letting her take his weight, being connected to her in a way he couldn't ever remember was so tempting it made his whole body ache.

"Yeah?"

"I would be willing to take…you, I mean. If you wanted to give."

His head dropped to his chest. There it was. Such a perfect invitation. She was offering. He wasn't seducing. There would be no guilt. Only pleasure. For him certainly. For her hopefully.

Mark went to her and crouched in front of where she sat on the couch. So still. So brave.

He reached up and cupped her face, then dropped his hand to her neck and rubbed the evidence of her conviction to remain removed from the world in a very significant way.

"Please, I have maybe an ounce of goodness in me. Let me use it tonight. Let me be noble."

"You look so…lonely. So lost. I don't like it."

It felt like a sharp blow to his chest. Because she was right. He was lonely. But he did that to himself.

"And you would keep me company?"

After a pause, she nodded slowly.

"JoJo Hatcher, you are the most amazing woman I have ever known." He raised himself so he could press his lips to hers. They were soft and giving and her taste was everything he remembered. But he had to let her go. He had to. For his own sanity. "But you're not ready for this and there is that last ounce of goodness. I will see you tomorrow."

"Okay."

He nodded and straightened. "Okay."

"Mark?"

"Yes."

She shrugged. "I think you have more than an ounce."

It wasn't a night of unbridled passion, but it made him feel like a king nonetheless.

He brushed his fingers against the softness of her cheek and somehow, somewhere in what he thought was a cold and unfeeling heart, found the strength to walk way.

CHAPTER FIFTEEN

JoJo STARED UP at the ceiling, seeing nothing. Sophie was sound asleep in the bed next to her making deep-breathing noises that came close to snoring, but were too gentle.

JoJo hadn't heard that sound in thirteen years.

Thirteen years since she'd lost her sister, her best friend and eventually her entire family.

Not to mention her ability to ever have a family in the future. To have a family you needed to be willing to have a relationship with a man. To have children you had to be willing to risk loving someone unconditionally.

She'd set herself up as an outcast and thought that was the way she wanted it. A single room in college, spending all her money on a one-room loft in the city instead of trying to live with someone. Keeping all her professional colleagues at a distance.

Even keeping all the people she called friends at a distance.

She thought she was content with how she was living her life, and maybe she was, until she met Mark. Now she knew that it could be different. If she wanted it to be.

"What a joke," she whispered to the ceiling.

Sophie took another breath and gurgled another release of breath. JoJo closed her eyes as tears leaked out and dripped down into her hair.

She hadn't even realized, hadn't considered…how much she had missed that sound.

The sound of life. So close. So connected.

When Mark suggested the sleeping arrangements, she hadn't even balked. Thinking about it now, that was odd for her. Yes, it made sense for her to stay with Sophie so she could provide around-the-clock protection, but she could have asked for a connecting room. But no, it had to be total protection. That it wasn't even awkward was a testament to how well they got along.

It should have been.

They weren't friends of the same age. JoJo was her father's employee. It should have been incredibly odd for both of them to get changed into their pajamas while the other was in the bathroom brushing her teeth. Sharing shampoo and toothpaste.

And mascara, as JoJo had noticed that Sophie's eyelashes had thickened earlier this afternoon.

Even when they changed hotels, not sharing one of the suite rooms had become unthinkable. They were officially roomies.

JoJo turned her head and stared at the lump on the bed. So completely trusting. No thoughts about anyone bad in the world who wanted to hurt her. Someone who had followed her to Chicago to send another note. JoJo wanted to shake Sophie until she woke and tell her how wrong she was. How there were so many bad people who could do horrible, horrible things to a teenage girl.

Instead JoJo let her sleep. The burden of knowing what was out there was hers to hold alone.

No, she thought. Not just hold. Clutch. Imprison. Lock away. Until all the pain and all the fear and all the knowledge of what could be comprised the sum total of all her parts.

Had she actually offered herself to Mark? Did she for a second believe he would take her up on it? In truth, she knew he wouldn't. He liked to imagine he wasn't the best man in the room. That he was darker and harder than anyone else. But he wasn't. That was only one side. One side of so many, and all of his sides added up to yield a good man.

He'd looked so lost when he'd headed to his bedroom. As if he had nowhere else to turn and no one else to go to. As if he'd failed. Not just to protect Sophie, but to be the man he obviously wanted to be for his daughter.

She'd thought about holding him, comforting him. Letting him take comfort in her. She thought doing so would be noble.

Hell, she thought she was a damn sacrificial virgin.

That wasn't entirely true. When he was being noble and refused her, that was what he didn't realize. He didn't understand that deep inside she wanted to be sacrificed. She wanted to be seduced. It would have been so easy, to have the decision taken away from her.

She wouldn't be betraying Julia, she would simply be succumbing to charms of an impossibly sexy man. How could she be blamed for that? How could she let the guilt interfere with what she imagined would be incredible pleasure?

This time, when she closed her eyes there were no tears. Just the image of what Mark would look like without his shirt. Or his pants. How he would feel under her hands. What it would be like to have him touch her.

No, JoJo didn't think that giving herself to Mark would in any way be a sacrifice. The problem was, he'd given her no out, no wiggle room to let him take control of the situation. Any choice she made was hers to own.

JoJo tossed back the covers of the bed and swung her legs around until her bare feet were touching the carpet. She could see the mound under the covers breathing deeply, if a little less quietly. She tried to imagine what Sophie would think if she knew that they had more in common than Sophie could possibly imagine. Two virgins: one girl, one woman.

No doubt that if Sophie knew, the girl would think her less fierce. Certainly less brave. Because there was a certain amount of bravery involved the first time. Knowing there would be pain, but choosing to act despite it.

JoJo wasn't exactly certain when she had become such an extreme coward.

Standing, she felt as if her body was suddenly acting on its own accord. Like it knew where it wanted to go and what it wanted before she did. Soundlessly, she made her way across the room, opening and closing the door behind her without so much as a click of the knob.

Moonlight broke through the curtains and made patterns on the furniture and carpet as she walked the distance to the door to Mark's bedroom. Standing in front of it, she could feel her heart rate accelerate. She couldn't tell if it was from fear or excitement.

It wasn't the sex that excited her. As good as he made her feel with just a kiss or a touch, she didn't imagine the actual act would bring much feeling beyond some discomfort. It wasn't the physical act, it was the idea of being changed. Of becoming more normal. Of maybe someday coming to understand that sex was okay. Pleasure was okay.

Being connected to someone, intimately, was okay.

JoJo opened the door and stepped into the room. This time she didn't worry about the sound as she closed it behind her. She imagined she would need to wake him. Maybe even need to shake his arm or tug on his blankets, depending on how soundly he slept.

But as soon as she closed the door, his head turned in her direction. She could see his eyes in the moonlight, open and alert, staring at her.

"I want to do this." Her voice was low, nearly broken. She tried again. "Please don't send me away. I want to do this."

For a moment he didn't say anything. Instead he moved over to the other side of the bed and lifted the covers in invitation. She walked to the bed and, looking down on him, she felt a crazy need to groan a little.

He wasn't wearing a T-shirt. His chest was covered with dark hair that swirled around his nipples and the defined muscles of his pecks and abs.

"Are you wearing shorts?"

"No."

Which meant he was naked. All the way. Under the blanket. She'd never acted like such a virgin in her life. She even crossed an arm over her stomach and took hold of her other wrist.

"Take off your clothes."

Right, she thought. Because that was how it had to happen. Him all the way naked. Her all the way naked. She shuffled her feet.

"I don't want you naked so I can look at you," he said, even as he reached over and turned on the light. "Although I will very much enjoy seeing you. This is for you. You need to come to me naked. No barriers, Jo."

Reaching over, she turned off the lamp. But when she straightened, she pulled her T-shirt up and over her head. With no bra, she knew he could see her shape. The curve of her breasts. Then, before she could think about it, she pushed down her cotton pajama bottoms and stepped out of them, too.

She didn't like wearing underwear to bed, so there was nothing. Just the curve of her waist, the weight of breasts. Her bottom and thighs. The dark blond swirl of curls between her legs, which always reminded her she wasn't a brunette.

"You're beautiful."

She shrugged and swallowed and wondered whether he would chase after her if she ran from the room. Probably not. So instead of running she kneeled on the bed and stretched out on her side, facing him.

She could see his nose and his eyes and his chin. She could instantly feel his body heat. Or was her nervous agitation causing her to flush?

She saw his hand move and wondered what he might touch first. His palm rested on her cheek. For the briefest moment, she thought she felt his hand trembling. Oddly, it gave her some comfort.

"Are you sure?"

"Yes. One hundred percent." It wasn't a lie. She felt trepidation, anxiety and anticipation. She still wasn't absolutely certain she wasn't going to run, but she knew without a doubt that she wanted this.

Wanted him.

"I don't know…how good it might be for you.…"

Mark chuckled. "Sweetheart, I'm not a virgin. And even if I was, here is a nasty little fact. It's always good for men."

"I just meant…"

"I know what you meant. Now hush and let me handle this. I've never taken a virgin before and I'm scared out of my mind."

She cupped his cheek in her palm. "Don't be scared. You can do it."

His eyes met hers and she saw a promise in them. One that excited her. Then his gaze was moving up and down her body, but more with an assessing manner than an admiring one.

"I'm not a turkey you're going to carve up."

"The beginning is the same. It's a question of where to start on such delicious flesh." He moved toward her and she was overcome again by the heat of him. As if he was a living fire that would consume her.

One hand slipped over her waist and settled on her back. The other he used to prop his head on his fist. She waited for him to start but he seemed to content to let his eyes drift over her face. She was about to force some kind of action when he bent down and placed a gentle kiss on her lips.

She liked that. Then he teased her lips with his until she opened her mouth and his tongue was dipping inside. She wasn't sure what to do with her hands, so she kept them to herself. One under the pillow, the other laying along her side. But she figured it was appropriate to touch him and after fifteen years of curiosity, now was a pretty good chance to find out what a man felt like. The first place she wanted to go was down low.

She was finally about to meet the Penis.

As she reached down, he broke the kiss and turned onto his back. "Hold on."

She waited a few breaths, hoping he would turn back toward her. When he didn't, she grew worried. "You're not chickening out, are you?"

"No," he groaned, his forearm covering his face. "Will you just give me a minute? This is a big deal."

"Yeah. For me!"

He turned back to her, his face serious. "Is that what you think? That this isn't a big deal for me, too? Then you're wrong. It is. I'm just… I'm really… I don't want to scare you."

"I'm a virgin, not an idiot. I know what's down there."

"Yes, but you don't know how much. Let's try this first."

He took her hand and placed it around his back. She could feel his body tighten and then relax. Then he circled her waist again and nudged her closer until their knees touched, then their thighs, then their middles. Until her breasts were pressed into his chest and his lips were nuzzling the spot under her ear while she took in the depth and breadth of him.

His erection pressed against her belly. Long and thick and hard. Yes, maybe this was a better way to meet the Penis. She could let her body get used to it before she had to deal with the reality of it being inside her.

Her legs shifted and so did his until one heavy thigh was between her legs. He pressed it firmly against her and the pressure of his body there was thrilling, even more thrilling than his hand had been.

He rolled her slightly onto her back, but not all the way, and she was glad. She wasn't ready to feel what it meant to have someone on top of her, covering her completely and pushing her into the mattress. Instead they were still mostly on their sides but her shoulder was turned away, which gave him access to her breasts.

He brought his hand up around her body, skimming her buttocks and back and stomach until it settled on her breast. He cupped her right boob and played with it. Stroked it and let his fingers dance around it until her nipple was hard and aching. She wanted him to touch that pointed nipple, pinch it. She'd read enough in books, seen enough in movies, she knew what was supposed to happen and she wanted to know how all of it felt.

But instead of feeling his fingers, he dropped his head and she felt his mouth. His tongue licked the hard flesh and her body shuttered in response. She could feel his thigh again right in the center of her. So firm and unforgiving. His penis, now slightly less foreign and mysterious, was still pressed into her belly like a massive elephant in the room that neither of them had any intention of discussing.

His mouth drew on her, sucked her in, and she could feel it all the way down her stomach and between her legs. Until his mouth shifted and he was sucking on her other breast. Lips and tongue. So wet and soft. But then there was the rough edge of his teeth. It was better than she'd imagined. So different from touching herself, when she knew what her moves would be in advance.

Mark was unpredictable. Where he touched her, where he kissed her, where he licked her.

Where he sucked on her.

Restless, she twisted her body to take in more. Her leg locked around his one heavy thigh and she pressed herself against him. It felt so good to do that she did it again, until she found an even rocking rhythm that matched his mouth on hers. The thrust of his tongue against hers.

Her hand clutched his upper arm for support as she tried to angle her body in a way that brought his thigh into even better contact with where she wanted it. But then he was shifting back, moving that wonderful, delightful thigh away from her.

"No!"

"It's okay. Listen, sweet, I'm going to make you come first. Okay."

"Yeah." She agreed like it was something that happened every day. Like he was offering to clean the dishes or put away laundry.

I'm going to make you come first.

Sounded like a plan.

This time he arranged her so she was more fully on her back. He kneeled between her spread legs and she missed the warmth she'd felt when they were closer. But now she could look up at him and take in his broad chest and tight middle. She could see the thrust of his erection standing between his legs, but it didn't scare her as much as she

thought it would. In an odd way it seemed familiar. Like
this was how it was all supposed to be. Like her body was
completely okay with everything that was happening even
though this was the first time it was happening.

This time when she reached out her hand, he let her
touch him.

Hello, Penis.

She heard the small gasp, followed by a low moan, as
she tightened her grip. Wow, he felt good. Really hard and
really hot and sort of thick. And smooth. Or maybe fluid.
She couldn't really summon the right word, but instinctively her hand wanted to circle his length and stroke him.

She watched HBO. She'd seen naked men before, but
she'd never touched this part of a man and once again reality was far better than her imagination. After a second
he moved her hand away.

"You first."

She wasn't exactly sure what that meant until his hand
drifted down her center over the small roundness of her
belly and between her legs. She could feel and hear the
slickness of her body as his fingers toyed with her first
before he plunged one deep inside her.

"Oh!"

"Good?"

"Yes," she confirmed. She knew what an orgasm was,
too. There had been a few times when, as much as she
tried not to touch herself, tried to deny herself that fun-
damental pleasure, that she couldn't stop her body from
convulsing on its own. Sometimes it happened in a dream
and she could indulge it because she couldn't be accused
of betraying Julia then.

But Julia wasn't here now. She wasn't in this bed. There
was no guilt as she pressed herself into his hand, as his
finger slid deep. None when he added another finger, then

used his other hand to tweak her nipples. Pinching them until they stood up in sharp attention.

Finally his thumb slid between her folds and pressed against her clitoris. It was all her overstimulated, sex-starved body needed. She threw herself into the tremors of her climax, twisting and stretching, pulling every delicious sensation out of it. Eventually the feelings subsided and she relaxed against the bed, her arms to the side, her legs spread wide with Mark still kneeling between them.

Beautiful, magical Mark. Her brain registered a non-organic sound and she rustled up enough effort to open her eyes. His fingers were sliding a condom down over his firm erection and suddenly it occurred to her that this wasn't over.

"I'm going to take you this way first, okay. It will be easier."

She didn't have enough sense left to either agree or disagree. She simply acquiesced as he shoved one, then another, then another pillow under her ass. Forcing her into an almost bowed position as he took his cock in his hand and began to press it into her body.

Her first thought was pressure, her second thought was a burning painful sensation like he was ripping into something even though she knew she didn't have a hymen. And it continued as he pressed farther into her, not once stopping despite her whimpering.

The word *no* surfaced quickly, immediately followed by the word *stop,* but she clamped them down. She knew it wasn't going to feel good, not the first time. This was the bravery part. Accepting the pain, accepting that he was the one giving it to her, and then hoping he would also be the one to deliver her from it.

Their breathing was harsh now and it filled the room with the noise of a loud engine. He pushed again and she felt him so deep inside her. She used her hands to push against his hips, trying to back him off and lessen the extreme fullness.

"Just get used to it a little," he said gruffly, his hands now tightly wrapped around her hips as he held himself still inside her body.

"Used to it? Little?"

He leaned down and nipped her breast. "You're doing fine. This is sex, baby. The pleasure and the pain of it. You're getting good and laid."

He had the audacity to chuckle and she wanted to hit him for it, but then he was easing out of her body. Like a wave slowly receding, the relief of it was enough to make her moan. Only without warning he started to push back inside. This time she really was going to stop him, but before she could register the heft of him, he was slipping away again.

And that was how it went for what felt like an endless amount of time. Him pushing into her too high and too hard, then him sliding away. Again and again.

"Better?"

"It's okay." And it was. The burning sensation was gone and she liked the feel of him sliding away so much that she was willing to tolerate the heavy fullness when he was deep inside. "I don't think I could…uh… I don't feel what I felt before."

Then he leaned down over her, his hands on either side of her head, caging her, but not letting her take his full weight.

"That's because you have to learn what you like, what your body wants. We're going to roll now, baby."

He did it as soon as he said it. He shifted their position without leaving her body, so that he was on his back and she was lying on top of him. She settled her knees on either side of his hips and experimented by putting her hands on his chest and using her own weight to spear herself on his cock.

When the pressure got to be too much she could ease up on her own. She liked that. She really liked that.

"But what about you? Is this frustrating? Don't you want to…"

He laughed again. "Yup. Frustrating as hell. Keep it coming. You can do this all night, baby. I never come on my back like this, so play to your heart's content. After you come again we'll worry about me."

Play. That did sound like fun. Here was this incredible man underneath her legs, inside her body, and she could do whatever she wanted. Take him deep or shallow. She sped up her movements and he growled. She liked that, too. Liked the fast in-and-out motion. Then she tried it slow again and that was good.

She wasn't sure when it had changed, but the pressure definitely became a pleasure. And she wanted more of it. More of him. She sank down and forced her body to take all of him until their bodies were pressed tight.

"Jo, yessss. That's it. So good."

She leaned forward and rubbed against him, feeling the friction of his hard stomach pressing against her mound even as she forced his cock deeper. "Ahhh…"

"Don't push it, baby. Take only what you want."

But that was the crazy thing. She wanted all of him. She wanted him so completely inside her that she wouldn't forget him. That he would be tattooed forever inside her body.

"Mark. Mark." It was a chant that left her body as she continued to move on him. Up and down in her own relentless rhythm. "I don't know how to…get there. Help me. Please help me."

She saw his eyes open, felt his body tense, and she knew that she was no longer in charge of this ride.

CHAPTER SIXTEEN

HELP ME. PLEASE help me.

The words tore through Mark like an electric shock. Yes, he wanted to help her. Yes, he wanted to give her everything she needed. He wanted to be everything to her. Her savior, her ravager. Her pleasure.

He sat up and it shifted his cock inside her body, which made her gasp.

He decided making her gasp could be his new life mission.

He grabbed her ass and pulled her closer, her legs shifting so they wrapped around his waist. He could feel the tips of her nipples agitating his chest, making him remember how they felt in his fingers, on his tongue. Her arms wrapped around his neck and she let her head fall back, accepting the switch in control. Then he started to thrust his hips, even as he was pulling her down hard on his erection, going deeper than she had taken him on her own. But her soft cries told him that she welcomed it.

There was no finesse in this. His body was jerking and shoving at hers while she was trying to get closer, holding him even tighter so that place where they were connected was the center of both their universes.

He thought about trying to use his fingers on her clitoris. He thought about trying to kiss her again. He thought of so many clean—and maybe even a little dirty—ways to bring her more pleasure, but he couldn't make himself stop. He could feel the rush in his balls and knew what was coming, what he could no longer hold back.

"Mark!"

There it was. Her body squeezing around his, her insides squeezing around his cock in the tightest, hottest grip he could imagine. He thrust once, then again, then again, letting his orgasm overtake him, feeling his come spill out and crazily wishing that there was no condom between them. That he could be leaving himself inside her to become a part of her.

Then all those crazy thoughts left him as he pulled her down with him, into the bed. Her legs stretched out alongside his, her cheek pressed against his chest. There was a pleasure in this he didn't think he'd ever felt before. Her body filled with air and then released it in time with his own quick breaths. Like they shared a heart and lungs.

Eventually he would need to separate himself from her, deal with the condom and the realities of sex, but for five more seconds he simply wanted to hold her.

"I thought you said it didn't happen for you in that position. I'm no expert or anything, but that felt like something happening."

It usually didn't. Not since he'd been a teenager when a girl looking at him the right way was enough to get him off. He liked to be on top, controlling his own tempo in order to orgasm.

There hadn't been any control in what they had just done. His climax had hit him like a shot to the base of his spine, exploding out of him.

Shit, that had felt good.

But then reality intruded and he remembered why he'd wanted JoJo on top of him in the first place. He should have been softer with her, but he couldn't summon the decency to be ashamed of himself.

He could, however, be a gentleman now. Cupping her bottom he held her steady as he slipped out of her.

"Nnnnn…"

"I'm going to interpret that sound as regret."

"Half regret, half…I'm not sure what."

He rolled her again so that she was on her side and then left the bed. He could feel her eyes on him, following him. He had the urge to ask her if she liked what she saw—the first time in his life he'd ever cared about that.

He went to the bathroom, dealt with the condom, then he grabbed a washcloth and turned on the water. Bringing it back into the bed, he didn't hesitate before pressing the cold cloth against her sex.

"Yeow!"

"Hold still."

"It's cold."

"It's supposed to be."

"I thought you said you never had a virgin. What makes you think you know what you're doing?"

"It's common sense. Cold will settle the inflammation. This way maybe we can do it again without it being too painful. I'm going on record to say I really, really want to do that again."

"Well, then, this makes all the sense in the world."

A niggling worry clouded over his good humor. "Was it too much this time?"

"Too painful?"

He nodded. He knew it hadn't been painful enough for her to want to stop. He also knew he'd brought her pleasure at the end. But he hated the possibility that what had felt so completely right, so inherently good to him, had brought her pain instead.

"No. It hurt a little in the beginning and I wasn't sure it

could ever really feel good." She smiled shyly then and it made his heart flip in his chest. "But then it did."

Mark took the cloth away and tossed it in the direction of the bathroom. Then he settled into the bed again and brought her against his body. Satisfied that he'd taken care of her as best he could, he took the time to appreciate how she felt pressed up against him. Her breasts along his side, her leg over his, shifting in a way to cause the most pleasant kind of friction.

"No bad thoughts," he said.

She propped her chin on his chest and for a second he could see she didn't know what he was talking about. Then her eyes widened, as if she was surprised at herself.

"No. I didn't think about her at all."

He felt her stiffen and instantly he wrapped his arms around her to hold her closer. "Good. She doesn't belong in this bed. You've held on for so long to what happened to her, I don't know how you can remember the good stuff. The good stuff is what's important."

"You're right. Sleeping next to Sophie, I remembered that Julia used to make the same kind of sleep noises. I hadn't thought of that in so long. It was a nice memory. I miss having nice memories of my sister."

Mark smiled. "Glad my daughter's snoring is a good thing."

"She wasn't snoring. More like snorting. Speaking of, I suppose I should go back. I doubt it would set a good example for her to wake up and see that I decided to change roommates. And be naked roommates."

"Right, I have to be responsible, don't I?" Fathers didn't let their daughters know they had sex. It seemed like a stupid rule. His daughter wasn't an idiot. Hell, she had even encouraged him to date.

Nancy. Not JoJo. JoJo, she had said, was strictly off-limits if they were going to be working together.

In the aftermath of awesome sex that also sounded like a stupid rule. He didn't want to fire JoJo. Didn't want her to leave either his bed or his business. He supposed the reason why mixing business with pleasure was so taboo was because ultimately, when things ended, it would be unpleasant. They would be more involved professionally, more involved personally. Dividing up clients and cases would be a battle. Figuring out which of the things in the apartment was hers or theirs or his could be a nightmare.

Intellectually it made sense. But when he looked forward and thought about the end, it was all blurry. It had never been blurry before.

"No, stay for a little while. This is the part women like best."

"It is?"

"Yeah, go figure, because orgasms are so awesome, but all women ever seem to want to do is cuddle."

"Well, maybe you weren't doing it right with those other women."

He sent his hand down her body and pinched her ass.

"Yeow!"

Mark laughed. "You deserved it."

"So are we going to do it again?"

This made him smile. "I don't know. I told you my position on the matter, but it's really up to you. Did you want to?"

A pause and then she said, "Yeah."

He had to work to keep the smugness out of his next question. "You liked it?"

"Yeah."

"You really liked it?"

"Now you're just feeding your ego."

"Let's give it a little time. I need to recover. I am a man after all." Although at the mere mention of *doing it* he could feel his sex swell. He needed to call on the nobility he had with her earlier this evening. She'd just gotten properly screwed and while he wasn't a woman, he could imagine her body needed time to process that. "Then we'll see how you feel."

He could feel her head plopping back onto his chest, rubbing her cheek against the mat of hair. "And we just stay here like this? Naked?"

"That's usually how it works."

"How do people sleep like this? You're naked and I'm naked and we're still touching and everything."

She was right. He'd swelled to a near full-on erection. Mentally, he told his body to chill out. What had happened between them had been pretty intense. While he obviously hadn't killed her desire for sex in the future, he didn't want to risk causing her pain. He wanted her to enjoy every second of their time together.

"Close your eyes and just listen to my heartbeat."

"That will work?"

"It will stop you from talking, which will let me sleep, and that's all I really care about," he said, laughing so she would know he wasn't serious.

He didn't try to evade it when her hand swept down his body. He felt her fingers on the side of his butt and when she gave him a really hard pinch, he yowled.

"You deserved it," she said, then did as he suggested and settled more comfortably into his body. In minutes he could hear her sleeping noises and they filled him with some kind of huge emotion.

She'd let him inside her body, she'd let herself fall asleep in his arms. She trusted him and Mark never wanted to lose that trust.

EARLY IN THE morning she stirred against him. Her hands moved over his body and he returned the favor. It was so slow and easy. So simple to roll her onto her back and kiss her breasts while she moaned softly in his ear and ran her hands up and down his back. Then he moved his body lower and found her soft stomach and her belly button, which while not designed for piercing, was perfectly adequate for him to dip his tongue into. When he did it, he made her squirm.

Then he moved lower and waited for a beat to see how she would react. She had to know his intent. While she'd never had sex, only the youngest of children or most sheltered of adults could avoid knowing what it was all about. Still, he had to remember that everything was new to her. It only made sense that she would be hesitant to let him have whatever he wanted. And he was completely fine with that, as long as she let him have what he wanted eventually.

Because what he wanted, what he really wanted, was to make her scream with pleasure.

Finally, her legs shifted apart and she arched her back and gave him everything.

He felt like a king when he pressed his tongue against her slick folds. Like a god when she cried out his name as he brought her to climax. Like a man with his cock throbbing, desperate to be inside her.

He had enough sense left to grab a condom from the nightstand where he'd stashed some just in case. When he was ready to enter her body, he forced himself to take it slow and easy. She was so snug, but this time there was less resistance to his entry. It was like she'd been welcoming him into her body all her life.

He put his weight on his forearms on either side of her head and just rocked his hips into her in a steady, even beat. She kissed his chin, his cheek. She pulled her legs up and wrapped them around his hips. They kissed and made love and when she tightened around his body he held himself still and reveled in the feel of her climax before taking his own pleasure.

This time there was no talk afterward. He took care of the condom and got back into bed. They repositioned themselves. He spooned her into his body and they fell back asleep like the lovers they now were.

MARK HEARD A sound but it didn't register immediately. As he forced himself awake he had to work to recall where he was. Not in Afghanistan—he was too damn comfortable. Really comfortable. Like he could lie in this bed with this person for the rest of his life.

That was right. He was with JoJo. They were lovers. Everything made sense.

"Mark? Are you in there?"

He wanted to tell whoever was knocking to go away, that he and JoJo were still sleeping. Then it occurred to him that the person on the other side of the door was his daughter.

Oh, shit.

Mark turned and saw JoJo still soundly sleeping on her stomach, her face turned toward him. The dark tattoos on her neck stood out in stark contrast to the white pillow. So hard and unforgiving, when she was anything but.

He couldn't wake her. He couldn't force her to hide in the bathroom. It would somehow make what had happened between them last night wrong—and there was nothing wrong with what they did. It had been perfect.

He rolled out of bed naked and snatched up his robe. Then he went over to open the door and deal with whatever reaction Sophie was going to have to the change in their sleeping arrangements.

It was one more reason not to bother hiding the situation from her. He had no intention of going to bed tonight without JoJo next to him.

Sophie looked anxious, which instantly worried him.

"What's up?"

"Did JoJo say anything about having to do something this morning? I woke up because I wasn't feeling well and her bed was empty. It's been a few hours and I just thought…"

Mark walked out of the bedroom and shut the door behind him. "JoJo's asleep."

"No, that's what I'm saying, she's gone."

Mark used his chin to indicate the room behind him. "It's okay. She's with me."

"With you?"

He watched his daughter's face as understanding dawned. She said she hadn't been feeling well and he could see it. Her cheeks were red, but there were dark circles under her eyes. She looked worn and tired.

"Hey, I'm thinking we should find you a doctor. You really don't look good."

"I'm fine. It's just the flu or something," she said tightly. "So are you serious? Are you two doing it now?"

Having absolutely no idea how to have this conversation with a teenager, let alone his daughter, he thought back to when he was her age and what he would have wanted to hear.

The truth, he suspected.

"JoJo and I are sleeping together, yes. But it's not going to change anything."

"Bullshit!"

"Watch your language."

"Oh, please. Spare me your fatherly disapproval. I can't believe you."

"I don't get why you're so upset by this. You like JoJo.

You like hanging out with her and you even said she was my type."

"Yes, and then I said it was too bad because you couldn't do anything about it. She works for you. Remember?"

"I don't think that has to change," he said stubbornly, his thoughts from last night returning. Why couldn't they work together, eat together, sleep together? Why couldn't he have everything he wanted?

"Of course it's going to change! You're freaking screwing her now. Everything is going to change. You'll get tired of her like you did with Mom and then she'll leave. She's been, like, my only real friend and you just ruined it. But maybe you don't care about that. I mean who cares if she leaves, right? Who cares if you leave for that matter."

"Leave?" The idea was crazy to him. She was his responsibility from now until, well, forever. "Sophie, where the hell do you think I'm going?"

The door behind him opened and Sophie backed up a few steps, her glare and derision now fully transferred to the woman behind him.

"Sorry. I heard you guys talking. Sophie, what's happening between me and Mark doesn't have to change anything between us."

"Right," Sophie snapped. "Whatever. It doesn't matter. You were probably just being nice to me so you could get into his pants."

JoJo moved to stand front of him. "That's not fair. You know me better than that. You know I wouldn't use anyone. Certainly not you. What happened between me and Mark…just happened."

"Like I said, I don't care. But don't even pretend we know each other, okay. You're nothing to me. You're just someone who my dad fu—"

"Hey!" Mark barked. "That's enough. I don't know what

bug crawled up your butt. You need to get over it. JoJo and I are together now."

"Together," Sophie huffed. "You don't know what *together* means. I'm out of here."

"You're not going anywhere, young lady."

"Screw you...*Dad.*"

Mark reached out to grab her arm, but she pulled away and bolted for the door. He ran after her, but she was fast and disappeared down the hallway in a blink. He pulled up when the elevator door closed behind her and cursed when another elevator opened. People got off, gaping at him as he stood there in his robe and bare feet.

Then he heard the sound of feet pounding the floor behind him. While he'd been chasing Sophie down, JoJo had changed into a pair of jeans and a T-shirt. Her sneakers were unlaced as she came up beside him and hit the down arrow.

"I'll follow her."

"If she gets down to the lobby she could get a cab, go anywhere."

"Go get dressed. Start calling people at the other hotel. Nancy, Bay. She'll likely go there."

"JoJo," Mark said, taking her arm and wondering if she understood what had just happened. Sophie was out there in the city without him. "Find her."

She flashed him a smile as she kneeled down to tie her sneakers. When she stood, he could see the determination in her expression. "I won't let anything happen to her. She might be pissed at me right now, but she's the only friend I've made in a long time, too. I'm not letting her go."

The elevator dinged and JoJo stepped in. As the door closed, she gave him the thumbs-up sign and for some strange reason he felt relieved. JoJo wasn't going to let anything happen to his daughter. Tightening the sash around his robe, he made his way back to the hotel room only to realize he had no key.

What had started out as a great morning was turning into a real shit of a day.

CHAPTER SEVENTEEN

"No, SIR. SHE's not with me. Of course. As soon as I see her I'll call you."

Bay hung up the hotel phone and Sophie closed her eyes with relief and gratitude. She hadn't been sure that when it came to either choosing her or doing the right thing that Bay would pick her. He was a traditionalist that way.

"You know this is temporary, right? You're going to have to talk to him eventually."

"Eventually," Sophie repeated. "As soon as I get the image of them doing it out of my brain. Which could require a lobotomy."

Bay sat on the opposite end of the queen-size bed where she was stretched out. He was probably trying to show her that while he had no problem sitting on a bed on which she was lying, the closest they were going to get was two body lengths away.

"Did you actually walk in and see them, you know, doing it?"

The way she had previously told the story might have been slightly exaggerated. But it felt like she had caught them in the middle of something tawdry. Even though Mark hadn't tried to hide it. Not really. Just came right out and said it.

We're together.

What he forgot to add was…*for now.*

STEPHANIE DOYLE   237

"Not exactly. I mean, I wasn't in the room with them or anything."

"You're really that upset about it?"

Yeah, she was really that upset about it. What bothered her was that she couldn't exactly pinpoint why she was so upset. She felt betrayed by both of them. Like neither one of them thought about how she might feel about them sleeping together before they went ahead and did it.

"I think they sort of fit together."

"What do you know about them?" Sophie snapped. Then she bit her tongue. She was supposed to be getting him to like her enough to make out with her. Snapping at him like she did with Mark was probably against the rules of flirting. Unfortunately, it seemed to be a pattern she'd developed. All someone had to do was tell her something she didn't want to hear and bam, she turned into royal teen bitch.

Sophie hated being so predictable. She decided to blame her attitude on her cold.

"I know that she's badass with her tattoos and all. The way she hopped up on the stage and took on the maestro for you, that was cool. Plus your dad's already a badass just by being in the CIA. All I'm saying is I get why they like each other."

"Maybe."

"Plus she's hot."

That had Sophie sitting up on her elbows, glaring at the opposite end of the bed. "You think she's hot?"

"Uh…yeah. Not pretty…hot. More like smart Goth-chic hot."

"Is that what you like? In a girl?"

"Me?" Bay laughed. "No. My parents would kill me if I brought some girl home with piercings and a bunch of tattoos."

Sophie smiled, very pleased to hear that. She'd only

met the Tongs once when Bay introduced her to them after opening night. She knew he didn't do it because he wanted her to meet them. Only because they had asked to be introduced to her. She tried not to hold that against him. At the time she felt like they had approved of how she handled herself onstage and off. To a pair of longtime stage parents, that meant something.

While she understood why she and Bay couldn't officially *date,* she still had this idea that someday soon he would bring her home with him for a break or maybe even a holiday. Then the Tongs would get to know her and realize how mature she was for her age. Then Bay would be less freaked-out by the almost three-year age difference.

Then…

Sophie thought of her logical progressions like they were runs on the piano. It was part of what she loved about playing, each note leading to another note. Each sound building on the other. Starting low and then getting a little higher, a little higher, a little higher.

That was the way she thought of everything.

Get through the night after the police let her know her mother hadn't survived the car wreck. Get up the next morning and don't break down in front of her grandparents. Get through her mother's funeral. And then…get on with her life. Alone.

Get Bay to notice her. Get Bay to talk to her. Get Bay to like her. Get Bay to make out with her.

Get Bay to have sex with her. To be her first.

Always so nice and orderly. Every note in her life in its perfect place.

"Bay, do you mind if I use the bathroom?"

"Go ahead. But seriously, you need to call your father or JoJo. The whole letter thing probably still has them freaked-out. You can't hide out here forever."

"Sure. I will."

She rolled off the bed but stilled herself when a wave of dizziness swamped her. Stupid cold. If it didn't let up, tonight's performance was going to suck. She wasn't really worried about how she would play. She knew once she got onstage the adrenaline would kick in and overtake her. The sucky part would be afterward, when she would totally collapse. Which would make getting up for the next performance that much harder.

But none of that mattered. She and Bay didn't have to be at the theater until close to five. It was only ten in the morning. They totally had time to do it. Maybe they could even do it twice. Because she knew the first time would probably really hurt.

Sophie looked at her reflection in the mirror. Immediately, she lifted her hand to her mouth and started biting through her clear polished nails. This time she didn't try to stop herself but suffered through the horrible taste because she needed the comfort.

Her hair was in a ponytail. She wasn't wearing any makeup and she was wearing the jeans and black T-shirt she'd thrown on that morning. A black T-shirt with a big treble clef on it. She sighed. No wonder Bay thought she was a kid. She took out the twist band and tried to fluff her hair. Then she took off her T-shirt and stared at herself in just her bra.

It was black. Another Victoria's Secret bra that she had totally overpaid for, but she thought this one made her look bigger than she actually was. If she just walked out there without her shirt, then he would have to do something. Right?

He was a guy. She would be almost naked. If she didn't give him a chance and just walked up to him and started kissing him, then he would kiss her back. She was sure of it. Then once they started kissing she could entice him into going all the way. Guys wanted to go all the way all the time.

And today she did, too. She was tired of waiting. Tired of playing by the rules.

What did it get her anyway? Her mother was dead. Mark didn't care enough about her to keeps his hands off her friend. And JoJo? JoJo was just using her. She wasn't sure what hurt worse.

She had been starting to feel, like, close. To both of them. But they didn't care about her—all they cared about was getting into bed with each other.

Proof that sex was probably even a bigger deal than she realized. Proof that no matter now *noble* Bay wanted to be, he wouldn't be able to resist.

All she had to do was go out there.

Maybe she should take off her pants. Sophie reached for the top button and pulled them down.

Okay. No way. She had on Snoopy underwear. Which was cute in the packet when she bought it. There was actually a Linus pair. But she couldn't walk out there in something that made her look more like a kid. Instead she took off her bra, unhooking it and letting it slide off her shoulders before she could think about it.

Her stomach started to flutter and she could feel her face flush. She forced herself to keep her hands at her sides and let her hair fall behind her back. Actually, her breasts looked better in the bra. Definitely bigger.

"Yo, you okay in there?"

Sophie scrambled to put her bra back on, even though she doubted Bay would open the door. "I'll be out in a second."

This was it. She could do this. "Bay," she said softly to

the mirror. "I want you to be my first. I swear I won't tell anyone."

Turning toward the bathroom door, she took a deep breath. She could do this. She was ready. She wanted this. She wanted this with him. She wanted to be important to someone. Sex would change everything between them.

When she put her hand on the doorknob, she saw that it was shaking. She was such a pansy. It was just sex. Girls her age did it all the time. And he couldn't reject her. Not with her in a black bra. He was a guy. They had absolutely no control.

Opening the door, she forced herself to walk out into the room. He was flipping channels on the television.

"Hey, I thought if you want to hang out we could watch a movie."

"Bay." Her voice cracked. "I swear I won't tell anyone."

He turned and his eyes got big and his jaw dropped. "Sophie…"

"Please don't say…say…" *Oh, this wasn't happening.*

Completely out of her control, she bent over and hurled on the carpet in front of him.

"ARE YOU GOING to tell Mark?"

JoJo removed the cool cloth she'd placed on Sophie's head and replaced it with a fresh one. The cloth apparently had tremendous healing power because Sophie was finally speaking.

She knew what Sophie was asking, but she wasn't sure what the right answer was. When she got to the hotel JoJo had gone straight to Bay's room, knowing not to trust what he'd told Mark on the phone. She knocked on the door and shouted "house cleaning," which apparently he was desperate to have right at that moment because he immediately opened the door.

JoJo had pushed through and found Sophie on her knees in front of a pile of sick wearing only her jeans and her bra and sobbing hysterically.

JoJo feared Bay might have developed a permanent stammer, given the amount of stuttering that accompanied the excuses he'd been trying to offer while she helped Sophie to the bed. First JoJo got the girl back into her T-shirt and then she had brought her back to their hotel suite.

Thankfully, Mark was gone. He'd gone to the theater to try to track her down. When JoJo called him, his relief had been palpable—until she told him to go for a walk for an hour.

He'd pressed her for information but all JoJo offered up was that they needed *girl time*.

Men didn't mess with *girl time*.

He agreed, but only for the forty minutes it would take him to walk back to the hotel from where he was.

JoJo hoped it was enough time.

"So are you?"

JoJo shrugged. "I don't know. I'm not really good at this. I guess he should know, so he can talk to you about sex and stuff."

Sophie closed her eyes and groaned. "Please do not make me talk to Mark about sex."

JoJo thought about the conversations she had with her father about sex. Decidedly not fun, but she knew it wouldn't be like that with Sophie and Mark. Mark didn't know how to be judgmental as a parent. He didn't have enough practice. JoJo guessed he would simply lay out the facts and talk to her about contraception. At least, after a little blustering about the fact that Sophie wasn't ready yet.

Deciding she wasn't ready to have Sophie stop talking to her quite yet, she changed topics. "You really freaked Bay out."

"You think? What part? Flashing him with my bra or puking at his feet? I'm never going to talk to him or look at him again."

"Well, that would be a shame. You guys are friends."

Sophie shook her head, her eyes once again welling up with the tears that seemed endless. "I blew it."

"Isn't that the best part of being friends? You can blow it and still be cool."

Sophie's eyes narrowed. "Was that code for an apology?"

JoJo took the now-warm cloth off her head and chucked it toward the bathroom. She sat on the bed, facing Sophie, and had this crazy urge to smooth the damp hair off her forehead.

Did she want to apologize? No, that really wasn't the question. The question was, did she blow it?

"I'm not going to apologize for sleeping with your dad, if that's what you're after. I…I like him. I trust him and I haven't trusted anyone in a really long time. And, well, he's important to me."

Sophie closed her eyes. "Then I'm sorry for you. Mark's not exactly the settling-down type."

"Maybe not."

"Which means you're just going to leave and find the next guy. I know how this works."

JoJo smiled at that. Such confidence from someone so young. She thought about telling Sophie the truth and considered the thousand reasons why she shouldn't. Because it was private and personal and a little embarrassing. Because Sophie had enough on her plate without having anyone add their baggage to hers. Because she hadn't shared anything with anyone since she'd lost Julia.

Until Mark. It seemed like there were a lot of firsts happening for her lately. And the members of the Sharpe family were responsible.

"I'm not going to find the next guy, at least not right away." JoJo couldn't really say what had changed by having sex. She didn't know if suddenly all her fears had been magically lifted. That now she could go on a string of one-night stands if she wanted. Somehow she didn't think so.

Being a virgin had been more about keeping to herself and less about sex. While she trusted Mark and while she enjoyed making love to him, she didn't feel fundamentally changed. As if she was ready to open the doors and shout her secrets to the world.

Just to him. And to Sophie. That was all.

"You need to know…I want you to know that what your dad and I did wasn't something that just happens for me, okay. It was special because—" JoJo took a deep breath "—he was my first."

That had Sophie sitting up on her elbows.

"Yeah, right."

JoJo shrugged. "It's the truth. I had a lot of hang-ups about sex and so I avoided it. But I…I really like your dad. So I did it. For the first time."

Now Sophie sat up completely, her face a mix of shock and horror. "Really?"

"Really." JoJo could feel herself compulsively swallowing and her stomach clenched. She was having a conversation she was about ten years too old to be having, but at the same time she was strangely delighted to be having it.

How many times had she been forced to listen to her friends in high school detailing their first time, all while rolling her eyes and putting on her *beentheredonethat* face.

"Was it… I mean, did it hurt? Oh, God. Oh, gross. I can't ask you these things. You were doing it with my dad!"

"Sorry." JoJo winced. "It does add a creep factor. Not that I'm going to tell you details anyway. This is just the point where I tell you when you decide to do *it* for the first time, it should be with a really great guy. Who you trust more than anything. And you should want to do it for the right reasons. Certainly not because you're angry at me or your father."

Sophie's eyes dropped and JoJo knew she had at least scored that point.

"I was so tired of playing it straight, you know? Always doing the right thing. Study hard, practice hard, perform well. Don't break the rules, ever. I did everything right and my mom still died and my dad didn't come home to see me until after she was dead. The guy I like thinks I am a kid instead of someone he wants to have sex with. I thought I could push him into it. I figured all guys lose it at the sight of a bra."

"Trust me, Bay lost it a little. Not just because you got sick, either. When he opened the door his face was as red as a stoplight."

Sophie chuckled, then dropped her head into her hands. "Ugh! I can't believe I have to see him tonight."

"If he says anything, just play it cool. You feel better and let's just forget what happened—that kind of thing."

"If he even speaks to me. He might completely ignore my existence. I wouldn't blame him."

JoJo considered the young man she'd gotten to know. "I think he'll speak to you. I think he's a good guy. He still talked to you after your dad grilled him about the notes. That shows courage. He let you hide out, even though he knew your dad was looking for you. That shows loyalty. Maybe also a smidge of stupidity, but all the same. I say you two are going to get through this. As friends."

"I hope so. I really do like him. I mean I don't know if I was actually ready for…you know. But if I had to trust anyone I think it could be him."

"So in three or four years you should be golden."

"Uh, hello? That would like make me the oldest virgin ever." Sophie winced as soon as the words came out of her mouth. "Oh. Sorry."

"No offense. I'm pretty sure I was in the running. Now there is a nun somewhere in France who probably holds the title."

Together, they laughed.

"We cool?"

Sophie nodded. "Yeah."

"You cool with your dad?"

"Not exactly sure yet. But it's not about you or anything. It's still about us. Sometimes I don't think I get who we are and who we're supposed to be. Does that make sense?"

It did. It sounded like two people who were in a relationship where they were both trying to establish the rules. Mark wasn't exactly sure how to be a father. So Sophie didn't exactly know how to be a daughter.

"Yep."

"Right. You would know. I mean what are you guys? Like boyfriend and girlfriend. Or employees with benefits?"

That was a very excellent question. "I don't know. Give me a break. It just happened."

"Just tell me that he was nice to you. I would hate to think that Mark was a jerk like that."

JoJo smiled. "He was nice to me."

Sophie retuned the smile. "You know you keep saying how much you like him."

"I do."

"Yeah, but you pause every time. Like you want to say something else but you stop yourself. If you fall in love with him and he breaks your heart, just know I totally have your back. We're girlfriends, right? We have to stick together."

JoJo nodded. "Yeah. We're girlfriends. We stick together.

Now you rest. You've got to be at the theater in a few hours. Do you need me to get you any cold medicine or anything you think might help?"

"No. I'm not really stuffy or anything. Besides, medicine could make my performance sloppy. I'll be fine."

"Okay. I'll come get you when it's time."

JoJo got up and left the room, shutting the door behind her. Mark was back and pacing at a pretty fast clip in the living room. He stopped as soon as the door shut.

"Well? Want to tell me what this was about? I practically jogged back here and the door was closed and I could hear you talking, then laughing, so I didn't feel like I could barge in… This sucks. This absolutely blows."

"What part? Fatherhood? Concern for your daughter? The sick worry that every parent feels on a daily basis for their child?"

"All of it." He sighed and sat down on the couch. "Okay, I take it back. I actually kind of like it. Most days. Today was not one of those days. I've got Ben hunting down every angle back in Philadelphia. We're trying to find any spare cousin, relative, next-door neighbor who might be connected to the Andersons, but we're coming up with nothing. Then she runs off and I don't know where she is and it was freaking me out."

"She was with Bay."

Mark turned his head toward JoJo. "Do I want to know what she was doing with Bay?"

"No." JoJo figured she could spare Sophie that. If need be, she could have another talk with the girl about being ready, and when she was ready, to make sure she always used birth control. They were friends after all. "But if you're worried something happened, then you shouldn't be. She wasn't feeling well and I brought her back here. I explained to her what happened with us…"

"Not in detail?"

She smiled at his aghast expression. "Yes, I told her exactly the way you went down on me. Will you please give me a little credit."

"Sorry."

"Anyway, she is cool with me. She is cool with us."

"Is she cool with me?"

"Can't help you there. That's between you two."

"I'm so worried. If someone hurts her…I don't think I could take it."

"Then we'll have to make sure no one hurts her."

"Who is doing this, Jo?"

Thoughts had been going through her head when she was running to the other hotel. Whoever sent the last note delivered it in person, which meant they had followed them to Chicago. "I feel like it's someone close to her."

"That's not a lot. You, me, Bay, the conductor, maybe the producer, the other musicians…"

"Nancy."

Mark's eyes zeroed in on her. "You think something is there?"

"I'm throwing darts. I'm just trying to list the people who were with her in Philadelphia, who had access to where you lived and who also knew you would be in Chicago and at what hotel. Nancy falls into that category of people. When did you hire her?"

"A few weeks before this started, maybe even longer. Her other tutor went on maternity leave. So nothing fishy there. Nancy was the only one I interviewed, and I hired her because I liked her off the bat. Calm, no hassle. I thought she would be a good influence on Sophie."

"Yes, but when was that? In relation to the Anderson case."

Mark shook his head. "I did a background check on the

woman. My kind of background check. There's no connection between her and the…"

"What?"

Mark tilted his head. "She was adopted. Later than usual, as an older child. I can't remember exactly what age. Nothing that sounded any alarms. The adoption was sealed. I didn't think to pry that far. But like I said, she'd been with us for weeks before the first note showed up. Why wait?"

JoJo shook her head. "Don't know. It's a long shot. She's done absolutely nothing to warrant suspicion."

"But you're suspicious anyway."

"We were both suspicious of Bay. You followed up."

"I'll have Ben break the seal on the adoption records. We'll see if anything turns up."

"In the meantime, Sophie has a show to do and she's sick. So lay off yelling at her at least for today, okay?"

"She's sick?"

"Flu probably."

"I should help her." Mark stood as if ready for action, but JoJo laughed at him.

"Going to fight the flu now, too?"

"If I have to."

She walked over to him and rested her hands on his chest. Then lifted herself enough to press her lips against his. It had only been hours and she hadn't forgotten how completely marvelous it was to kiss Mark.

"Like I keep saying, you're a good dad. Don't ever doubt that."

She started to step away but he wrapped his hand around her neck and pulled her closer for another kiss. "And what kind of lover am I?"

JoJo smiled. "Now, that would really be hard for me to answer as I don't have much to compare you to."

"Trust me. I'm awesome."

JoJo laughed. She couldn't disagree.

"She knows we're going to be shacking up?"

JoJo turned her head toward the room where Sophie was hopefully resting. "Do you really think that's a good idea? If you hadn't let me sleep, all of this drama could have been avoided. It's called discretion and I'm pretty sure you're supposed to have some around your teenage daughter."

Mark bent his head and gave her another kiss. "Yeah. I could have. But here's the thing, I like sleeping with you. Just sleeping. All the other stuff, too, don't get me wrong. I don't know why. It's stupid because I'm asleep, too, right? But I like it."

JoJo liked it, too. She must have or she never would have slept so deeply. So soundly. Like there was no one in the world who could hurt her anymore. But it was probably something she shouldn't get used to.

Sophie wasn't wrong about Mark. He wasn't the settling-down type. Hell, she wasn't the settling-down type. While they shared this attraction she planned to enjoy it, but she had to remember that it was temporary.

Just like every other love she'd had in her life.

CHAPTER EIGHTEEN

"CAN YOU SEE NANCY?"

"She's in the third row on the left," JoJo whispered to him. "Stop worrying about it. It's not like she's going to pull a gun out."

For this performance they were standing in the back of the auditorium rather than behind the curtains onstage. Mark was too anxious to sit down. Plus, he was waiting on a call from Ben and might need to step into the lobby. He knew that if he did, they wouldn't let him back into the auditorium. But at this point getting information was the priority. JoJo stood with him and it helped to calm him. He gave her credit for being more rational in this moment. He couldn't fly off the handle because she wouldn't let him.

But every moment the phone didn't buzz was agony. How stupid he'd been not to dig into Nancy's past a little deeper.

You didn't because she wasn't suspect. She was someone you were even considering dating.

Mark sighed. The voice in his head was always so damn right. When he hired Nancy there had been no reason to do anything more than he'd done. He kept circling back to the thought that she'd been tutoring Sophie for almost a month before the first note showed up.

Why wait if she was behind it?

It didn't matter. Ben would find something or he wouldn't. If he didn't, then they would move on to the next suspect. An investigation of everyone in the orchestra. Potentially someone onstage now, moving a bow in perfect synchronicity, was somehow connected to Anderson.

Mark felt an irrational urge to storm the stage and stop the performance so that he could shake down each person up there. Find out who would dare to harm a hair on Sophie's head. Instead he stood in the back, his arms folded over his chest as he scanned the crowd. The music played on.

"She's off tonight," JoJo muttered.

He knew. Having listened to his daughter play on a regular basis in practice and during performances he knew what was perfection and what wasn't. What was her all and what was not. He might have even given the maestro permission to yell at her after this performance if he hadn't known she was struggling with the flu.

She'd been sick while getting ready backstage, not that there was anything left in her stomach. He'd asked her again if she could handle going out onstage. The lights, the heat, the energy it would require. It all seemed too much to ask of her.

But she'd straightened, smoothed her hair, took a few sips of water and a deep breath and walked to her mark on the side of the stage, waiting to be introduced. The crowd's applause was loud and supportive. As his daughter sucked it up and did her job, Mark couldn't imagine being any prouder a parent even while his heart went out to her.

When he'd asked JoJo if he was cool with Sophie earlier, he hadn't really expected her answer. A simple "yeah, sure," was all he needed to be reassured that Sophie wouldn't be slamming any doors in the foreseeable future. Until he screwed the next thing up.

Can't help you there. That's between you two.

Mark frowned as he considered what that meant. He

thought things had been getting better. They talked, they even laughed. He was completely cool regarding her crush on a kid who was too old for her. He hadn't even grilled her about what happened while she'd been alone in Bay's hotel room.

Nor had he gone to the other hotel to have a strong *conversation* with Bay about allowing Sophie into his hotel room ever again. Even though the kid had lied to him on the phone.

He and Sophie were going to be what they were going to be. He needed to accept that. JoJo needed to accept that, if she was going to stick around for a while. Sophie was probably never going to forgive him for leaving her mother. And he was never going to be grade-A father material. Despite what JoJo said. There were too many things he didn't know. Too many ways to slip up.

For example, while JoJo had been telling him what a great dad he was, he was wondering if he could get her back in bed for another hour or two. Some dad.

No, real dads had this crazy sick feeling for their kids. Real dads didn't run away scared from that feeling. Real dads didn't hate or resent the constant anxiety their children put them through—they accepted it as part of the job.

Real dads went all the way. Full-on love and commitment.

The only thing Mark had ever committed to was his work. Yet, when Sophie made that crack about him leaving, he rejected the idea so fundamentally. He wasn't going anywhere. Was that the same as commitment?

He looked over at JoJo, who was staring at the stage with intense concentration, her brow pinched together with what he assumed was concern. She'd known his daughter only a few weeks and he could tell their bond was already strong.

How was Sophie going to feel when they ended things?

Mark cursed silently. That was what she'd been trying to tell him that morning. That was why she was so mad when she realized they were sleeping together. Sophie and JoJo had connected in a sincere way and now he'd started them on an inevitable path toward separation.

Because eventually, they would break up. Like he'd broken up with Helen. Like he'd ended any sexual fling he'd started. Eventually people just got tired of one another.

A rush of heat flooded him as he remembered what it felt like to be inside JoJo, to be on top of her, to have her on top of him. Tired of that? He couldn't fathom it. At least not now. But wasn't that how it always went? The chase, the game, the excitement leading up to the big moment, then the sex. Hot sex. Passionate sex.

Then okay sex. Then boring sex.

Then he was gone. Or she was.

Inevitable.

The thought irritated him. He didn't want to be so damn predictable. He didn't want to look at JoJo and see a time when she wasn't going to be there. At least that was different. When he compared JoJo with the other women in his life, there was more than just sex with her. More than the chase and surrender.

They worked together. They protected Sophie together. He trusted her.

The truth of that was like a knife to the gut. He didn't trust. Period. Not people in general because most of them lied. Not women specifically because he'd trusted Helen once and she'd done more than lie. She made him into a bad father by making him choose.

But with JoJo trust just happened. Like he'd never had a choice.

So what the hell did that mean?

The sound of a discordant note echoed in the theater.

He heard the reaction of the crowd, gasping, muttering. He focused his attention on the stage and watched as Sophie tried to lift herself off the piano bench.

Her hand crashed down on the white and black keys. The notes clanked and the surprise of it froze Mark for a second. He'd never known his daughter to make a sound with that instrument that wasn't absolutely lovely.

"Mark, something is really wrong."

JoJo's words didn't register. He was already jogging down the center aisle, and some people started to stand. Doctors maybe, getting ready to help. He pushed his legs to go faster. No one was going to beat him to his daughter. She was his to take care of. His to protect.

He leaped onto the stage and heard more gasps from the audience. Sophie was bent over, legs buckling, her hand on the piano the only thing holding her up. When he reached her, he saw the sweat pouring down her face, dripping off her nose.

"Dad…I'm gonna be sick…."

"I got you, baby."

Then she fainted into his arms.

THE NEXT FEW hours were a blur to Mark. He hadn't been able to form any coherent thought other than his daughter was sick, his daughter was sick. Fortunately, he hadn't needed to. JoJo had called 911 as soon as he'd run for the stage. Together they rode in the ambulance with Sophie, who was groggy but awake as they hooked her up to an IV.

She cried when she realized she had ruined the performance by cutting it short with her dramatic exit. But Mark didn't give a shit about a crappy performance. They reached the hospital and Sophie was assigned a bed in the emergency room, with nothing more than a curtain on either side separating her from a knife wound and a heart attack.

Her feistiness was intact, though.

"If I don't see a damn doctor in the next five minutes…"

"Relax. Your impatience isn't going to help, Sophie."

"I don't need a doctor. I have the flu. I can't believe you took me to the hospital," Sophie huffed.

Mark looked at his daughter, her cheeks so pink she must be filled with fever. Her formal green dress such a stark contrast to the thin white hospital sheet that only half covered her.

The flu. A bad cold. Certainly the lights onstage wouldn't have helped. A plausible explanation. He might have even been convinced if he hadn't received notes that threatened her life.

"Five minutes," Mark growled. "Then I'm going hunting."

"Ooh, Sophie. Did you hear that? Your dad is going to hog-tie a doctor for you. You should be flattered."

"This isn't funny," Mark snapped. "She's sick."

"She is and she's in the hospital. A doctor will be by shortly. Going rogue commando on us isn't going to help. It's only going to piss off the staff."

Mark wanted to throttle JoJo, who looked completely calm sitting in the chair beside Sophie's bed. He wanted to rail at her. She wasn't a parent, she didn't understand this gut-wrenching awful feeling that his child was in danger and he was without the power to help her.

If only she wasn't so damn right. Going crazy wasn't what Sophie needed right now. Sophie thought they were overreacting to a normal condition. Sophie didn't understand that Mark suspected something else.

Finally the curtain was pulled back and a short and harried-looking man stepped into the crowded space. He had short curly dark hair and massive circles under his eyes. His appearance screamed resident and Mark wasn't having anything of it.

"No, not you," Mark protested. "I want your boss or your chief or whatever you call the real doctor on call."

The man sighed. "I'm Dr. Fishman and I assure you I am a real doctor. Now can I please look at the patient?"

"Mark, don't be a jerk," Sophie commanded.

He looked to his daughter and nodded tightly. He would hold his tongue until the doctor was finished and then he would find the man's boss.

Fishman leaned over Sophie and smiled. "I saw you once. In New York. You broke my heart with your playing."

"I'm sorry," she said weakly.

"Forgiven. These your folks?"

"He is. Sort of. She's my friend but she also works for him. They are sleeping together."

JoJo gasped and Mark swallowed. "She's a little out of it, Doc."

"I am," Sophie said. "Like I can't focus."

"It's probably the fever," Mark suggested. "Isn't that what happens if it gets really high? She might be delirious."

"Yeah, that might explain it if it wasn't for one pesky little thing," Fishman said as he read her chart. "She doesn't have a fever."

"She doesn't?" JoJo popped out of her seat. "But she's completely flushed. She's been like this all day. Mark, go find someone else."

Fishman held up his hand. "Look, I could put a thermometer in her mouth and prove it to both of you, but—oh, that's right—I'm a doctor not a lawyer and all I care about is finding out what's wrong. Not proving the facts. Now both of you back off and let me do my job."

Mark crossed his arms over his chest and JoJo sat down with a hard thump.

"Talk to me, Sophie. How do you feel?"

"Dizzy. Fuzzy, I guess. Totally nauseous. I got sick on Bay. Onstage I felt like I couldn't breathe right."

Mark's eyebrows rose when she mentioned what happened in that hotel room, but he put it away and said nothing. Even he understood that now wasn't the time. Fishman continued to study her. He checked her eyes and ears, used his stethoscope on her chest and lungs, asked a few more questions, then wrapped the stethoscope around his neck and shoved his hands into his pockets.

"I'm going to admit her overnight."

"No…" Sophie wailed. "I have to perform tomorrow."

"Not going to happen," Mark interjected. "You're sick. Deal with it. They will reschedule the shows. This shit has to happen to other performers, doesn't it?"

"Not to me."

"Yeah, well, tough. He says you're staying, you're staying. Now it's my turn to tell you. Don't be a jerk."

"Whatever."

Fishman nodded. "We'll find her a room. I want to run some more tests."

Again JoJo popped out of her seat.

"What kind of tests?" she and Mark asked in unison.

Fishman shook his head. "Sophie, are you sure they're not your parents?"

She smiled but didn't seem to have the energy to fire back. Fishman took a few steps away from her bed and Mark followed him like he was on the trail of a terrorist leader. JoJo was immediately behind him.

"What tests?"

"Look, it's not the flu. Or a cold. She has no fever, no congestion. I would say maybe dehydration, exhaustion is a possibility.…"

"That's possible." Mark jumped on the idea that all she

needed was rest and some water. "She's been… This whole year, she's been through a lot. And she doesn't let up. It's practice, then rehearsal, then performance. In between all that she gets A's on all her schoolwork. She's…she's amazing."

Fishman nodded. "I get it. Look, we'll find out what's going on. But she's been on the IV for a while and she's still a little confused. It's why I want to watch her. At least for a night. I'm going to take some blood samples to see if it's something chemical."

Mark froze. Blood samples. He felt JoJo grip his arm, her fingers tight around his wrist.

"Oh, God, Mark. Anderson's daughter…"

Mark didn't need for her to finish. They both understood what might be happening.

"You need to listen to me. I'm a private detective. In Philadelphia. Lately I've been receiving notes of a threatening nature. Nothing overt, but notes that I might interpret as being from someone who wants to harm Sophie. Either myself or JoJo has been with her around the clock, but if these notes are saying what we think they might…" Mark gulped. He couldn't get the words out. Couldn't imagine that his fears could be true.

"Doctor, we want you to check for poison," JoJo said. "Any type of toxin, anything that might be out of the ordinary."

The man's eyes widened. "You think someone poisoned that girl? Why?"

"Me," Mark said, closing his eyes. "They want to hurt me."

"Please just check."

"Yeah, okay. If we do find anything I'll need to let the police know."

"Yeah, that's good. We'll need their help once I find out who did this."

The doctor nodded and left them. Mark clutched his head with his hands. "Jesus, JoJo. If we're right..."

"We can't speculate. Not until we know. Don't let your emotion cloud the facts."

"The facts are," he said in a harsh whisper, "my daughter is in a hospital bed with an unidentifiable condition. We know Anderson poisoned his daughter. We know someone broke into their house, stole a car off the same street and came after her. We know someone wants to take Sophie from me. What other facts do I need to know?"

"We've been with her around the clock. If it is poison, then how did they do it?"

"Not around the clock. Not when she was in that damn hotel room. I'm going find that kid. I want to know if he gave her anything."

"She was already sick by then...."

"Mark, JoJo!"

Mark turned at the sound of his name. Nancy was rushing down the corridor, bundled in a scarf and winter coat. "How is she? Is she all right? I got here as soon as I could."

"She's resting," Mark said carefully. Instinctively he reached to check the phone in his pocket. No missed call. No message from Ben.

"It was so awful. I felt so helpless just sitting there watching her. What did the doctors say? Is she going to be okay?"

Mark felt every muscle in his body clench. Was it her? Had she sent the notes? She'd had the opportunity. She ate with Sophie on a regular basis. How hard would it have been to put something in her food?

The silence must have gone on too long, or maybe it was

his expression, because he could see Nancy's face change. She actually took a step back.

"Maybe I shouldn't have come. I just…when I saw her faint I got so worried."

JoJo stepped in front Mark. "The doctor is going to admit her. He thinks it might be dehydration mixed with exhaustion."

"Oh, well that doesn't sound too bad. I can certainly scale down her tutoring sessions. She probably doesn't need a full three hours. Especially with her grades…"

"Did you do it?" Mark asked. He was done waiting. Done searching. Done investigating. He wanted to know who wanted to hurt his daughter and he wanted to know that answer now.

"I don't know what you mean. I thought we agreed on the time…."

"The notes. Did you send the notes?"

Nancy's face scrunched up in a picture of confusion. "Notes? I don't know what you're talking about."

Mark pushed JoJo aside and stood over Nancy, using every inch of his height advantage over her. He could see her cower, could practically feel her shrinking in on herself. This was what he'd wanted in a girlfriend? Someone nice? Someone respectable? Someone safe?

JoJo would never have let him do this. JoJo would have kneed him in the balls by now. But Nancy wrapped her arms around her waist and pushed her shoulders together.

"Mark, if you think I'm somehow responsible for her exhaustion, that's a little unfair."

"I want to know about the notes, Nancy."

"I don't know what you're talking about."

"What about Jack Anderson? Do you know what I'm talking about now?"

"No. Who? Mark, I understand you're upset about So-phie."

"Yeah, I'm upset. And when I find the person responsi-ble for this I'm going to show that person how upset I am."

"Okay, back off, Mark." JoJo pushed her way between him and Nancy.

"What is he talking about? I don't understand any of this. I just wanted to come and see how Sophie was doing."

Tears were dripping down Nancy's face.

Mark wanted to tell her that he'd seen coldhearted ter-rorists cry, just like that. Pretend they were innocent, pre-tend they were simply part of the village. Cry and protest, all while plotting to kill him.

Tears didn't move him.

"Nancy, maybe you should go," JoJo offered. "It's been a rough night. Obviously, he's upset."

She nodded, shifting her purse up over her shoulder. Wiping her tears away with the sleeve of her heavy coat. "If you want me to leave Chicago...quit...I'll do it. I don't know what I did, but I don't think I want to work for you anymore."

JoJo put her arm around the woman and squeezed her. Mark wanted to squeeze her, too, squeeze her until the an-swers he wanted to hear came out of her mouth.

"Look, Nancy, just give us time to cool off. Okay? I'll come find you tomorrow. Explain everything."

Nancy kept her eyes focused on JoJo. "Okay."

"Sophie's going to be fine. We all need some rest."

"Okay."

"I'll see you tomorrow?"

Nancy turned to Mark, who didn't have it in him to re-spond. He simply stared at her, trying to see if her pupils were dilated, if she was sweating or showing any of the telltale signs Greg might have used to determine whether she was lying.

Finally she turned and walked back down the hospital corridor. It took everything he had not to follow her.

"You shouldn't have let her go. If it is her, she'll be on a plane tonight."

"Uh, yeah. If it is her, she now knows we suspect her. Way to go, spy man."

"Don't."

JoJo shoved him, hard enough to force him back a step. "No, you don't. You need to get your head out of your ass now. If Nancy is responsible you've just tipped our hand and yes, she could be headed to the airport right now."

"You let her go," Mark snarled back.

"With my phone in her purse, you jackass. I have a tracking app. If I get to a computer I'll be able to see where the phone is located. You stay with Sophie and call me when you know something."

"How? You gave your phone away, remember."

"I'll pick up a go phone. Let me see your number." She took his phone and memorized his number. "As soon as I have the phone I'll call you. Tell Sophie I'll be back."

"Don't lose Nancy. Not until we know for sure."

"Trust me."

Mark grabbed her arm. "I do. I trust you with everything."

JoJo nodded.

"Then I guess I better not let you down."

CHAPTER NINETEEN

JoJo WALKED INTO the Chicago hotel with a sense of urgency. She'd been able to pick up a GoPhone at a pharmacy not far from the hotel and had called Mark to give him her number. Then she stopped at their hotel room for the extra security measure Mark had brought, just in case. Assuming Nancy hadn't bolted directly for the airport, but had taken time to pack, JoJo should catch up with her. Assuming the woman had reason to run.

Heading for the computer room, JoJo brought up a Google page and activated her find-a-phone app. As she waited for the signal to hit on a map, she considered calling Mark again. But she doubted he would have an update after only five minutes had passed since she'd last talked to him. Now it was all about waiting.

Waiting on Sophie's doctor to find something conclusive.

Waiting on Ben to see if he could learn more about Nancy's adoption.

A map with a green dot appeared on the screen and JoJo zoomed in. The phone was in the hotel. Nancy had come back. Which meant she was either not panicked by Mark's questions or she was completely innocent.

Or she'd found the phone in her purse and ditched it.

Leaving the room, JoJo headed over to the concierge desk. A dapper man in a gold vest smiled as she approached. She smiled back and watched his smile dim a bit as he took in her appearance.

She was wearing a black cocktail dress and low-heeled pumps with a black wool overcoat that was open down the front. Mark had said she looked pretty in her dress, a word she wasn't used to hearing describe herself. It pleased her and made her feel like a girl. Which, she admitted, was the point.

She'd bought this particular dress for the orchestra performances because she thought it did what Mark said it did. Make her look pretty. She couldn't remember a time when that had mattered to her. Yet another sign of how Mark was changing her. She would think about what that meant later.

Now she had to deal with the concierge, who had at first seen a woman in a sophisticated black cocktail dress, but who now saw a woman with serious neck art and a shiny nose stud. It was the only jewelry she owned.

"Can I help you?"

"I need to make a call to a room, but I'm afraid I've forgotten her room number."

"The guest's name?"

"Nancy Burke."

"One moment." The concierge tapped at his computer. JoJo knew he wouldn't give out the room number and she didn't need it. She simply needed him to step away when he passed her the phone.

"Yes, I have her. I can dial the room for you." He picked up the receiver and JoJo smiled.

"Great, but I have to warn you this isn't going to be pretty. I'm certain my girlfriend is cheating on me with a man. She thinks she can hide in this hotel and that's fine, but she is going to get a piece of my mind."

The concierge nodded and handed JoJo the phone. He then surreptitiously checked around, as if looking to see if any other guests had an immediate need for him. He nodded. "If you'll excuse me. I believe I'm needed at the check-in desk."

"Sure. I have everything I need."

JoJo put the phone to her ear. On the third ring, Nancy picked up.

"Hello?"

"'Scuse me, mees. 'Ousekeeping."

"Yes?"

"Towel? More towel for you?"

"No, no thank you."

JoJo hung up the phone. Nancy was in her room, and from the cracking sound of her voice, she was still upset about the confrontation with Mark. Which meant she could be completely innocent.

They had nothing. The only warning sign, if it could even be called that, was a late adoption. Nancy had had complete access to Sophie long before JoJo showed up. If at any point she had wanted to hurt the girl, she could have done it.

JoJo sighed. They were panicking. Sophie was sick with something the doctor couldn't immediately identify and they had started grasping at straws. How was Mark going to explain to Nancy that when he'd asked her about the notes, he'd essentially been accusing her of nefarious intent toward Sophie?

He was probably going to need to get a new tutor. Simple Nancy. Nice Nancy. Had they both been crazed by the need to find something there? To find anything that might stop this.

They weren't even sure what was wrong with Sophie.

JoJo found a seat in the lobby and planted herself, prepared for a long night. If it wasn't Nancy, there was nothing she could do without more information. If it was, Nancy wasn't leaving this hotel without JoJo being aware of it.

Her phone rang and JoJo reached into her coat pocket. "Anything?"

"They did a blood tox screening."

"And?"

"Cyanide. It's effing cyanide."

The phone fell out of JoJo's hand and onto the carpet.

She remembered this feeling. Knew what it was like for her heart to stop for a beat and to feel as if the world had suddenly shifted and she was still in the same place but everything around her had moved.

"JoJo? JoJo!"

She could hear his shouts coming through the phone but she couldn't move. Her body wouldn't move. Someone had tried to kill Sophie. Someone had tried to take Sophie away from her. Just like Julia. It was happening again.

She shouldn't know people. She shouldn't know anyone again. She was a jinx, a curse. Hadn't her father said that once? That she was the reason bad things happened. Everything she touched turned to ash.

"JoJo, answer me. Now!"

The sharp command jolted her into awareness. No, this wasn't because of her. This was because of someone else. Someone wanted to hurt Julia. No, Sophie. Someone wanted to hurt Sophie, kill Sophie. Only this time, she wasn't going to let it happen.

She bent down and picked up the phone. "I'm here. Tell me everything. Does he know how the cyanide was delivered? Did she eat it? Absorb it through her skin? What?"

"No, they don't think it was ingested—her symptoms would have been more acute. They found traces of some chemical called aceta...notrile...something. When it metabolizes in the body it becomes cyanide. She wasn't pink because she had a fever. She was pink because the cyanide messed with the oxygen in her blood."

JoJo took Mark's words and tried to focus on the facts. She couldn't get emotional. She needed to think about what he was telling her so that she could feed the facts into her brain and ultimately find the answer. Before she could do any of that, she had to know.

"What's going to happen to her?" She whispered the question as if she couldn't bear to give the words sound. It made it too real. Too loud in her head.

"She's going to be okay. We caught it before it had a chance to do any damage to her organs. They're going to do a CAT scan to be sure. She'll need to stay in the hospital for a few days while they flush it out of her system, but then she should be fine."

"She's going to be okay?"

"Yeah. That's what they're telling me."

"Not like Julia."

She could hear him breathing over the phone. Then he said, "No, she isn't going to be like Julia."

"Okay."

"Where are you?"

"I'm at our original hotel. I checked. Nancy is in her room."

"She didn't bolt? Then it's not her. I'm going to owe her one hell of an apology. If she will even listen to me. I wouldn't blame her. I was crazy. Why don't you come back, then? Sophie's sleeping now, but I could use the company. I feel like I've gone ten rounds with an Ultimate Fighter."

JoJo could only imagine. She knew how she felt and what Mark was going through had to be so much worse. The fear of a parent.

The fear her parents had felt when Julia was taken.

JoJo had always thought it was the same as what she'd felt. She never wanted to give them credit for hurting more than she did. It might have been too easy then to forgive her father when he started to get abusive.

His pain was worse. His grief was deeper. It wasn't his fault he lashed out at those close to him. He wasn't himself. It was the argument her mother used to make for him before JoJo told her mother to stop making excuses. She was tired of listening to them.

Only in this moment, she could see that maybe it was worse for him. Mark was Sophie's protector. *She* was Sophie's protector. He wasn't just hurting because his daughter was sick, because someone tried to hurt her—he was hurting because he failed to stop it.

JoJo felt that pain, too.

"Hey, you still there?"

"I'm here."

"You'll come, then?"

"Not yet. Text me the name of that chemical the doctor said was in her system."

She heard him sigh and thought about how he needed her to be there with him. To hold his hand, to rub his back and to remind him that Sophie wasn't going to end up like Julia.

"Babe, it's late. I was wrong about Nancy, so you don't have to watch her. We'll start over again in the morning. Together."

She wished she could. She wished she had it in her to be a normal girlfriend, or lover, or whatever she was to him. If she was different she wouldn't think twice about getting into a cab and joining him. It was what he wanted. It was the least she could do for him, considering what he was going through.

But she wasn't. She was the JoJo that the people who took Julia and destroyed her family made her into.

"I'm sorry. I have to go to work."

MARK STARED AT his phone. He couldn't be mad at her for wanting to help his daughter, something that he was currently powerless to do. He wouldn't leave Sophie, which meant he was dependent on others doing the work for him. It was an intolerable situation.

He texted JoJo the name of the chemical the doctor gave him, spelling it phonetically as best he could. If she had access to a computer, it would be enough.

"Dad?"

He shoved the phone into his pocket and turned to his daughter on the bed.

"Where am I?"

"They moved you into a private room," he said, sitting on the edge of the bed and taking her small hand in his. "You remember the ambulance and the E.R.?"

"Yes. I was really out of it. And really scared."

Of course she was. He forced a smile. "Nothing to be scared of now. They found out what is wrong and are fixing you up."

Her eyes narrowed. "That was so lame of you. What is wrong with me? I'm not a kid. I know it isn't the flu. I've never felt that way before. It was like I couldn't even think."

He hated to do it. He hated the idea of forever shattering his daughter's sense of personal safety. If only she were the type of kid who could settle for a pat on the hand, a smile and assurance that everything was going to be all right.

Then she probably wouldn't be his kid.

"It was a chemical. Somehow it got into your system and when it did it acted like a poison. The doctor is trying to find out how that might have happened."

"Poison? Wow. Do you think it was the person who sent the notes?" She started to sit up, but Mark put a hand on her shoulder to keep her still. He used the remote to move the bed into a more upright position instead.

"Don't try to sit up on your own, you're still going to be dizzy. As for the notes, I don't know. JoJo's out there now trying to find that out."

That seemed to relax her and she settled back against the bed. "I remember thinking I was going to be sick and wanting to get off the stage before I did. But when I stood up, I was so dizzy."

"They are all symptoms. Dizziness, difficulty concentrating, nausea, erratic behavior…which I'm sure explains why you were so pissed off at me."

"No way. That wasn't the poison, that was you."

Now wasn't the best time to have the conversation. She was still weak and needed to sleep, but he felt like they had come to this impasse and maybe now was the time for them to talk. Because it was not lost on him that he'd heard her call him *Dad* twice in the past few hours.

"Are you really upset that JoJo and I are together?"

She sighed in the manner of a world-weary adult trying to explain something to him he simply didn't get. He wanted to get it. For her.

"It's not about you guys being together. It's that you didn't think about me and how it would affect me. You're a parent, Mark. You're supposed to do that."

"A couple of minutes ago you called me *Dad*."

She frowned. "That was probably the poison."

He laughed and as soon as he did, tears rushed to his eyes. He used his thumb to brush them away. "You are so amazing, you know that? I use that word all the time to describe you to people. Amazing. But it's not enough. And not for the obvious reasons that you're smart and beautiful and talented…."

"Jeez, Mark.

"No," he said, stopping her. "Let me finish. When I heard about your mom I told you I had already been thinking of coming home to you. That's the truth. I had this idea in my head of us getting to know each other. Spending time together. Then that changed and I knew I needed to step up for Dom and Marie's sake. For your sake. I knew then that this wasn't going to be a weekend thing. Or a once-a-week, dinner-out deal. This was going to be real."

"You said that's what you wanted."

She sounded defensive, so he squeezed her hand with assurance. "It was. But I had absolutely no idea what that meant. I don't know even know how to say this. When I met JoJo I had this instant reaction like she wasn't going to be good for us. If I was going to find someone to be in my life she was going to be someone I would want you to have as a role model, right? By rejecting JoJo at first sight, I thought I was thinking of you, but I didn't really know what that meant, either. Now I do. You're right. I should have talked to you about her first.

"I should have said that not only do I really like her, but I like how much she likes you. I like how much you like her and I would never want to be with anyone who you couldn't get along with. I should have asked what you thought and then tried to convince you if you didn't agree with me. But I suck as a parent."

"You don't completely suck."

"No, full-on truth. I don't know what I'm doing ninety-nine percent of the time. But I know something now I didn't before. That this thing between you and me isn't about two people living together. Getting along. This thing between us is real. I was too stupid to even understand what having a daughter and being a father really meant. That's how amazing you are. I thought I loved you, Soph. I didn't know what love was. Now I do."

It was her turn to cry. "I didn't want to even like you. I

thought I would be betraying mom if I did. Like she was dead and she didn't matter anymore."

"Oh, hon, you're not betraying her. She liked me, too, you know, once upon a time."

Sophie nodded. "She didn't talk about you much, but she used to say I got your smart mouth."

Mark chuckled. "I'm sure she is somewhere in heaven laughing at the idea of you using it against me."

"I miss her."

"I miss her, too. The girl I knew. I see a lot of her in you and I love everything I see. I promise to always make sure she's a part of us. Not just a part of you. Okay?"

Sophie nodded. "I really do like JoJo. I hope you don't screw it up."

Mark winced. "I hope I don't, either. I've never not screwed it up—I'm not going to lie. But JoJo's different. I feel differently about her. I think that's because of you, too. I love you, kid. I think you cracked something open and now it's all spilling out. I'm probably going to start crying every time I see you and start sending JoJo greeting cards with hearts and flowers on them."

"Mark, just because you're in love doesn't mean you have to be a sap."

"That is excellent advice."

A knock on the door made them turn their heads. Mark checked the clock on the wall: it was after ten. Well after visiting hours. But a nurse or a doctor wouldn't have knocked.

He got up and opened the door to find Bay on the other side. The kid was still dressed in his white tie and black tux. He look frazzled and worried. "I know it's after hours, sir, but they wouldn't tell me anything downstairs. Her status is still listed as critical and I just...I had to know.

So I waited until the admin person got up and I found her room number."

"Well, that's tenacity. She's okay, Bay. Let me see if she's up for company."

When he turned around he saw her smoothing her hair down. Mark stepped back and let him inside. "You get ten minutes. I'm going to go find a bad cup of coffee. When I get back, you are gone."

"Yes, sir."

Mark was about to leave, but then stopped and wrapped his hand around the man's arm. "You also don't leave her alone. Anyone who doesn't look like they belong doesn't get through that door, you understand?"

Bay turned to him with an expression of true intensity. "Yes, sir."

"Be gentle with him, Sophie. The boy looks frazzled."

"Mark! He's not a boy."

"Remind me again what happened to *Dad*."

"Fluke. Get used to it."

Mark left the room with his head down, but he didn't go beyond ten feet so he could keep an eye on the door.

SOPHIE FOUGHT THE urge to bite her nails. Instead she kept her hands in two fists by her sides. In one way the last person on the planet she wanted to see was Bay. She'd managed to avoid him completely before curtain call by hiding in her dressing room with JoJo. Only now it was perfect. She had a totally good explanation.

Mark said one of the symptoms of the poison was erratic behavior. She could tell Bay she wasn't herself earlier today and be done with it. A person who had been poisoned couldn't be held accountable for her actions. Everyone knew that.

"Hey."

"Hey," she said with a brief smile.

"How are you feeling?"

"Better." It was true, too. Or maybe she didn't feel bad. She was realizing that she'd been feeling off for a while. It was hard to remember the last time she had felt physically good.

"I figured it was the flu or something but the hospital status has you listed as critical and I didn't know what to think."

Perfect. He had given her the opportunity she needed. The best part was that it was almost like she wasn't even lying. Maybe she had done what she did in his hotel room because of the drug. Or at least she didn't have to examine it too closely, which was fine with her. "It's kind of crazy. Apparently I was exposed to some chemical that acted as a poison. It's why I was sick and it causes really erratic behavior."

"Oh."

"Yeah, how crazy was this morning? Totally not me at all. I'm so sorry I put you in that situation but whatever this chemical is, it was messing with my head. A lot."

"Oh."

Sophie wasn't sure what to make of either of those *oh*s. He was still standing by her bed, his expression difficult to read.

"Anyway, I'm really sorry."

"Sophie, I don't care about what happened this morning. I care that you're going to be okay."

"Yeah, Mark says I'll be fine. I'm hooked up to all these tubes, so something must be working."

"Then that's all that matters."

"Good. Then we can forget about this morning?"

"Yeah. Sure. You were sick and everything."

"Not myself at all," she insisted. "Like this completely different person."

His lips twitched. "I don't know. I don't think I buy that."

"No, it's the truth. It was the poison in my system messing with my head."

"I just mean you were pretty brave. Doing what you did." He lowered his voice. "Taking off your shirt and everything. To me it's exactly something you would do. You want something and you go for it."

Sophie closed her eyes with embarrassment. No doubt her face was back to a shade of red, which was getting typical these days.

"Well, it's not going to happen again. So you don't have to worry."

"It can't, Sophie. I'm eighteen."

"I know. I'm sure it was really awful for you and everything. Me standing there in my bra…"

"No," he spat out. "That part wasn't awful. That part… was actually pretty awesome. We both know it can't happen again, but there is no point in lying."

"Really?"

"Really. You puking up right after that…that was the awful part."

She couldn't help it. She started to laugh. So hard she made a snorting noise through her nose, which could have been humiliating all on its own if Bay wasn't also laughing as hard.

"Friends?" he said finally.

"Yeah."

"Cool."

It was cool. It was actually better than cool. Bay thought she looked good without her shirt on. He was going to have no chance against her when she finally turned eighteen.

CHAPTER TWENTY

"Mr. Sharpe, a word."

Mark looked up from the watercooler where he was pouring a second cup of water. He'd lingered for a little longer than ten minutes and was about to tell Bay his time with Sophie was up. Today had been a long day for her and he wanted her to try to sleep, which would be hard in a hospital. Harder still if she was thinking about her current crush.

Mark looked at the man approaching him and immediately knew he was a cop of some kind. He had swagger mixed with authority and since he was dressed in jeans, a flannel shirt and a lined leather jacket, Mark pegged him as a detective.

Mark felt overdressed, still wearing his suit. At least he had ditched the tie.

"I'm Mark Sharpe." Mark held his hand out and the man shook it.

"Detective Milton. I got a call earlier from Dr. Fishman. He said he let you know we would be contacting you."

"Yes. It's about my daughter."

"I understand she was poisoned. Is that right?"

"Partly. She ingested a chemical that broke down into cyanide in her system."

"Dr. Fishman indicated you fear this may be intentional."

"I do." Mark spent the next ten minutes catching the detective up on the events of the past several weeks. "The hit-

and-run was reported to the police in Philadelphia. I told the officer who filed the report about the notes, as well. You can verify that."

"Can you describe these notes?"

"The notes are vague, as I said. An implied threat. No evidence of any kind that might reveal who sent them. I'm speculating that they may have come from someone involved in my most recent case, but that's all it is at this point. Speculation. It's also circumstantial to connect her condition to the notes. However, I'm not willing to take any chances."

"Understood."

"So what happens now?"

"I'll file a report. I'll wait for morning to talk to your daughter and this partner you mentioned. Then we'll take it from there."

Mark nodded. While he appreciated the detective's attention on the matter, he already knew there was nothing to find. Certainly nothing that could be proved in a court of law. Mark's interest was not justice. Only safety. For his daughter. Who every once in a while called him Dad.

"There you are, Mr. Sharpe."

Dr. Fishman was walking in their direction. Mark introduced the detective to the doctor. "Detective Milton will be investigating this from Chicago. Detective, I'm assuming you can transfer any information you learn back to the Philadelphia police?"

"If the poisoning happened in Chicago it's our case."

"I don't think it did," Dr. Fishman interrupted. "Looking further at her levels and the chemical involved, and given the slow progression of her symptoms, I'm fairly confident in saying this has been administered in small doses over a couple of weeks."

A slow steady poisoning. It was exactly what Jack Anderson had done to his daughter, Sally. To cover up the fact that he had been molesting her for years. It had to be connected. It had to be.

"I have a list of products this chemical was actually used in before anyone knew about its toxicity. Some of these are fairly innocuous. It's a wonder more people didn't die from this stuff, but then again most of this isn't ingestible." Dr. Fishman read from the list. "Cleaning solvents, some cosmetics. I guess with skin absorption that could be an issue. Some nail polishes, but they've all been taken off the market. Nail polish remover, as well..."

"What?" Mark took the list from the doctor's hands and scanned the items again. "Holy shit. It's in the nail polish. It was absorbing into her skin and she was ingesting it."

"Excuse me? Why ingesting it?"

"She bites her nails," Mark snarled. "It's a really bad habit."

JoJo LET OUT her breath when she read the list of products that contained the chemical known as acetonitrile. Any nail polish containing the chemical should have been removed from the shelves, but what if someone had an old bottle? Something that didn't look that old. Something clear in color.

JoJo stood and left the computer room. She made her way to the check-in counter and didn't bother with any pretense or story. "Can you please connect me to Nancy Burke's room?"

"Yes, ma'am."

JoJo took the phone and listened to it ring. On the second ring, Nancy picked up.

"Hello."

"Hi, Nancy, it's JoJo."

"Hi."

"Can I come up?"

There was a pause before Nancy finally said, "I don't think that's a good idea."

"I just want to talk, Nancy. Don't you think we should talk?"

"I suppose you're going to want to know why I did it."

"Yep. But I also know you're sorry. You said so in your last note."

"I am," the woman said on a broken sob. "I'm really sorry."

"Tell me your room number. I'll come up. We'll just talk."

"Don't lie. You're going to bring the police."

"I am. Not right away, though. It can just be the two of us for a while. I think that will help you, Nancy. I really do."

"It's 742." Her voice was small and tight. JoJo could hear the panic, but she didn't think Nancy had any plans to run. In fact, running or fighting back were the last things she feared Nancy would do.

As JoJo hung up the phone, the cell in her pocket started ringing. She picked it up and thought about how Mark was going to react to the news. He probably wasn't going to like what she planned to do.

"JoJo, it's Nancy. It was in the damn nail polish she gave her."

"I know."

"I take it she hasn't tried to leave or you would have spotted her. But she has to be thinking about running. Let the hotel security know that all exits have to be watched. You need to find out what her room number is and stay posted outside her door. The police are on their way and I'll be there as soon as I can. If the staff needs confirmation they can call the Chicago P.D. and ask for..."

"I have her room number. I just talked to her. She's still there."

"What do you mean you talked to her? Did she confess?"

"She did, but I already knew. I realized it when I saw the list of products that contained the chemical. Mark, I think she's going to hurt herself."

"Then. Let. Her."

It was the anger talking. Or maybe not. Mark had lived a different kind of life abroad in which emotions like compassion and forgiveness were in short supply. He'd lived in a kill-or-be-killed environment and she didn't judge him for that. But she hadn't lived that life and she couldn't let Nancy do what she suspected the woman wanted to do.

"I can't. She knew we would find out. She knew when you confronted her about the notes. It was only a matter of time. She didn't run for a reason. I think I can talk to her. I think I can convince her I know how sorry she is."

"JoJo." There was a moment of silence and she imagined him taking a breath and doing what she'd yelled at him to do earlier that night. To think logically and rationally. "That woman is unstable. That woman tried to run you and Sophie down with a car. That woman tried to kill Sophie. You are to wait there until the police arrive."

"I got your gun. I stopped at our hotel room first before I came back here. I can't believe you thought you needed it but I guess you were right to be prepared."

"JoJo, I swear to God…"

"I knew you had it because I saw you show airport security your papers. Former CIA but you still get to carry concealed on an airplane. As an American citizen I'm not sure how I feel about that."

"JoJo…"

"Why didn't you have it on you?"

"Truthfully, I forgot about it. If you remember, I was a little rattled this afternoon."

She smiled then. Poor Mark. He'd gone from taking her virginity, to getting screamed at by his daughter, only to have her run off. Yeah, she could see why he'd been rattled.

"Please don't do what you're thinking of doing."

"I know how to handle a gun," she assured him. "I've also had training in hostage negotiation."

"Who the hell is the hostage?"

"Nancy is. At least her life is. You've seen my training, you know I'm as qualified as any police officer to confront her. If I don't act now, she's going to find a way to take her life. I can't stand by and let that happen. I have to try."

"JoJo. Please. Please don't do this. I'm coming. I'll be there in minutes. Let me do this with you."

"She won't want to talk to you. She'll be too afraid. I'm going to hang up now. Please don't hate me when this is over."

"I will," he shouted back. "I will hate you. Do you hear that? Are you listening to me? I will hate you!"

JoJo hung up the phone and then left it on the desk. She could hear it ringing again as she made her way to the elevators. Nancy was seven stories up. Waiting.

JoJo STOOD IN front of the door and considered what she was doing. She didn't know how Nancy planned to take her life. Only that she was going to. There was no other reason for the woman to stay. Even now she could be suffering from the effects of an overdose or bleeding out from cuts to her wrists.

Or she could be armed.

JoJo fought through her fear and realized that if the woman was going to live, JoJo was her lifeline. She knocked on the door and in seconds Nancy opened it.

"Come in."

Cautiously, JoJo walked into the room. She didn't see blood, and Nancy didn't appear to be suffering from a reaction to drugs. She was only a second late in registering the gun in the woman's hand before Nancy was pointing it at her own temple.

JoJo had her gun out and pointed at Nancy in less than a blink, but the woman only laughed.

"What are you going to do? Shoot me?"

"Nancy, put the gun down. It's why I came here. I want to talk to you."

The woman, who was only a few years older than JoJo but who looked so much older, so much more worn down by life, shook her head. "There is nothing to talk about. I tried to kill an innocent young girl. There is no forgiveness for that. Only a life in prison."

"It's still life. Your life. I'm sure there were circumstances. You just need to tell people why."

"I thought I had to. I thought it was my penance."

JoJo hated having her gun trained on the woman, but didn't dare lower it. As long as Nancy's gun was engaged, so was JoJo's weapon. She thought about taking a shot at her arm, or hand. Ultimately, she had to hope that Nancy would choose life over death.

Rather than ask the hardest question, the one she knew Nancy would hesitate to answer, JoJo kept it lighter, easier for the woman. "Where did you get the gun?"

"Gun show this week at the Chicago Convention Center. They've really got to do something to close those loopholes, don't you think?"

JoJo didn't bother to engage the woman on a gun debate. "What about the nail polish? That must have been a really old bottle."

"I found it in my mother's house. In an old makeup kit. I

had researched all these poisons and then when I found the nail polish I thought, well, Sophie has that horrible habit. I sent a sample away to be tested. I told the company I was concerned that my nail salon was using a banned product and the lab confirmed that the chemical was present."

"It was a good plan." An evil and horrific plan. "But I know you're sorry."

"I am sorry," the woman nodded, tears barely held in check surfacing again. "You know that, right?"

"Yes, you sent the note."

"I wanted to tell him. So that he would know. I didn't mean for any of this to happen. All of it was my fault. From the very beginning."

The gun dipped a bit and JoJo didn't move. "I understand. You made a mistake, but we all make mistakes. Don't let this be another one. Put the gun down and we can sit and you can tell me everything that happened. Oh, Nancy, I know you want to. Please, talk to me."

"You really are nice. Even though you look that way with the tattoos and the nose piercing. It's really very off-putting, to be honest. So harsh."

"I appreciate you letting me know that. I don't want to put you off, Nancy. I want to try to be your friend instead."

"But I tried to hit you with the car."

"I know, but you didn't hurt me. A bump on the head. What's that? Nothing."

Nancy's eyes drifted and again JoJo watched the gun dip. She might consider tackling the woman, but the risk that the gun could go off was too great. Better to keep her talking.

"I could see he liked you and I thought I'm always second. Never first. Always second. My whole life. Why is that? Everything was working so well, but then you showed up and I just got mad. Really, really mad."

JoJo nodded. "I get that. It makes sense. Nancy, who is Jack Anderson to you?"

Instantly Nancy refocused on her and her hand started to shake. JoJo tightened her hold on her weapon, her finger resting on the trigger. If Nancy made one startling move, JoJo was going to have take her down.

Please don't make me do that.

Time was passing. The police were on the way. Mark was on his way. She was running out of time to end this peacefully.

"He was my father. My real one. But my mother... Mommy...gave me away. Sally they kept. Sally was first. I was second and they sent me away."

"I don't understand," JoJo said, truly confused.

"She said she was protecting me. She said Daddy would hurt me. I can only assume it was their compromise. He would let me go and she wouldn't report him? I'll never know. All I remember her telling me was that she had no choice. She was crying and I thought...but there was a choice. She could have sent Sally away."

She could have sent her husband away. To jail. JoJo considered a mother who would give away a daughter. A mother who knew what was happening to her oldest but wouldn't stop it. Thinking her only option was to try to save her other daughter. She hoped the woman was on some seriously good drugs in the mental health facility where she had been committed.

"And your brother? Sean. Didn't he wonder..."

"He was only two. But Sally was older and she told me it was going to be okay. I thought we were moving to a new house, we were so excited. But then Mommy gave me to this couple and said I was going to be their little girl. That I was going to be safe."

"You understand why she did that now, don't you? You know your father hurt Sally."

"I know," Nancy snapped. "Sally and I were *sisters!* Sisters. They couldn't break us up. I knew my name was Anderson. When I was old enough I found out where they moved. They were only in the next town. I went to Sally's high school and found her there. She told me I had to stay away. She told me what Daddy was doing to her. She wanted to scare me."

The pieces started to fall into place for JoJo. "Then she got sick."

Nancy shook her head. "I didn't know. I didn't know he was hurting her that way, too. She just got sick, but she was so scared. The last time I saw her I could tell something was really wrong. The way she said goodbye to me... But she wouldn't have killed herself. I know that. She wouldn't have left me!"

"You sent the anonymous letter, didn't you? To Mark, telling him to look into her death."

"I saw his ad in the paper. How he specialized in cold cases. I thought maybe someone should look. Even after all these years...nobody looked after she died and she was so scared."

"You did a really brave thing." JoJo didn't know if Nancy could hear the sound of footsteps in the hallway outside the room. Too many to be a guest. The police were here. A small force was outside the room, waiting to make their move. In minutes the phone would ring. A police specialist would be on the other end of the line ready to take over the job that JoJo wasn't getting done.

"But I didn't! I ruined everything. My father killed himself, my mother had to be institutionalized. If Sean remembered me a little and knew I what did, he would hate me. My only family would hate me. Because those other people weren't my family. They were never my family. They were just the people I lived with until I could get away. I needed to do right by *my* family. I needed to make it even."

"By hurting Sophie?"

"I almost didn't because I didn't think it would matter. When I first got the job, I saw that Mark and Sophie could barely stand each other. I was going to quit and just leave it alone, but then I could see things changing. They were starting to like each other. Laughing and joking and it wasn't fair. It wasn't fair that my family was ruined and his was just starting."

JoJo watched as Nancy's hand dropped steadily through her explanation until it rested at her side, the gun now barely gripped in her hand.

JoJo took a step closer. "Drop the gun, Nancy. Let's end this. Once you tell people how sorry you are, you'll see how it will be. They'll understand everything. Yes, you hurt Sophie, but you also brought justice for Sally. For your sister. Think about her. Wouldn't she want you to live? Live the life that she never got to."

The thunk of the gun hitting the carpet was the sweetest sound JoJo had ever heard. "Take a few steps back for me, Nancy."

The woman did even better and went to sit in the single chair provided in the hotel room. JoJo picked up the gun and pocketed it. "I'm going to open the door, okay. The police are going to come in and take you away. You'll need to get a lawyer."

Nancy nodded but JoJo didn't know if she really heard her.

"I didn't want to die, I guess. Not really."

"Nobody does."

JoJo opened the hotel room door to find four, five maybe

six SWAT team members armed and ready to take the room. "She's unarmed and compliant. Go easy, okay, guys."

JoJo handed Nancy's weapon over to one of the officers and walked a bit down the hallway. She listened as Nancy screeched, knowing she was forcibly being taken to the floor, her arms jerked behind her, then cuffed, then lifted from the floor as the officers read her rights.

She didn't watch as they took Nancy down the hallway toward the elevators. There was nothing left to see but a broken woman who had a broken life. There was no satisfaction to be had from anything that had happened tonight. Unless she counted Nancy's survival.

Would the woman have killed herself if JoJo hadn't intervened? She didn't know. She only knew she would wake up tomorrow after sleeping with a clean conscience tonight. JoJo put her head back against the wall and closed her eyes.

It did raise a very good question about exactly where she would be sleeping. Forget letting her back into his bed, would Mark even let her back into the hotel room? He would probably leave her stuff outside in the hallway and let her make her own way back to Philadelphia. Was she supposed to believe what he said? That he hated her now.

The sudden fear of that, the fear of losing him, was shockingly intense.

"See, this is why I avoid relationships. There I was in the deserts of Afghanistan hunting down Taliban tribal leaders, no fears or worries. Not a care in the world. Then I come home and these women enter my life and it's danger around every turn."

JoJo opened her eyes to find him leaning against the opposite wall of the hallway. The police had taken Nancy away and were processing her room as a crime scene. JoJo wouldn't have much quiet time before they started to question her about what had happened. It was going to be a really long night.

"She was Jack Anderson's daughter."

"Yep. Ben called me."

JoJo shook her head. "How sick do you have to be to give away your youngest daughter because you know your husband is molesting your oldest?"

"Very sick. Now it's clear she didn't protect him because she was in denial about what he was doing. Jack Anderson was a monster, but Regina was worse because she let the monster thrive."

JoJo looked at him then, not asking the question she really wanted to. Until finally, she couldn't hold it back. "Do you hate me?"

"For talking her off the ledge, no. For aging me ten years while I stood outside the door, a little."

"I had to do it. Had to try."

"Debatable. But as she's alive, I'll concede the point."

"How's Sophie?"

"She was freaked-out, which made me ache even more. But the doctors say she's going to fully recover in a few days. Then Bay came to visit and when he left she had this really goofy smile on her face. I didn't tell her what you were doing. She didn't know to be scared for you."

JoJo would have to find out what that was about tomorrow. A goofy smile equaled a positive conversation. That is, if there was a tomorrow for them.

No, that was already determined. There was going to be a tomorrow for her and Sophie. It was nonnegotiable. Sophie was part of her life now, and JoJo was part of hers. That wasn't going to change, no matter what happened between her and Mark. She would need to make sure Sophie understood that.

"Ms. Hatcher. Do you have time to talk now?"

"That's Detective Milton," Mark said, pointing his thumb in the direction of the man approaching them. "He's handling the case on this end."

"Yeah. I'm ready." She pushed herself off the wall. Suddenly, she seemed to weigh three hundred pounds, but there was no putting this off. Nancy's story had to be told.

She started to walk and saw Mark kept step with her. "You're coming with me?"

"I am. When we're done you can come back to the hospital with me. Sophie's got a private room so we can move in two cots." He stopped walking, which forced her to stop, as well. She didn't want to miss anything he had to say. "If that's what you want."

She smiled. Strange, when only a few minutes ago she didn't think she would ever smile again. "That's what I want."

"Good. Then let's get this show on the road."

As they started to walk again, JoJo reached into her pocket and handed him his gun. Mark took it without a word, put the safety on and shoved it into the back of his pants, mostly hidden by his suit coat.

"I guess you don't hate me."

"I guess I don't."

"That's good because the whole time Nancy was talking and I was hoping she didn't kill herself or try to kill me, something occurred to me."

"What was that?"

"I think I'm in love with you." She didn't think it. She knew it. But it was best to hedge her bets with a man like Mark. Not let him hold all the cards at once.

"Yeah. I figured it out when I was shouting at you that I would hate you. I could only be so mad at someone I loved."

"That's pretty messed up."

His brushed her tattoos. "Yeah, because you are a ringing endorsement for normalcy."

"We all have our issues."

He wrapped his arm around her shoulders and brought her close to his body. It felt really good.

"So, do you think two messed-up people can make a relationship work?" he mused.

"The chances are fairly slim."

"I thought so, too."

Sophie opened her eyes slowly. She waited to see if the dizziness would still be there but fortunately it was gone. Sitting up, she actually felt fairly normal. Maybe that meant she could get away with only two days in the hospital instead of the three the doctor had predicted. Then she was going to have to talk to the show's producer to reschedule the performances. She hoped he agreed that included rescheduling her crappy collapsing performance. Not an impression she wanted to leave in the minds of those who had attended.

Looking around the room, she could see the cots filling up the open space. Mark was on his stomach snoring and JoJo's hand had fallen off the side of her cot. Sophie smiled; she bet the nurse loved having to tiptoe around these two to take her vital signs.

"Hey, guys. Wake up."

Mark's head jerked and as soon as he moved JoJo woke up. She ran her hand through her cropped hair and immediately stood. "What is it? Do you need anything?"

"A toothbrush," Sophie said. "But that can wait. What happened with Nancy? Dad told me she was responsible when they came in to take the polish off my nails. Is she like totally sick?"

"Totally," JoJo agreed. "The police have her in custody."

"Nancy. She was so normal. So nice and plain. The whole time she wanted me dead. I'm sorry, that's completely freaky."

"She's gone," Mark said coming to stand on the other side of the bed. "That's all you need to know about her."

"Won't I have to testify and stuff?"

"Not if she pleads guilty, which I think she might do. She didn't run when your father blew it and tipped our hand. I think she wanted to be caught. What she did was horrible, but what's crazy is that I really believe she is sorry she did it."

"Do I have to get another tutor? Mark, I can make a case for having been traumatized."

"Clearly." Mark snorted. "Yes, you will have another tutor, but the next one will have top-level government-security clearance."

"So what happens now?"

Neither Mark nor JoJo said anything and Sophie had this sense that they probably didn't know.

"I guess we go home," Mark suggested.

"We'll need to come back for the makeup dates."

"Not until you're completely well, but then sure. I guess you can go back to your routine."

"What about you two?" Sophie wanted to know. "Are you going to date?"

"No," Mark said. "She's going to move in with us."

"I am?"

"No way," Sophie said. "That's way too fast. You have to date for at least three months."

"Three months!"

JoJo nodded. "Yeah. I like the idea of that. And you have to do nice stuff like bring flowers."

Mark looked perplexed but eventually he conceded.

"Fine, three months, then she moves in. When can we get married?"

Sophie considered that. "Well, you are kind of old—"

"Hey, I am not."

"Maybe like six months if things are working out," Sophie said.

"Fine," Mark agreed.

Sophie thought JoJo looked pretty freaked-out, but she didn't say anything. "So if everything works out and you guys get married, then we'll be, like, a family."

"Oh, wow. I think I'm going to be sick," JoJo muttered.

"Suck it up," Mark demanded. "If I can handle it, you can handle. We should consider what we're all going to bring to this family of ours."

"I'll bring my uncanny knack to pick the perfect restaurant."

"That's a good one," Mark agreed.

They looked at JoJo, who was kind of pale. Sophie reached out and took her hand. "It's okay. I know we're freaking you out."

JoJo squeezed her hand back and smiled. "I'll bring my risotto."

Sophie and Jojo both turned to Mark.

"I'll stay."

Sophie could see his face was suddenly really serious. He met JoJo's eyes, then Sophie's. Like he was making an important vow.

"Forever. I'll stay with both of you forever. I'll never leave."

JoJo shook her head. "You can't promise that."

Mark reached over the bed and took her free hand. Then he took his daughter's hand and Sophie could feel the power of his words. Could feel what the three of them might actually become someday. It was a risk. She and JoJo knew it, because she and JoJo knew that people didn't stay forever. Even when you wanted them to.

"Try me."

Sophie nodded. "It's okay, JoJo, I think he means it."

"Forever," she whispered. "Okay."

"Great, now let's seal the deal with Sharpe on the three."

"My last name isn't Sharpe," Sophie pointed out.

"Yeah, and I don't know how I feel about taking the man's name. It seems a little archaic—"

"Oh, for Pete's sake."

"And are we really the type of family who cheers together?" Sophie asked.

"I agree. I think we're more of a noncheering bunch."

"Forget it," Mark grumbled.

Then the door opened and an aide brought Sophie her breakfast and they all sat together on the bed and teased each other, and laughed, and were…together.

Forever.

EPILOGUE

Six months later

"Ahh! Oh, my God this hurts."

Mark clutched JoJo's hand. "You're doing great, babe, hang in there."

"Sophie give me your other hand, I need to squeeze on both sides."

"Uh, no way." Sophie held up her hands. "I'm a professional. These are my tools, remember?"

"No help," JoJo growled. "You are no help."

"Hey, we all have our roles. I'm deciding where we're going to lunch afterward."

"Oh, man, please stop!"

The doctor standing over JoJo paused. "You need to stay still or it's only going to hurt worse."

"You need to be kicked in the balls over and over again so that you know what this feels like."

"Okay, that's borderline abusive."

Mark waved him off. "I'll give you a tip, Doc. Just keep going."

Once more the doctor lowered the laser over JoJo's neck while she struggled to stay still. Mark tried not to smile in the face of her misery, but it was hard not to. Because he knew what she was doing, she was doing for him. Because she loved him that much.

After three months of dating and three months of living together she had finally accepted his offer of marriage.

But to get the ring, he told her she needed to lose the tattoos.

At first she fought him, wanting to cling to her crutch, but then he showed her the diamond. It was a big one.

"How much longer?"

"They're almost invisible," Mark said. "Last side, last wire."

"I can't believe you talked me into this."

"No more walls, Jo. Not even the symbolic ones. It's the price you pay for letting people in and having them love you."

"This is love?" she screeched as the doctor continued to wave the laser over her neck.

Sophie moved around the table so JoJo could see her. "Look at it this way, you don't want to be walking down the aisle in this beautiful white dress with black tattoos around your neck. It would totally spoil the pictures."

"We're getting married in a courthouse and you're fired as my maid of honor. Done."

"Please. As if you could get someone at this late date. You're both taking too many cases. I've had to handle everything, make all the arrangements for the reception. If I didn't force you to go dress shopping, you would be standing in the courthouse naked."

"Now that might be interesting."

"Can it, Mark," JoJo growled.

"All I'm saying is you need me. This wedding is like my baby."

"Yeah, a baby you are paying for with my credit card," Mark grumbled. "What was the last five hundred dollars for?"

Sophie dropped her gaze to the floor, a habit that had replaced biting her nails. Not once since they had removed the toxic polish had she ever been tempted to bite them again. Now she conveyed nervousness, and what Mark knew was also guilt, by simply not looking at him.

"Sophie…"

"Shoes," she admitted.

"Five hundred dollars for shoes?"

"What the hell am I wearing, gold?" JoJo squeaked.

Sophie rocked on her heels. "Actually they are for me. They're Michael Kors and they are totally cool."

"No way. Unacceptable. They go back."

"Daddy, *please.*"

"Oh, no, you didn't. You did not invoke the Daddy card." The shame of it was, it pleased him inordinately to hear it. For the most part he was still Mark to her. But every once in a while, when she wanted him to know that he was okay, she would use the big *D* word. This, however, was the first time she had ever used it to manipulate him.

Sophie smiled very wide.

Yeah, it would probably work. "Fine, but your dress better be cheaper than dirt."

"Okay, can we focus on me here? You're both supposed to be offering me support."

"Right. You're almost done. Actually, I have no idea if that's true. Doc?"

The doctor stood and turned off the laser. "Take a look." He handed JoJo a mirror and Mark watched as she rediscovered herself. She'd dyed her hair back to blond and in the past few months her natural color had taken over. It was a stunning gold-and-caramel blond and it highlighted the blue in her eyes even more than the jet-black color.

This was JoJo Hatcher. The woman she was supposed to be. Mark didn't know he had this much love in him, until each day he found more for her. More for his daughter.

For a man who thought he'd been so content without it, he hadn't realized he had no idea what happiness truly was.

"I know that girl." JoJo smiled as she checked out her neck. While red, it was devoid of ink.

"She's hot," Mark confirmed.

"Stop, you'll embarrass me."

"You mean that hasn't already happened," the doctor said, putting away his equipment. "I have to say, you guys are one...unique...family."

"Yeah," JoJo agreed. "But they are mine. My family."

Mark narrowed his eyes. "Are you going to cry again? 'Cause I have to say you've been like a faucet. Crying when I propose, crying when you ask Sophie to be your maid of honor..."

"Mark, I love you, but shut the hell up."

He leaned in to kiss her. "Yes, ma'am."

* * * * *

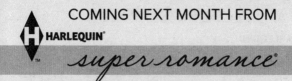

On the anniversary of her sister's death, things
aren't going well for Miranda Sinclair—especially
after losing out on a big promotion. So she's
determined to forget about it all tonight. But the
stranger who walks into the bar might not be a
stranger for long....

Read on for an exciting excerpt of
the upcoming book

That Reckless Night
By **Kimberly Van Meter**

"You're as stubborn as your old man and just as mean," Russ,
the bartender, said, setting up her drink. "Why do you do this
to yourself, girl? It ain't gonna bring Simone back."

Miranda stilled. "Not allowed, Russ," she warned him
quietly. "Not allowed." Today was the anniversary of her
youngest sister's death. And most people knew better than to
bring up Simone's name.

This, Miranda thought as she stared at the glass, was how
she chose to cope with Simone's death, and no one would
convince her otherwise. What did they know anyway? They
didn't know of the bone-crushing guilt that Miranda carried

every day, or the pain of regret and loss that dogged her nights and chased her days. Nobody knew. Nobody understood. And that was just fine. Miranda wasn't inviting anyone to offer their opinion.

Russ sighed. "One of these days you're going to realize this isn't helping."

"Maybe. But not today." She tossed the shot down her throat. The sudden blast of arctic air chilled the closed-in heat of The Anchor, and Miranda gave a cursory glance at who had walked through the front door.

And suddenly her mood took a turn for the better.

A curve settled on her mouth as she appraised the newcomer. The liquor coursing through her system made her feel loose and wild, and that broad-shouldered specimen shaking the snow from his jacket and stamping his booted feet was going to serve her needs perfectly.

"Hey, Russ…who's he?" she asked.

Russ shrugged. "Never seen him before. By the looks of him, probably a tourist who got lost on his way to Anchorage."

A tourist? Here today, gone tomorrow. "He'll do," she murmured.

But what if the stranger is not a tourist?
Find out in THAT RECKLESS NIGHT
by Kimberly Van Meter, available November 2013
from Harlequin® Superromance®.
And be sure to look for the other books in
Kimberly's The Sinclairs of Alaska series.

REQUEST YOUR FREE BOOKS!
2 FREE NOVELS PLUS 2 FREE GIFTS!

HARLEQUIN®
super romance®

More Story...More Romance

YES! Please send me 2 FREE Harlequin® Superromance® novels and my 2 FREE gifts (gifts are worth about $10). After receiving them, if I don't wish to receive any more books, I can return the shipping statement marked "cancel." If I don't cancel, I will receive 6 brand-new novels every month and be billed just $4.94 per book in the U.S. or $5.24 per book in Canada. That's a savings of at least 14% off the cover price! It's quite a bargain! Shipping and handling is just 50¢ per book in the U.S. and 75¢ per book in Canada.* I understand that accepting the 2 free books and gifts places me under no obligation to buy anything. I can always return a shipment and cancel at any time. Even if I never buy another book, the two free books and gifts are mine to keep forever.

135/336 HDN F46N

Name _____ (PLEASE PRINT)

Address _____ Apt. #

City _____ State/Prov. _____ Zip/Postal Code

Signature (if under 18, a parent or guardian must sign)

Mail to the **Harlequin® Reader Service:**
IN U.S.A.: P.O. Box 1867, Buffalo, NY 14240-1867
IN CANADA: P.O. Box 609, Fort Erie, Ontario L2A 5X3

**Are you a current subscriber to Harlequin Superromance books
and want to receive the larger-print edition?
Call 1-800-873-8635 or visit www.ReaderService.com.**

* Terms and prices subject to change without notice. Prices do not include applicable taxes. Sales tax applicable in N.Y. Canadian residents will be charged applicable taxes. Offer not valid in Quebec. This offer is limited to one order per household. Not valid for current subscribers to Harlequin Superromance books. All orders subject to credit approval. Credit or debit balances in a customer's account(s) may be offset by any other outstanding balance owed by or to the customer. Please allow 4 to 6 weeks for delivery. Offer available while quantities last.

Your Privacy—The Harlequin® Reader Service is committed to protecting your privacy. Our Privacy Policy is available online at www.ReaderService.com or upon request from the Harlequin Reader Service.

We make a portion of our mailing list available to reputable third parties that offer products we believe may interest you. If you prefer that we not exchange your name with third parties, or if you wish to clarify or modify your communication preferences, please visit us at www.ReaderService.com/consumerschoice or write to us at Harlequin Reader Service Preference Service, P.O. Box 9062, Buffalo, NY 14269. Include your complete name and address.

HSR13R

Don't miss the first book in The Legend of Bailey's Cove trilogy!

In the sleepy, picturesque town of Bailey's Cove, Maine, restaurateur Mia Parker and anthropologist Daniel MacCarey discover each other while dealing with a two-hundred-year-old skeleton found in her wall. The attraction between Mia and Daniel is immediate and irresistible, but an unyielding darkness from his past stands between them and love.

Better Than Gold
by **Mary Brady**

AVAILABLE IN NOVEMBER